An ancient order.
A deadly conspiracy
A race against time.

MW00479136

When Jake Crowley rescues Rose Black from assailants on the streets of London, the two find themselves embroiled in a mystery that could cost them their lives. People are dying, and all the victims have one thing in common with Rose: a birthmark in the shape of an eagle.

From beneath the streets of London, to castle dungeons, to the heart of Christendom and beyond, Jake and Rose must race to stay alive as they seek to unlock the secrets of the *Blood Codex*.

Praise for David Wood and Alan Baxter

BLOOD CODEX

A Jake Crowley Adventure

David Wood
Alan Baxter

Adrenaline Press

Published by Adrenaline Press
www.adrenaline.press

Adrenaline Press is an imprint of Gryphonwood Press
www.gryphonwoodpress.com

This is a work of fiction. All characters are products of the authors' imaginations or are used fictitiously.

ISBN-10: 1-940095-58-1
ISBN-13: 978-1-940095-58-5

PROLOGUE

*Near the City of York
Kingdom of Northumbria, England
October, 867 CE*

Leather-armored men with bloodstained hands forced Aella to his knees, raised his arms wide and high, and tied his hands to posts of weathered wood. They used knives to strip away his remaining clothes, and left him shivering and naked, kneeling on the wet grass. Aella lifted his head to stare into the face of Ivar the Boneless as the huge, muscled son of Ragnar Lodbrok approached, and poured all his hate out through that steely blue gaze. Fear knotted Aella's stomach, made his veins run with ice, but he would be damned before he would let Ivar see that terror.

"I am a king!" he roared.

Ivar bared his straight, white teeth and shook his head slowly. His long braid hissed against his leather armor with the movement, audible despite the crackling fires all around. "Not for much longer."

The Northman's breath steamed in the cold autumn air, the night sky a vault of glittering stars without a single cloud to mask them. Sparks and smoke spiraled up into the night, twisting in the frozen breeze, the fire-glow competing with silvery moonlight that bathed the grass all around.

Aella's hair hung unbound, disheveled and filthy as it lay draped around his bruised face, his beard matted with blood and dirt from the beating he had sustained. But his pride remained intact.

Men and women stood scattered about. Aella's own people were on their knees, in the custody of Ivar's men, or dead at the hands of those same warriors. Aella smiled crookedly, proud of his own forces, who had stood and fought and died, and now stood before the gates of heaven, their sins washed in the blood of their noble sacrifice against the pagan invaders. But he was beaten, he knew that, his land wrested from his grasp. His people would be released soon enough, to carry on serving under a new king, but Aella himself would not live to see it. All that remained for him was how he died. And he would die a warrior's death--strong and defiant.

"You have two choices, *Highness.*" Ivar, his voice strident to draw the attention of all, twisted the honorific into mockery.

The crowd of warriors closed in, leather and mail glistening with blood and sweat in the firelight, blades of swords and axes glinting. Their mutterings and conversations faded to silence, enthralled now to watch a king beg for his life.

Aella's smile deepened, despite the terror twisting his heart and gut. He would not give them that pleasure.

Ivar tipped his head back and laughed. "You face your death stoically, I'll give you that. But it can be swift."

"Make it as slow as you like," Aella growled. "I. Am. A. King!" He gritted his teeth, against the fear more than the cold, hoping his trembling could not be seen.

Ivar's face twisted in rage. "You murdered my father!" he roared. "You threw the mighty Ragnar Lodbrok into a pit of snakes to die in writhing agony, denying him the glory of a death in battle. You will die slower and be equally denied! While you've squabbled with Osberht over this land, my Great Heathen Army, as you call us, has only grown stronger. While you've lounged in that great city of York, growing fat and lazy with the blood of Ragnar Lodbrok on your hands, I have marched. My father's revenge will finally be found. You are no longer a king, Aella."

Aella swallowed the rising bile of terror. He had no fear of death, but was not ready to go yet. Life became suddenly the most precious thing in the world and he despised this Ivar who stood about to take it from him. Not to mention the method, which was truly frightening. "Your father knew the risks of his actions. Ragnar Lodbrok was twice the man you'll ever be."

"And yet here you are on your knees before me." Ivar smiled again, controlling his anger. "But like I said, this can go one of two ways. You know the blood eagle torture, Aella? I will open your back with knives and lay aside the flesh. I will use an ax to separate your ribs from your spine and pull your lungs out to lie upon your shoulders like an eagle's wings. And you will live through it all to die in slow agony and suffocation. I would warn you that if you cry out even once you will be denied entry to Valhalla, but you are no Northman. Your Christian god died his own pitiful death, so perhaps your screams will be pleasing to him." Ivar leaned in close, his sour, ale-soaked breath hot on Aella's cheek. "And you will scream, Aella. You *will* scream."

Aella met the other man's gaze and bared his teeth in a wordless snarl, not trusting his voice to be strong if he spoke.

Ivar stood straight again. "But there is another option. Just tell me where it is and your death will be swift. Valhalla's doors will stand open for you, welcoming."

Temptation rippled through Aella, the thought that all this could be over with one swift stroke of an ax and his soul set free. But he could never possibly let Ivar find what he sought. He only hoped God would forgive him for being tempted by the power. In the end, he had given it up. That had to count for something, didn't it? He found his voice and was pleased it came out strong. "You can do your worst, Ivar, you fetid dog. I will never tell you where it is and I will never scream."

Ivar's eyebrows rose. "Truly, little king? You *really* think so?" He leaned forward again. "Tell me where it is!"

Aella gathered saliva and blood in his mouth and drew all his breath to spit it full into Ivar's face. Ivar roared again and dragged the back of his hand across his nose and mouth. He pulled a long, gleaming knife from his belt and strode around behind Aella.

The deposed king gritted his teeth as cold steel bit into the flesh of his back. Hot fire lanced down his spine and the pagan horde inched closer, eager to watch the bloody spectacle.

"Tell me where it is and this ends quickly." This time, a touch of urgency tinged Ivar's words-- one final chance to get the information he wanted.

Aella forced a laugh. "Take your sorry time, son of Lodbrok!"

With a hiss of rage, Ivar drew the knife point down. Aella ground his teeth together and promised himself he would not scream.

Chapter 1

London, England

Danny Bedford walked with *Alice In Chains* blaring in one earbud. He'd kept the other ear free of interference since a close call with a speeding taxi some months before. It didn't pay to cut off one of his most important senses, even on a quiet night when a person might expect to have the city to himself. He wore a black woolen cap pulled down tightly over his shoulder-length coppery red, curly hair, and kept his hands thrust deep into the pockets of his puffy green jacket.

Tiredness clawed at him, hung heavy off his eyelids. He appreciated the extra income from double shifts at Great Ormond Street Hospital, but the work of an orderly was physically demanding, and wearing him down. Still, he had two full days off coming up and he planned to spend them on the couch mainlining seasons of television shows he'd got stacking up on the hard drive.

He turned off the main street into an alleyway that stank of stale urine and rotting garbage. A streetlamp at the far end illuminated the wet cobblestones underfoot, made them glisten like eyes staring up from the dark road. Clouds had closed over the night and Danny smelled more rain in the air. He didn't mind that; the city of London needed to be washed regularly, in his opinion.

The thought brought to mind his tub and the idea of a hot bath. His aching muscles would appreciate that. Footsteps echoed off the building walls either side of him. Danny stopped, glanced back. No one there. It was late, the streets mostly deserted on his walk home as they often were when he finished a late shift in the early hours of the morning. He pulled the ear bud free to listen with all his hearing, looked up and down the alley again. Nothing. With a shake of his head he continued on, but his ears were alert, the tiredness pushed away by a slight surge of adrenaline that made him suddenly jittery. He had nearly reached the end of the alley when the footsteps came again, perfectly matching his own tread.

Danny spun quickly around, mouth already opening to

issue a challenge. No one. He swallowed, licked strangely dry lips, looked up and down the narrow gap between the tall buildings. He was completely alone.

"Hello?" His voice sounded childish, fearful. He felt five years old and that in turn made him angry. "Who's there?"

Of course no answer came, and Danny huffed a short grunt of annoyance and carried on along his way home, walking at a determined pace. He stepped out of the claustrophobic alley and turned left along Southampton Row, heading for the bus stop and the night bus that would take him slowly through the brightly lit city toward his home in Shepherd's Bush. Traffic moved along the busier road, the comforting signs of life altogether more obvious, and the quiet pursuit in the alley became an instant memory, some strange dream moment trapped between the waking hours of Danny's life.

He shook his head, put the earbud back in and began nodding to the opening strains of "Heaven Beside You". As he passed Catton Street on his left an arm shot out of the shadows and grabbed him. The man hauled hard and Danny staggered, unable to prevent the motion, and stumbled into the shadows under a stand of unhealthy city trees. Cars crawled by not ten feet away, their drivers and passengers oblivious as four angry-looking men thrust Danny up against the worn, grubby trunk of a tree. They wore blacks and grays, faces partially concealed by hooded jackets casting deep shadows.

"What do you want?" Danny asked loudly, his voice high with panic.

"Just stay calm," one man said. "Don't do anything stupid."

Danny drew breath to scream, to yell for help, but the cry stuck in his throat. Who would hear him anyway? Who would help if they heard?

The man stepped forward, his fingers digging painfully into Danny's arm, and another man took hold of the other side. They spun him around, pressed his face up against rough bark. A series of rapid, terrifying thoughts rushed through his mind, horrible possibilities of what they might be about to do to him. He thrashed, desperation breaking through the bonds of fear, and yelled out. "Get off me! Leave me alone! Help!"

Someone cuffed Danny across the temple. Dizziness swept his brain. His knees buckled and he probably would have gone down if the two men weren't holding him up. A third set of hands grabbed at the back of his jacket and hauled it up, along with his shirt tail. Cold night air swept across the bare skin of his back. Despite his giddiness, Danny thrashed again and drew breath to scream, when the man said, "Yep, he's the one." He let the jacket drop back down.

Confusion killed Danny's cry before it even began. "What is this?" Something cold and wet slapped over his face, covered his nose and mouth. His eyes went wide, real panic setting in as a sharp, cloying chemical odor flooded his senses and then everything closed to a dark tunnel and went black.

CHAPTER 2

Natural History Museum, London

"As you can imagine, many mythologies and superstitions have arisen around birthmarks over the centuries, from the comedic to the malevolent. They have been considered marks of luck and of evil, of witches and of prophets. As with many things slightly to the left of what most would consider 'normal', there are almost as many varying stories surrounding them as there are people to tell those stories.

"Take this human skin, for example, preserved in the permafrost of Siberia and recently on loan to this special exhibition. That birthmark is unusually dark and some consider that it might be the reason why the body was interred in such an extravagant grave, that perhaps the mark gave the person special standing in their ancient society."

Jake Crowley zoned out while the museum guide continued her monologue to his class of fourteen-year-old history students. He let his gaze roam the "Blue Zone", the Human Biology section of the Natural History Museum. A giant model of a human cell, a journey through reproduction, birth and growth, all kinds of interactive displays. He loved this place, had since he was a kid. The building itself mesmerized him, a mixture of Gothic Revival and twelfth-century Romanesque-style architecture, in line with Museum founder Sir Richard Owen's vision of creating a 'cathedral to nature'. Inside, the exhibition spaces were wonderfully high, serried arches and vaulted windows, bright skylights, wide staircases and shining marble floors. And the museum's contents were truly mind-expanding. Taking his classes on field trips here was probably the most satisfying part of his often thankless job.

The group shuffled forward and Crowley's eyes returned to the museum guide as she continued her guided lecture. He drank in her shining black hair in a neat bob, her smooth, lightly ochre-tanned skin. She was clearly of East Asian extraction, but Crowley thought maybe half-Chinese and half-white European. He enjoyed guessing the heritage of people and was right more often than not. She stood a little taller than he considered most

Chinese, though several inches short of Crowley's firmly muscled six-foot frame. And she looked fit and strong, lines of muscle clear on well-formed arms, hard calves showing beneath a straight skirt. She was quite a stunner, and clearly as smart as any university lecturer. Her delivery was alive and passionate, far from the rehearsed speeches so many guides went through in robotic fashion day after day. Then again, this woman wasn't just a guide, but an employed historian at the museum, taking time out from a busy research program now and then to talk to interested groups. Crowley was pleased his students might benefit, perhaps absorb some of her enthusiasm for the subject. Then again, maybe not. Teenagers had a strange resistance to things they might learn from unless it was something they chose to investigate. History rarely fell into that category.

Crowley permitted himself a moment's fantasy, imagined walking arm-in-arm with the beautiful historian, a fine contrast to his perpetually pale skin and slightly angular features. As the thought drifted through his mind, her eyes locked with his for a moment and he had the strange sensation she could hear his inappropriate desires. His cheeks flushed hot and he thought he saw the slight twitch of a smile on her mouth as she looked away, not breaking stride with her lecture for a moment. She was saying something about fertility rites and one of his less focused students, Maxwell Jenkins, made some ribald remark about the rites he was planning to take out on some poor hapless female classmate. She snapped a justified obscenity at him and Maxwell's perpetually obsequious friend barked a dutiful laugh. Neither lad realized Crowley stood directly behind them until he clamped a hand to each of their shoulders and steered them away from group.

Sometimes Crowley wished he was still in the army, so he could slam them down and give them fifty push-ups on the spot, while he yelled at them about respect and not being smartasses. But as a teacher, main force was not an option. His military training often helped. The voice he had developed along with his impressive physical presence meant he had a much easier time keeping his students in line than many teachers did. And there were other ways he could make these two boys suffer later on.

"Aw, Sir, I was just joking," Jenkins complained, his outrage slightly marred by the cracking of his puberty-stricken voice box.

"And you know very well I won't stand for that kind of

talk, in class or out of it," Crowley said. "When we get to rugby training after school this afternoon, the three extra laps of the pitch and subsequent push-ups will be down to you. You'll be kind enough to let the rest of the squad know that, won't you?"

"Sir, that's not fair!"

"Life isn't fair, Jenkins, but it's a lot easier if you don't act like an animal. You're smart boys underneath all that testosterone, so maybe the extra rugby training will help to reveal it, eh?" He enjoyed being their rugby coach as well as their history teacher for the variety of influence it provided him. They weren't bad kids. Just teenagers.

Jenkins and his friend screwed up their faces in disdain but were smart enough to keep their mouths shut. Crowley pushed them back to the group as the guide was finishing up her talk.

"No matter what superstitions and stories are told around subjects like these," she said with a smile, "here at the Natural History Museum we focus as much as we can on facts. But check the information panels by the exhibits as there are some fascinating stories that *have* been corroborated and are well worth your time."

"You've all got fifteen minutes," Crowley called out, his strident voice ringing in the large space. "Do not leave this area and we'll gather by the blue whale at exactly eleven forty-five. Off you go. Try to learn something!"

The students drifted away in their cliques and groups, chattering about anything except the exhibition and what they had just heard. Crowley approached the guide, offered her a warm smile. "Thanks very much. Great talk." He saw her name badge read Rose Black. She noticed him glancing at her chest and he quickly lifted his eyes, offered his hand to shake. "You're Rose," he said lamely, trying to explain why he had been looking down. "I'm Jake Crowley."

She flashed that subtle half-smile again, and shook his hand. Her touch was soft and warm, a tingle of something quickly passing between them. Or was that just wishful thinking on his part? "Nice to meet you, Jake." She nodded back toward the milling students. "I'm really never sure how much attention any of them pay."

Crowley was pleased she had smoothly changed the subject from his embarrassment. "You know what, the ones who are genuinely interested take it all in quietly and the others do tend to absorb more than you might imagine. Either way, this is a particularly interesting special exhibit. I never realized there was such a history to something as simple as birthmarks!"

Rose nodded and glanced around the space. "They're anything but simple, really, in a historical context. And as part of the greater history of human biology they've had some interesting effects on society."

"You have any birthmarks of your own you're hiding?" Crowley asked, and instantly felt like a fool. Who was the idiot teenager here really?

A strange expression flitted across her face, partly concern, partly curiosity. Then that soft smile was back. "You know, you should at least buy me dinner before asking a question like that."

Relief flooded Crowley that she wasn't offended and he took a deep breath and dove all the way in. Fortune favors the bold and all that. "That's a tremendous idea," he said. "It's a date. Are you free tonight?"

CHAPTER 3

Rose Black watched Jake Crowley head off across the restaurant floor toward the bar. He cut a tall, strong figure through the crowd as he went. She leaned back on the sumptuous red vinyl couch under arched white ceilings, pleasantly full from a fine dinner. It was strange furniture for a restaurant, one long couch shared by several tables, with curved wooden chairs on the other side. But the place had a great vibe, the food was good, the cocktails excellent. Crowley knew how to pick a place for a first date.

She watched the people eating and talking and laughing. One couple sat deep in a serious conversation that had all the hallmarks of a break-up while another couple, only two tables away, stared into each other's eyes, lost in the early throes of all-encompassing love. The rich variety of life endlessly fascinated Rose. Crowley returned only a minute later with two drinks and sat in the pale tan chair opposite her.

"Told you it would be quicker than trying to catch the waiter's eye again," he said, handing her a tall, condensing glass of caprioska, ice rattling against the rim. "They've got really busy all of a sudden." He raised his bottle of Corona beer in a toast.

She clinked, took a sip, enjoying the sweet sugar and tart lime behind the taste of good vodka. She'd developed a taste for the drink several years ago while dating a Brazilian. These days she drank it long, with soda water. "It is busy. I'm surprised we got a table on such short notice."

Crowley grinned. "I know people."

"Really?"

"Yeah, it's true actually. Nothing very exciting. The head chef is an old army buddy and always gets me in. But I rarely have reason to take him up on the offer."

Rose could see the military bearing in Crowley's demeanor; he wore his strength and confidence plainly but without pride or swagger. "Were you in the army long?"

"Long enough. Quit after my second stint in Afghanistan."

Rose frowned. "You must have seen some pretty terrible

stuff."

"Yeah. Most of it best forgotten, if only that were possible. But it's okay, you know. A lot of guys really suffer with it, but I'm all right. In many ways I was pretty lucky, in service and out."

"So why did you decide to leave?"

Crowley pursed his lips, thoughtful for a moment. "The real truth is that I probably shouldn't have joined in the first place. My dad was a soldier, in the SAS, a real hero. But he was killed in the Falklands War in eighty-two, while my mother was pregnant with me, so I never knew him outside the stories everyone told me."

That cut somewhere deep in Rose's heart. "That sucks."

Crowley shrugged. "Yeah, but it's all I've ever known. The army was great to my mum. Afterwards, I was raised by her and my grandmother, my father's mother, I was well looked after. I always idolized my dad, had his picture in my room in his uniform, all that stuff. I knew I was going to follow in his footsteps. Quit school first chance I got and signed up, pushed through. I was a good soldier. Started working my way toward the SAS and was about to move into it when I had this... I guess it was a revelation."

"It wasn't what you really wanted after all?"

"Exactly. I was doing it all for my dad, which was fine, but I had issues with the government, with the tight discipline, with the things we were being ordered to do. I saw things in Afghanistan that made me realize I was doing the wrong thing. Wrong for me anyway."

Rose sipped her drink, smiled. "So you became a history teacher."

Crowley laughed. He had an open, honest smile, no artifice. She liked that. "Not right away. I was in my mid-twenties when I demobbed, young and stupid, full of freedom and irresponsibility. I ran into a few London hoodlums, got into some dodgy stuff. Nothing really terrible, but when I nearly ended up in prison, I stopped and had a hard look at myself. I've always loved history. War taught me that people make the same mistakes over and over again because they refuse to learn from what went before. So I went to college, trained up as a teacher, and here I am."

Rose lifted her glass in another toast. "You're a smart and driven man, Jake Crowley. Good for you. You'll have to tell me about your dodgy hoodlum days some time."

"Let's save that for another date." He grinned cheekily.

She flicked her eyebrows up, unable to resist toying with him. "We'll have to see how this one goes first."

He actually blushed a little. "You're pretty smart yourself; a historian." He was clearly trying hard to change the subject.

She decided not to feel bad about embarrassing him. He was a big boy. "But not nearly so interesting."

"I bet that's not true. What's your story?"

She laughed. "I'll give you the short version. My mother emigrated from Guangzhou with her parents when she was only a child, so that side of my family is very traditional Chinese. Mum married a London taxi driver, about as London as you can get, in fact, much to her parents chagrin, so that side of my upbringing is as English as it's possible to be. I grew up loving it all, went to university reading history and ancient cultures, got a job at the Natural History Museum, then you asked me out for dinner."

Crowley laughed again. "Man, that really is an abridged history. There must be a lot more to you than that."

She smiled softly. "Maybe I'll tell you on another date." Before he could reply, she added, "Assuming this one goes well."

"You're mean."

Rose checked her phone for the time, saw it was getting late. "I've really enjoyed tonight. I'm glad we had dinner. But I have an early start tomorrow."

Crowley's face twisted in genuine disappointment. "I suppose that's fair enough." He gave her that cheeky grin once more. "Can I call you again?"

"You have my number."

"Ah, maybe you're not so mean after all."

He caught the waiter's eye and mouthed, *The bill, please?* The waiter nodded and slipped away between the tables.

"You going to let me pay for half?" Rose asked. She didn't mind being treated to dinner, but equally she wanted to make no assumptions.

"If you insist, I won't be obtuse about it, but it would make me happy if you'd let me pay. I was the one who asked you out."

Rose tipped her head in acquiescence. "You're very kind, thanks. Maybe I'll get the next one."

Crowley grinned. "You have my number."

Outside the restaurant, Crowley looked up and down the busy King's Road. "Loads of traffic and not many cabs, like usual."

She frowned, mock outrage. "Don't let my dad hear you bad-mouthing the great London black cab!"

"I wouldn't think of it! But there are none right now, so you want me to wait with you?"

Rose shook her head. "I only live about a twenty minute walk away, just near Fulham Broadway. I'll enjoy the exercise. Especially after a big meal like that."

Crowley's brow creased in concern. "If you're sure…"

Rose jabbed one forefinger playfully into his chest. "Don't get a savior complex on me now. I can run fast and I've got a few years of Muay Thai under my belt. I'm more than capable of walking through Chelsea, mister!"

Crowley's frown melted into that honest smile. "Yeah, not exactly Kabul under fire, is it?"

"Not until the weekend, anyway." She pushed onto the balls of her feet and planted a quick kiss on his cheek. "It's been great, thanks."

"I'll call you."

"Look forward to it."

She turned and headed off down King's Road. She could feel Crowley's eyes on her as she went and smiled softly to herself, refusing to look back. Let him enjoy watching her leave. She was unsure how she really felt about him and was certainly in no place, mentally, to think about a relationship with anyone, not so soon after the debacle with Alison. But Crowley was an intriguing guy and she wasn't lying when she said she was looking forward to him calling her again. No point in over-thinking things now. Just let events unfold as they will.

She breathed deeply of London's unique aroma. It was often fairly horrible, sometimes nothing but exhaust fumes, but as the evening wore on it gained that quiet, resting scent of a city settling down to sleep. Not that London ever really slept, of course, but as the night wore on and most people found their beds, it revealed a little more of its true self. All cities had something unique about them in that sense. Hong Kong in particular held something special in Rose's heart, more even than her birthplace of Guangzhou. It had been too long since she'd been back for a visit. Much as she loved London, maybe it was time to set wings to her heels again and travel. She had some leave owing, so perhaps a few weeks off, take the long way around to Guangzhou via somewhere tropical and then Hong Kong before visiting her grandparents and extended family.

A hand closed over her upper arm with painful tightness and dragged her sideways into a shadowed alleyway. She began to cry out, but the assailant's other hand closed over her mouth and clamped the scream in. Two more men stood in the alley and the one who held her turned her to face them and wrapped his arm around her chest, pressing her back against his chest. His other hand remained over her mouth. The two waiting men stepped forward and Rose's anger surged up from her gut like a red wave, battling with sudden fear for supremacy. But terrified or not, no way would she take this assault without a fight.

She hadn't lied about her training. After so many taunts at school – *You're half Chinese, do you know half Kung Fu?* – she had eschewed martial arts until a friend a few years ago had got her into Muay Thai. It was a great supplement to her regular soccer playing and gym sessions. These guys had picked on the wrong girl.

She lifted one knee and drove a front kick hard into one attacker's stomach and, as he grunted and doubled over, she drove backwards against the guy holding her. She slammed him hard against the alley's filthy wall, got a satisfying whoosh of air out of him, but he didn't let go. She freed an arm and swung a punch at the third man as he closed in, scored a glancing blow across his cheek that made him take a step back, his eyes widening in fury in the shadows of his hooded jacket. She drove her elbow back into the gut of the man holding her and he lost his air again. This time he did loosen his grip and she pushed herself away, only to land in the grasp of the man she'd kicked.

She swung more punches and elbows, felt several satisfying impacts, but the odds were against her. Three strong men outgunned her fury and whatever training she could call upon. One of them grabbed at her short black denim jacket and hauled up the back of it.

"This is her!" the man said. "Hold her down!"

Panic washed fresh through Rose and she screamed out, her voice high and terrified.

"Shut her up!" the first attacker said, and then he grunted in pain and staggered sideways.

Crowley, his face a mask of righteous anger, sprang into the space between Rose and her attackers, knocking the men left and right with a flurry of punches.

The arms holding Rose slipped away and before that man could engage Crowley, she spun around and delivered her hardest kick across his leg, then threw a punch as he stumbled to one knee. Her punch missed and the man staggered up and backed away.

"Abort!" he yelled. "Abort!"

The other two attackers pushed back from Crowley, and all three ran back to the mouth of the alley, the one she'd kicked limping badly.

"Get back here, you bawbags!" Crowley yelled and made to give chase.

Still limping, the one Rose had kicked, drew a pistol from his pocket. The weak lamplight from the street gleamed on its surface, anodized a malevolent black. "You two ready to die?"

Crowley stopped, held both palms up facing the gun. Rose marveled at his bravery as he stepped between her and the attacker. "Be calm," Crowley said, his rage gone, his voice instantly level and calm. "Just leave us alone."

The man nodded. He and his companions disappeared out onto the busy street and hurried away. Crowley watched them go, then took one tentative step forward.

"Don't follow them, Jake," Rose said. She couldn't bear the thought of him getting hurt after they had been left alone. "Let them go."

He turned to her, brow creased in concern. "Are you okay?"

She took a deep breath and paused to consider the question. Despite the odds, she was unhurt. Shocked, scared, a little disheveled, hands and elbows slightly bruised from blows she'd struck, but essentially uninjured. "Yes, I'm fine. Thanks to you. Good thing you came along." She raised her eyebrows in speculation. "Were you stalking me?" She added a smile to show she was teasing.

Crowley smiled sheepishly. "You left and I realized I needed to go the same way as you to get the Tube. I didn't want to seem creepy, like I was following you, so I let you get a head start then made my way along. Thankfully I didn't wait too long, I heard you scream and came running."

"Did you know it was me?"

"No, but I could tell someone was in trouble."

Rose tucked her shirt back in and pulled her jacket straight.

She gingerly touched the knuckles of her right hand and winced. "Guy had a hard face."

Crowley nodded, a slight smile that she took for respect tugging at his lips. "Everyone does really. You handled yourself well."

Rose flexed her hand and realized it was shaking. "I've never had any kind of actual fight before. Not in the real world, anyway." Her stomach churned and her knees began to shake.

Crowley closed the distance between them and rested a hand on her shoulder. "There's a bench just out there on the footpath. Let's have a seat while the shock and adrenaline settles down, yeah?"

She nodded. "Good idea."

He guided her out into the streetlight and sat beside her. "And then maybe I should walk you home after all?"

She patted his hand gratefully. "Also a good idea. Thanks."

CHAPTER 4

Landvik leaned back in his expensive leather chair, letting it knock back against the huge mahogany desk as his eyes roamed the gray stone buildings and roofs opposite, visible through the large, multi-paned sash window. Dates and Latin names were engraved into the fascia of the buildings opposite, finely carved statuary stood in curved alcoves watching over the red and white lights of traffic busily moving to and fro through the night below. The hiss and rumble of a red double-decker bus drifted up to him as he ran a well-manicured hand over his ash blond hair, down over a neatly-trimmed salt and pepper beard.

He sighed. What was taking so long?

As if in answer, the phone on his desk vibrated in the quiet gloom of the otherwise deserted office. The tall man turned his chair around and snatched up the phone, tapped the answer button.

The voice on the other end was tight, breathless. "Mr. Landvik, it's Jeffries. You were right; she's definitely the one we're looking for."

Landvik sighed and shook his head. "So, bring her in."

"Well, there's a bit of a problem there."

Landvik pinched the bridge of his nose, closed his eyes. "A problem? You don't have her?"

"She fought back at first, but that was no problem, but then some guy came running to her rescue. Big bugger, he was, good fighter. Things were getting loud and messy, so I called the abort and we got out of there before we attracted any more attention. It was just bad luck, really. Before that guy intervened we had it all under control."

"Stop talking, Jeffries." Landvik took a deep breath and calmed himself while he considered.

"Yes, sir," Jeffries said, instantly disobeying the direct order.

Thankfully all Landvik heard after that was Jeffries' labored breathing. There was an edge of pain to it, and Landvik took some pleasure in that.

"This man who intervened, do you think he was some random white knight or someone she knew?"

"Actually, it was a guy she'd just had dinner with. She walked off on her own, so we took our shot. He must have followed her."

"Inconvenient."

"Yes, sir."

Landvik considered this turn of events. "Have you managed to establish where she lives?"

"Ah, no," Jeffries admitted. "She took a taxi from the museum to the restaurant, so we decided to grab her as she walked."

Landvik nodded to himself. It was a mess, but far from a lost cause. There were always hiccups in life and the trick was to move with them rather than let events control the situation. "So find out where she lives," he told Jeffries in a slow, measured voice. "If she's not there, grab her when she arrives at the museum for work tomorrow. This is only a short delay, yes?"

"Yes, sir. No problem."

"One way or another, I want you to bring Rose Black to me in one piece. And soon."

"So that last bloke wasn't the one?" Jeffries asked.

Landvik let out a harsh exhale. "Just find her."

CHAPTER 5

Crowley stood by the front door of Rose's flat. "So you're safely home."

Rose nodded. She still trembled and he didn't blame her. He was still buzzing as well. "Don't leave just yet?" Her tone framed it as a question, but she sounded a little desperate. Scared. And understandably so.

"I'm happy to stick around for a while."

She put her key in the lock and pushed the door open. Crowley followed her as she flicked on the lights and closed the door behind him. Her flat was bright and tidy, a polished rosewood table in one corner, red and white floral settee and armchairs facing a large television. It was roomy for a one-bedroom place, with doors leading off the main room to a kitchen, bathroom, and bedroom.

"I think I really need a shower," Rose said. "Wash that whole experience off me, you know? Can you stick around until I'm done?"

"As long as you like."

She gave him a grateful smile, dropped her light jacket onto an armchair, and went into the bathroom. He caught a glimpse of firm, smooth flesh as she peeled her shirt up before disappearing from sight. Crowley pushed away the thoughts that immediately arose, unbidden and inappropriate.

He wandered her living room. A couple of large images hung on one wall, slatted bamboo tied into a flat canvas for Chinese watercolors. One showed a red and white crane beside a waterfall, the other a stylized depiction of Zhangjiajie National Forest Park. Crowley smirked, shook his head. He couldn't believe he still remembered that name, but after seeing a documentary on the area of sharp peaks and deep forests he became mesmerized and researched it. One day he planned to take a vacation there. One day.

Pictures on the mantelpiece caught his eye. One showed Rose with two people who must be her parents, a small, determined-looking Chinese woman with kindly eyes and a tall man, dark-haired and slim-featured, with laugh lines at his mouth and eyes. They looked like a happy family. Not far from it was another photo showing a teenage Rose with her parents and another young girl. The family resemblance was readily apparent; it had to be Rose's sister. No other images of the girl were anywhere he could see. He wondered what the story might be there. Other photos showed her parents much younger on their wedding day, Rose with friends, Rose on a sleek red motorcycle. Crowley tried to imagine Rose riding the powerful machine rather than just posing on it and the possibility came easily. Maybe something else to talk about. He had often planned to take his test and get a bike, but had yet to get around to it.

He went into the kitchen and found the kettle, teabags, milk and sugar. He brewed two mugs of hot, sweet tea, the English panacea for all forms of shock and trauma. As he was stirring the sugar in, Rose emerged trailing a cloud of steam. Her hair was wet, flattened to her head and neck, her skin rouged with the heat of her shower. She pulled the rope belt of a towelling robe tight around her waist and smiled.

"Wow! A street fighter and a mind-reader!"

"I made it sweet," Crowley said. He hefted the carton. "You want milk?"

"No, thanks. Black and sweet is good."

She wrapped her hands around the mug and breathed in the steam first, sighed, and took a sip. "Thank you."

"Tea I'm good at. Just don't ask me to cook you a meal." Crowley added milk to his and took a gulp. The burning sensation in his throat and chest felt good.

"No, I mean thank you for everything. It terrifies me to think what might have happened if you hadn't come by." She nodded to a chair and sat in the other one herself.

As Crowley took his seat he said, "You'll torture yourself with what ifs. It's lucky I came along, but you weren't doing too badly for yourself."

"Not well enough. They had me beat."

He grimaced. "Yeah. But three strong guys is bad odds for anyone."

They fell into silence for a while, sipping their tea and staring at nothing in particular. The slow, drudging release of adrenaline felt familiar to Crowley, but he doubted it was anything with which Rose was well acquainted. "Don't be surprised if you feel a bit sick," he said. "The shock might make you nauseated."

She tipped her head toward the bathroom. "I nearly threw up in there, but it didn't quite happen." She lifted the mug. "This helps."

"Nectar of the gods."

They were silent again for a moment, and then Rose said, "Do you think they wanted to rape me? Kill me? They didn't seem to be robbing me."

The haunted, beseeching look in her eyes pained him. "No idea. Some people are broken inside, you know? I do wonder why they came after you. Maybe just a random choice?"

She made a noise that was almost a laugh, almost a curse. "I didn't have time to ask them, but I'll be sure to check next time." She threw him a crooked smile to show she wasn't being mean.

"Maybe you don't need to know. Best not to dwell on it."

"Hell of an impression for a first date," she said. "I'm not likely to forget this night."

Crowley made his eyes wide in mock outrage. "For all the wrong reasons! I'd hope to have made an impression without a potential... whatever that was."

"You did make a good impression, only more so after that." A strange look passed over her face, her words fading to quiet.

"What is it?"

"I just remembered something. One of them said 'This is her', like they knew me."

"How could they know you?"

She frowned, thinking, staring into her mug. Shook her head. "No, not like they *knew* me. One of them dragged up the back of my jacket and I thought they were going to pull my clothes off, to... you know. But then he said, 'This is her. Hold her down.'" She turned a quizzical look to Crowley. "Any idea what that meant?"

A chill rippled along Crowley's spine, the supposedly random attack suddenly seeming like anything but. "What might they have been looking for? Or seen? You got a tattoo back there or something?" He raised a hand. "Sorry, don't mean to get personal or pry."

Rose's mouth twisted in concern and confusion, a strangely vulnerable expression. "Not a tattoo, no." She stood, turned her back to him, and lowered the bathrobe.

CHAPTER 6

Crowley swallowed, wondering what he was about to see. Rose's smooth, lightly tanned shoulders gave way to a firmly muscled upper back. But as the robe reached halfway down her body, Crowley's attention was completely absorbed by the distinctive birthmark. A blood red line, maybe an inch wide with slightly undulating edges, ran down her spinal column and disappeared into the folds of the robe a hand's breadth or two above the swell of her hips. Almost at the top of the vertical mark a wavering horizontal line came off of each side, making a double downward-facing L pointing left and right, slightly rounded at the top.

"Wow," Crowley muttered, a little lost for words. He swallowed. "It looks a bit like…"

"An ugly eagle?" Rose slipped her robe back up and over her shoulders, to Crowley's subtle disappointment. "Pretty disgusting, huh?"

Crowley shook his head as she sat back down and faced him. "Not at all. It's quite beautiful, really, sort of like a stylized tattoo."

Rose sipped her tea again, looked away. "I call it my Blood Eagle after the Viking form of torture."

"Viking torture?"

She laughed quietly. "Aren't you the history teacher?"

"True." Crowley tried to sort through all the Viking lore and legend he knew from the syllabus, but no particular forms of torture were forthcoming. "You'll have to educate me on this one though."

She nodded. "You haven't watched the TV show?"

"*Vikings*? No, but people tell me I should."

"It's pretty good. They showed the blood eagle torture once. It's about as grim as it gets. The victim is tied with their arms out to either side, usually on their knees. Someone slices them open along the spine, makes two cuts sideways and opens the flesh out to either side exposing the back of the ribcage."

"Holy crap," Crowley muttered.

"That's not even half of it." She grinned at him. "Then they use an ax to hack the ribs away from the spine, lift out the lungs and lay them on the victim's shoulders like eagle wings. Hence the name. If the victim survives the pain and shock, they suffocate once the lungs are moved."

Crowley grimaced. "Let me guess. You love slasher films."

"No, actually. Hate them. But I love history." She made a cheeky face.

Crowley chuckled and lifted his mug in gesture of defeat. "Fair call." He logged away the information for future reference. He would study up on the practice and see where he might fit it into his lesson plans. Nothing like a bit of gore to get the teenagers' attention.

His mind wandered back to the issue at hand. "But how does the birthmark matter? And how would anyone know you have it?"

Rose shook her head, lips pursed. "No idea. It's not something I make public. Beyond my family and those who have seen me naked, no one really knows. I've always worn one-piece bathing suits rather than bikinis, because I'm a little self-conscious about it in public."

"I guess I can understand that, but you really don't need to be. It's kinda fascinating."

"I don't really want to be fascinating to people."

"Yeah, right. Sorry. I can understand that too."

She smiled. "That's okay." Her eyes widened. "I just remembered something else. I went to a birthmark removal clinic last year for a consultation, but they told me nothing could be done. I wonder if there's a connection there. When I heard about the possibility, I thought it might be worth checking out, though I didn't really have much hope."

"Why did you..?" Crowley stopped, didn't finish his sentence when he realized there wasn't a way to phrase it that didn't sound insulting.

Rose laughed. "You mean why didn't I care until I was almost thirty?"

Crowley shrugged. He'd actually been about to ask why she decided to get it removed at all, and decided it was none of his business. But she did make an interesting point. "I don't mean to pry," he said.

"It's embarrassing to admit," Rose said. "But I did it for a girlfriend."

A quick wave of disappointment washed over Crowley, with swirling crests of confusion. "Oh," was all he could manage. "Right."

"It was my first relationship with a woman. Her name was Alison. I kind of lost myself in it."

Crowley was embarrassed to realize that his disappointment had already transformed to relief. She described a situation that didn't preclude him and he was quite pleased about that. He shook himself mentally, throwing the thoughts away. It made no difference right now that she was attracted to men and he was a man sitting right here with her. The poor woman had just been attacked and the reasons for it were becoming potentially more sinister by the moment. "I guess I can understand that as well," he said, for wont of something to say.

"You're an understanding guy. Anyway, you don't want to hear my life story." Rose stood. "Give me a minute."

She disappeared into the bedroom and Crowley finished his tea while he waited. Her mug was empty, so he took them both to the kitchen, rinsed them, and turned them upside down on the draining board. Military training and neatness was encoded into his habits whether he liked it or not.

As he returned to his seat, Rose reappeared in a yoga pants and a baggy sweat top, carrying a laptop. Crowley sat quietly while she booted it up and tapped away for a few moments.

"The clinic was called The Holm Institute," she said, forehead creasing in a frown as she read.

Crowley leaned forward, concerned by her expression. "What is it?"

"Found an article here. It says the clinic recently had a data breach."

Crowley paused to think about that. "So if these guys are looking for you because of your birthmark, and they decided to hack into the records of a clinic that deals with birthmarks, they could have found your details there."

"But why are they so interested in my birthmark?"

"I don't know. Maybe for now, that's not the relevant issue. It seems they are, and we need to know who they are first and foremost. If they're likely to…" Crowley stopped, tipped his head to one side. Rose opened her mouth to speak and he held up one index finger to delay her.

Hairs tickled on the back of Crowley's neck. Not only

neatness was coded into his being, but awareness too. Years of training and months on the front lines of wars had hardened his senses into a state of sharp focus, something he couldn't turn off. He raised one finger, catching Rose's eye. She froze, her mouth opening slightly in fear.

A slight shadow moved in the line of light under the front door, the soft squeak of a shoe on the tiles outside, as of someone being deliberately sneaky in the hallway beyond. But not sneaky enough.

Crowley lowered his voice to a whisper. "Someone's out there."

CHAPTER 7

Crowley crept toward the front door, silent on Rose's carpet. A small wooden rack sat near the wall with a selection of footwear in two neat rows. He lifted a pair of sneakers, handed them over, and made a gentle *hurry up* gesture. Eyes wide with fear, Rose quickly put them on and tied the laces.

As she worked, Crowley put an ear to the door. Hushed voices outside murmured, but too quietly for him to hear the words. The tone was all intent and tight purpose. More than enough for Crowley to decide he wasn't being paranoid.

"Is there another way out?" he asked, his voice pitched low.

Rose was already on her feet. She grabbed her bag, slung it bandolier-style across her chest, and pointed to the kitchen. She headed for it and Crowley hurried after her. A small white table stood against one wall, opposite a stove, fridge and sink. Beside the table was a door. Rose reached for the handle just as a loud bang from the front room shattered the tension. Rose yelped in surprise as her front door slammed back against wall.

A man's voice, harsh and loud, barked out. "Nobody move!"

At the same moment, Crowley yelled, "Run!" and spun back to face the intruders.

He was pleased to hear Rose pull the back door open as he grabbed one of the white wooden chairs from beside the kitchen table.

"Come on!" Rose said, her voice strained with panic.

Crowley judged his timing as well as he could. "I'm coming!" Then he ran at the kitchen door, holding the chair out in front of himself like a lion tamer. His timing was good, meeting the intruder right in the kitchen doorway. The chair legs rammed into the man's arm, chest and face and Crowley threw his weight behind it, sent the intruder stumbling over backwards with a yelp of pain. The pistol in his hand boomed, but the bullet went high, bit a chunk of plaster from the wall above the cooker. Crowley slammed the kitchen door closed to buy them seconds, then bolted after Rose, slamming the back door behind him too.

Rose was already halfway down the cool gray concrete steps of the rear stairwell. Crowley hammered after her.

"Did he get you?" Rose called back. "Are you hurt?"

"I'm fine. He missed."

They swung on the banister to make the turn at the next floor at top speed when a bead of light appeared at the kitchen door of the flat below Rose's. Crowley didn't even pause. He ran at the wood, pushed it wide as he grabbed Rose by one arm and hauled her back to bring her with him.

A middle-aged man in a pale blue turban stumbled back into his kitchen, face crumpling into outrage.

"Don't make a sound!" Crowley said, injecting as much pleading into his voice as he could. He closed the man's door. "Lock that! Stay silent."

The sound of Rose's own back door came from above, banging back and echoing in the bare stairway. The turbaned man hurriedly locked his door, but Crowley was already moving, puling Rose along.

"We're so sorry!" Rose said as she stumbled past the shocked resident.

She shook her arm free, ran close behind Crowley as they crossed the living room and Crowley pulled open the front door. They hurried out, Crowley throwing a last apologetic look back to the turbaned man, who stood with his mouth open in stunned confusion. Crowley quietly closed the man's front door and Rose pointed to another door at the end of the hallway.

"Front stairs!" she said.

He nodded and followed, pleased she was so self-assured, so focused. She was clearly not the type to panic, immediately seeing his plan in the man's flat, working with him smartly, pointing out stairs rather than running for the elevator. As they hurried down the stairs, Crowley nervously glanced up, hoping the intruders didn't have anyone else in the building, waiting out front of Rose's flat. He'd seen at least one other man inside as he'd attacked with the chair, but there had been three in the alley. Could there be another one up there? Or outside on the street?

They flew down level after level, taking two or three steps at a time, using the bannister for control. Crowley followed Rose, marveled at her pace and athleticism. She looked good, sure-footed at every turn.

"Where do the back stairs come out?" he asked.

"Alleyway, other side of the block. Bins and stuff back there."

"So if they go all the way down, they'll have to come right around the building to catch up?"

"Right. There's a laneway almost directly opposite the front of this building. When we get out, run hard straight for it." Rose allowed herself a glance back. "You won't outrun me, so go hard. It'll take us directly away from them."

He saw fear in her eyes, but there was a fire of determination too. "You got it."

They barreled out of the stairway, across the lobby and burst out of the front doors. Crowley braced for a fight, quickly scanning left and right for the possible third attacker, but no one waited for them. A couple walking hand in hand on the footpath jumped aside, startled, as Crowley and Rose pounded across the street between a slowly moving red bus and a white panel van coming the other way. A heavyset, shaven-headed man leaned out of the van window to yell abuse as they sprinted away, zigging left and right to enter the laneway Rose had mentioned.

Crowley glanced back and saw no one in pursuit, then picked up his pace as Rose streaked away from him. She really did have a hell of a turn of speed. He wondered if maybe she was right when she said he wouldn't be able to outrun her. He'd taken it for rhetoric, but had to smile at the truth of her words.

The lane was mostly dark and they hammered through pools of wan light under small streetlights, then came out onto a much larger, well-lit street. Traffic was a little heavier, but no pedestrians traveled the footpath.

"Ease up," Crowley called. "I'm pretty sure we've lost them."

Rose slowed to a jog, but kept moving. Crowley respected that and ran along beside her.

"What now?" she asked.

"Well, those guys are clearly determined to get their hands on you."

She looked over at him, fear stamped on her features. "Those were the same guys from the alley?"

He nodded, put a hand briefly on her shoulder as they jogged. "It was. I'm sorry."

"So I ask again, what now?"

Crowley thought for a moment. "Well, you can't risk going

anywhere you would normally go. If they found your home they could potentially find anywhere else connected to you. For now, you'd better come back to my place. We'll settle down and figure out what to do next."

Rose nodded, then stepped up to the curb and waved at a black cab coming along the street, the light on its roof bright in the night. The cab pulled over and they climbed in, slumped gasping beside each other on the back seat. Crowley gave the driver his address in Deptford and the man gave them a brief salute over the back of his seat and pulled away.

Two burly men stood at the end of the alleyway behind Rose Black's block of flats and turned left and right, looking up and down the intersecting road. One of the men swore elaborately, slammed his fist into a wooden fence beside him, then shook the hand in pain and frustration.

"I can't believe they got away again!"

The other man shook his head, pocketed his small revolver. "Damn it, Jeffries, I told you we should have brought more men."

Jeffries turned on him. "Well, Patterson's knee is messed up from where that bitch kicked him earlier and there wasn't time to call in anyone else."

The two men stood indecisive for a moment, then Jeffries spat and stalked around the building, heading for their car parked half a block away out front. "Walter, we can't tell Landvik she got away again."

Walter followed, caught up in a few quick strides. "You're right there. He was mad enough already, yeah?"

"Cold fury," Jeffries agreed. "Really quiet and still, like, you know?"

Walter smirked. "Yeah. I know."

"Who the hell is that guy who keeps saving her?" Jeffries asked through gritted teeth.

"I don't know, but he's really starting to make me angry. We need to find out." Walter pulled a phone from his pocket, dialed a number. After a moment, he said, "Dean? It's Walter Brown. I'm here with Rob. No, we didn't get her. That bloody hero got in our way again and they legged it."

He paused listening. Then, "Well, I'll tell you exactly why I'm ringing you. I don't care how much your knee hurts, we have to find out who Rose Black's man friend is and we have to find out as much about him as we think we know about Rose."

There was the sound of a raised voice at the other end. Jeffries reached out. "Give me that." Brown handed it over and Jeffries slammed it to his ear. "You listen to me, Patterson. We need to get both these renegades in hand very quickly or a sore knee will be the least of your problems. Landvik will be wearing very personal parts of our anatomies as jewelry if we don't deliver them soon. So get dressed. We're picking you up in ten minutes."

CHAPTER 8

Holm Institute Laser Therapy Clinic, Dulwich Village

Rose walked along the main street of Dulwich Village, enjoying the sunshine and bustle of daytime after the threats and violence of the night before. Low rise brown brick buildings, wide footpaths and welcoming shops lined either side of the road, the area far more suburban than the tall, cramped city of London, yet only a twenty minute cab ride from Crowley's narrow Deptford townhouse.

Arriving at his place the night before, well after midnight, exhausted and nauseated from adrenaline, it had seemed like her life was irrevocably altered. And while that might still be the case, at least the light of day and pleasant tree-lined pavements did something to inject hope back into her thoughts.

Spending the night at Crowley's had been weird. The man was the next thing to a complete stranger, but Rose liked him. Trusted him. He was every bit a decent guy and had actually saved her arse twice. Then opened up his home to her. His place was neat and ordered, something of military precision about the sparseness, but it was homely nonetheless. He had two rooms upstairs, one a decent-sized bedroom, the other a study with a fold-out sofa bed. He had insisted she take his queen-sized comfort and he opened up the sofa bed for himself. She was sure she wouldn't be able to sleep, but once ensconced into the comfort of sheets and quilt, exhaustion had won out and she'd fallen into a deep, dreamless sleep.

Crowley woke her the next morning with tea and toast, offered her anything else she might want: coffee, eggs, cereal. He apologized for his lack of other breakfast choices. Rose smiled at the memory. He was a strange guy, hard and strong, but somehow vulnerable and nervous too. She had to admit it was almost certainly because he had taken a fancy to her, and she didn't really mind that. She certainly appreciated that he hadn't tried to act on it in any way, that he remained the perfect gentleman.

After eating and showering, she insisted that Crowley go to work, she would be fine. He tried to head her off, offer more help, but she pressed her case. Reluctantly he agreed, after ensuring she would contact him at the slightest hint of trouble. He offered to drop her off at the clinic, but she waved that off too and caught a cab after ringing the museum and calling in sick. She assured them it was only a virus or something and she should be back in a day or two. She desperately hoped that was true, though something made her think it really wasn't. Regardless, for the time being, she needed to be back in control, at least for a little while. Grateful as she was for his help, Rose wanted to feel like her own hand steered her ship for now.

She paused in the dappled shade of a flowering cherry tree outside a clothing store, tipped her face up to the late summer sun filtering between the green leaves. The air was still redolent with traffic fumes and refuse, but not nearly so strongly as it was in the city. She could smell the trees and various aromas of baking and cooking too. Much as she enjoyed life in Fulham, she often yearned to move somewhere a little more suburban like this, south of the river. More than an hour on two or three trains to get to work and back was less appealing. Her parents regularly hassled her to move nearer to them in Bromley, even further south. That would only make her journey to work more like an hour and a half on trains.

She shook her head gently, looked around. All this suburban speculation was no doubt born of the stress from the night before. Moving out of the city was unlikely to move her away from whatever violent men were chasing her, however much she fantasized. She needed to find out just what was going on.

Another hundred yards' walk led her to the front door of the Holm Institute Laser Therapy Clinic. It seemed like any other unassuming shopfront along the street, but was clinically bright and clean inside, modern and sharply decorated. A young blonde with a million watt smile sat behind a brushed aluminum reception desk.

"Good morning. How can I help you?"

Rose returned the smile, though hers dimmed in the presence of the effervescent receptionist. "I'd like a quick word with Doctor Zochowska if I may? I saw her last year and just wanted to follow something up."

"The doctor is in this morning. Just give me a moment to see if she's available. Your name?"

"Rose Black."

The blonde nodded, gestured to a series of white leather chairs along the window, dappled in light from a wide venetian blind.

Rose took a seat, thumbed through a glossy copy of *Country Living* magazine, shook her head at the ostentatious claims on the cover of the *House and Garden* magazine next on the pile. The receptionist murmured quietly into her telephone for a moment, then turned her smile back to Rose.

"The Doctor will be out in a moment, Ms. Black."

"Thank you."

It took a few more minutes for Zochowska to appear, but when she did she looked exactly as Rose remembered. Small, thin, severe angular features, ash-gray hair pulled back in what had to be a painfully tight pony-tail. She wore a white lab coat over a navy blue skirt and suit jacket. But for all her austere appearance, Rose remembered her as a warm and friendly woman.

"Miss Black." Zochowska offered a hand and shook with friendly firmness. "Good to see you again. I'm sorry we couldn't help you before. What brings you back?"

"I just had a few questions." Rose frowned, suddenly not sure where to begin.

Zochowska waved a hand back the way she had come. "Let's go into my office and sit down."

Once the office door was closed and Zochowska returned to her desk, Rose took a deep breath. Maybe start a little more generally. "Have you treated anyone else with a distinctive birthmark like mine?"

Zochowska's eyebrows rose. "Miss Black, lots of patients have distinctive birthmarks. But obviously I can't discuss them with you, or anyone, for confidentiality reasons."

Rose had expected an answer like that, but pressed on regardless. "But have you seen anyone with a birthmark like mine? You remember the eagle shape of mine, the size of it?"

"I remember it very well, Miss Black, and I have records of our consultations, but I simply can't discuss other patients with anyone."

Frustration boiled up in Rose, her volume rising with it. "Doctor, please, it's very important. Has anyone come to the clinic asking about a birthmark like mine?"

"Even if they had, I couldn't tell you. There are confidentiality rules and laws, Miss Black."

"Didn't confidentiality go out the window with the well-publicized data breach you guys had?" Rose realized she was shouting, her frustration giving way to fear that the men on her tail would catch up again, that she would have no further information, nowhere to turn. She had to learn something, find some way to protect herself.

Doctor Zochowska stood half out of her seat, shocked and surprised by Rose's outburst, her expression wide with concern. "Miss Black, please calm down. I would help if I could, but my hands are tied. Are you in some kind of trouble?"

"Yes, I could very well be! I really need to know, Doctor."

Zochowska went to the door, held it open. Her face had hardened again. "I'm very sorry, Miss Black, but I just can't divulge any information. If you are concerned about anything, go to the police. If there's something here that will help, and the police are involved, they may be able to request information. But confidentiality laws often block even law enforcement. I'm afraid my business hands are tied here."

Rose stood, paused half out of the office. "Maybe you need to spend more money on your systems then. Perhaps I'll get the information I need if I hack in as well, instead of asking nicely." She knew she was being unpleasant, irrational, but she didn't care. Fear and frustration made her want to lash out at Zochowska's calm, so-called professional, indifference.

To her credit, Zochowska looked away, unable to hold Rose's furious gaze. "I'm truly sorry I can't help," she muttered at the carpet.

Rose stomped from the office back out toward the reception area, mind whirling with confusion. As she reached the end of the corridor, she saw the sign for a toilet and went in. She leaned on the sink, took a few deep breaths to calm down. She certainly hadn't handled that very well at all. Could she have approached it differently? Short of holding Zochowska by the throat and threatening further violence unless information was forthcoming, she couldn't imagine any other course of action.

She cupped cold water from the tap into her palms and washed her face, trembling slightly with frustration. She had nowhere else to turn. Maybe she should call Crowley, ask if he had any ideas of further leads she could follow up.

When she emerged from the toilet, she glanced back down toward Zochowska's office and saw the door standing ajar. Narrowing her eyes, she crept quietly back toward it. The doctor wasn't there, the room empty and inviting. What chance might she have of quickly checking through the computer files, finding anything useful? She took a tentative step into the door when Zochowska's sharp tones made her heart slam in her chest.

"Is there something further I can help you with?"

Rose turned an angry glare to the woman, though she knew deep down it wasn't fair. None of this was the doctor's fault. But nothing in Rose's life seemed fair right now. "Just watch the news," she snapped, not sure what she really meant. She just needed to score some kind of juvenile points against the woman standing in her way.

Zochowska frowned, but said nothing. Rose turned and stalked back up the corridor to the reception area. She braced herself for the bubbly, blonde receptionist and the young woman's artificial good cheer.

But the receptionist's face was serious as Rose emerged into the sunlit area. Her eyes darted left and right nervously.

Rose opened her mouth to speak, but the receptionist shushed her and stepped forward and pressed a small fold of paper into Rose's palm with trembling fingers. The receptionist leaned close. "Don't read it until you're outside. And be careful."

She turned away, sat at her desk, and busied herself typing something into a Word document open on her computer screen. Rose stared for a moment, but the woman showed no signs of making any further eye contact.

"Thank you," Rose whispered, and hurried out, the bright, warm day unable to melt the chill running up her spine.

CHAPTER 9

Camberwell

The note had been quickly scrawled in blue ink, and gave nothing more than a street address in Camberwell, just off Peckham Road. Still south of the river and only a couple of suburbs away from the Holm Institute. Rose had used her maps apps to look it up and discovered it was a simple suburban area. Street view showed a non-descript townhouse, not unlike Jake Crowley's from the outside, but bigger, and the suburb a lot leafier and more upmarket than Crowley's inner-city Deptford address, where everything seemed to be gray concrete.

She called Crowley after that, while she sat drinking bad coffee in a Dulwich Village café. She told him all about the encounter with Zochowska, how poorly it had gone. He was skeptical of the receptionist coming to her aid, but agreed when Rose pointed out they had no other leads to follow.

"I finish at lunchtime today," Crowley said. "My last class ends at twelve-thirty and I normally spend the afternoon in the staff room, marking. But today I'll skip it and come to meet you. I don't like the idea of you going there alone."

Rose had been about to protest when a ripple of nerves in her gut gave her pause. Perhaps he was right, it might be too risky. What if the receptionist was on the side of the guys who had tried to abduct her twice now? What if the receptionist had aided the data breach? She hated the way her thoughts were going, the dark and paranoid possibilities she found herself considering. Rather than voice them, she simply said, "Okay. I'll text you a place to meet."

Rose then found herself with a few hours to kill and a desire to be outside, so she walked from Dulwich Village to Camberwell. It took her nearly two hours, but only because she rambled left and right, looking in shops. She could have made the journey in less than one hour if necessary, but the busy streets and inviting stores were a welcome distraction. The sheer normality of life around her was a balm to a soul battered by dark alleys and hooded attackers searching for birthmarks. Eventually she found another café on Peckham Road, a place of dark polished wood and blue velvet seating, with mirrors on the walls and stained glass lampshades hanging over each table to make rainbow pools of light. It felt safe, cozy, and was only about a five minute walk from the address she had been given. She settled in, ordered more coffee, and sent Jake a text message with the café's address. Then she tapped up an e-reading app on her phone. She opened a collection of Annie Proulx short stories she'd been meaning to read for months and let the talented writer carry her away on a sea of words, but she couldn't help keeping one nervous eye on the door, partly in anticipation of Crowley's arrival, partly in fear that someone else would find her here.

She was getting hungry by the time Crowley showed up, just after one in the afternoon, and slipped into the seat opposite her. She was inordinately glad to see him. They ordered sandwiches and more coffee. She wondered if she ought to cut it back, before the caffeine set her buzzing, but for now it seemed to calm her nerves. They ate while she brought him up to speed on all the details.

After they'd finished and paid, Crowley put a strong hand on her shoulder, gave a gentle squeeze. "Come on, then. Let's go and see who these people are."

The house stood among several others just like it, thoroughly non-descript. A nice enough place, the tiny piece of garden out the front well-tended behind its low brick wall, a Japanese maple tree in resplendent leaf. The front door was painted a deep maroon, the doorbell in the center of the upper panel a shining brass affair with curlicue back plate and faux-ivory button.

"Think it'll play *Für Elise* when you press it?" Crowley quipped, but his voice was tight.

Rose realized he shared her concern, but tried to mask it with levity. She threw him a quick grin and pressed the button. A muted *ding-dong* echoed from inside the house. Silence followed and Rose began to wonder if all her tension would be wasted on an empty residence when she spotted movement through the frosted glass panels beside the door. A gap appeared at the frame, then the door clanked to a stop on a brass chain. A woman's face appeared, maybe mid-forties, friendly enough under a mop of blonde curls. A large port wine birthmark covered one half of her face from forehead to throat, right over one cheek and entirely circling her left eye.

"Yes?" The woman's voice was taut with suspicion.

Rose swallowed, momentarily at a loss for something to say. The woman stared. Eventually, Rose said, "I was given your address. I think you might be able to help me."

"Help you?"

"Yes, I... Honestly, I'm not sure how, but I've got nowhere else to go. You're my last hope." Rose heard the fear in her voice and part of her loathed that she'd been reduced to begging strangers for assistance. But perhaps the genuine concern would convince this woman to open the door. Though Rose had no idea what kind of help she might be.

"Show me."

Frowning, unsure what help it would be, Rose held out the slip of paper with the Holm Institute receptionist's quickly scrawled handwriting. "I was given this address..."

"Not that. You're not getting in until you show me proof." The woman raised one hand, pointed to her purple cheek. "You want me to help you, so show me you need my help."

Crowley leaned forward, whispered in Rose's ear. "I think she wants to see your birthmark."

Rose nodded. "Yes, I realize that now!" The response had been snippy. She glanced back at him. "Sorry."

The woman crossed her arms and tapped her foot, waiting.

Rose turned and lifted the back of her shirt, her gaze darting nervously back and forth along the street beyond the wrought iron gate. What must this look like to anybody who happened to be passing?

The woman at the door gasped. She wore a horrified expression as Rose turned back to face her, then the door closed and she heard the clink of the chain being undone. Relief flooded her as the door opened again.

"Get in here." She grabbed Rose's hand and hauled her inside. Crowley stepped forward to follow but the woman put a palm into his chest to stop him. "Not unless you have a mark," she said doggedly.

"I'm with her," Crowley said, brow knitting in annoyance. "She's in all kinds of trouble and I don't plan to leave her alone in a strange house."

"You got a mark?" the woman demanded.

A liquid panic swelled in Rose's gut. Had she walked right into a trap? Was this woman somehow connected with the people who had been hunting her? Then again, the diminutive creature was really no match for Crowley should he choose to force his way in. Or Rose herself, for that matter.

A tall, thin man appeared along the narrow hallway, footsteps silent on the deep red Persian carpet. Rose jumped, but he put a gentle hand on the woman's shoulder, wisps of gray hair floating around his almost completely bald head. He looked to be of a similar age and bore a bright red birthmark over the back of his right hand. It ran up his wrist and disappeared into the sleeve of a linen shirt. "What's happening, Margaret?"

Margaret nodded toward Rose, her hand still pressed to Crowley's chest. "She has the same mark as Danny."

The man's eyebrows shot up. "The same? Really?"

"Exactly the same! And he insists on accompanying her."

"I'm not leaving without her, and you're not closing that door with her inside," Crowley said. He ignored the hand on his chest, but his voice had become dangerously hard.

The man raised both hands, palms out. "It's okay, no need to worry." He gently removed Margaret's hand from Crowley. "I'm George Wilson, this is Margaret. You'd both better come in."

CHAPTER 10

Camberwell

Crowley's breathing relaxed as he stepped into the house and closed the front door. The warm hallway smelled of roses and fresh coffee. A mahogany side table stood against the wall, with wallets and keys in a ceramic bowl on top. Alongside it stood a coat rack loaded with anoraks and scarves. At the end of the hall lay a kitchen bathed in sunlight; an inviting scene, all clean pine cupboards and gray marble benchtops. The place was as homely and unremarkable as anywhere he could imagine.

"I'm sorry," Margaret muttered before turning to follow the man. Her husband, Crowley assumed.

"It's fine," Crowley said. "I don't blame you for caution when strangers come knocking at your door."

She glanced back. "Well, we get quite a few, but things have been tense lately."

"Come in, come in," George said firmly before Crowley could question what Margaret meant by 'tense'. "I'll make us a drink and we can talk."

He led the way into a lounge room with a heavily padded floral sofa and armchairs. Glass-fronted wooden cabinets lined the walls, filled with all manner of souvenirs and knick-knack. It appeared that George and Margaret had spent many holidays in the Spanish islands, Majorca and Minorca memorabilia all over the place. A bookcase lined one side of the room, covered with novels and history books, atlases and dictionaries.

"This isn't what I expected." Rose accepted a seat in one of the armchairs.

Crowley took the other armchair, privately thinking he knew what to expect now, but he kept his silence. Better to let these people say what they would without prompting. He could press them for more information if he felt they weren't particularly forthcoming, but something told him that wouldn't be necessary.

"Can I get coffee? Tea?" George Wilson asked.

"No, thank you," Rose said. "I'd really just like to talk."

George nodded, sat beside Margaret on the sofa. "Who

gave you our address?"

Crowley watched as Rose bit her lip, clearly wondering how much to tell. He stayed silent. This was her issue. She would be more than capable of deciding what to say, what to ask. He desperately hoped they found some answers here. From a simple date the night before to this, it was insane how quickly things had spiraled away from any kind of normality.

Rose let out her breath. "Okay, here's the abridged version. For no reason, out of nowhere, people have started following and attacking me." She gestured to Crowley. "If it wasn't for Jake here they would have me already. For some reason, they seem to be interested in my birthmark. The only thing I know of that could have led them to me was a data breach at a clinic I visited last year to enquire about maybe having the thing removed."

"The Holm Institute?" George asked.

"The very same. So I went there, demanding information because I had nowhere else to turn. They were hardly helpful, but as I left, the receptionist told me to be careful and pressed a piece of paper into my hand. It had your address on it. So here I am."

George nodded, hands clasped. He tapped his index fingers against his lips for a moment. The he said, "We're a support group for people whose birthmarks have had a negative impact on their life. It started with a couple of friends and a private internet group and led to us meeting regularly here. We open our house for the meetings, lend mutual support, and people find acceptance here."

Margaret smiled, patted George's knee affectionately. "Sometimes we find more."

"So the receptionist sent me here to get support? Why did she tell me to be careful?"

"You mentioned that Rose has the same mark as someone called Danny," Crowley said, nudging the conversation in the direction he thought it should go.

"Yes," George said. "I imagine that's the connection. The receptionist at the Holm Institute is Claire Brady. She has a mark too, here." He ran a hand over his side, from ribs to chest. "She comes to our meetings, as did Danny."

"Did?" Rose asked. "What happened to Danny?"

Nerves rippled in Crowley's stomach. It was surely a very strange coincidence for two people to have the same birthmark.

He would never have considered it possible, let alone likely, unless Margaret here had said it were the case. So it seemed these people hunting Rose were not just after any mark, but a very specific one. He didn't doubt for a moment that Danny had met the same guys who had accosted Rose, only perhaps poor Danny had not managed to get away.

George spread his hands, then clapped them together again. "This is entirely speculation, of course, because we don't know anything for sure. Danny is a member of our group. Odd fellow, very interested in the occult and stuff like that, but a very nice young man. Friendly. Genuine. He was always talking about wanting to find the *Devil's Bible*, whatever that is. He said it was the key to understanding his mark, that there was a lot more to some birthmarks than simple skin irregularities. Anyway, a couple of weeks ago he didn't come to the meeting. It's not that unusual, of course, people don't come every week. But Danny was pretty regular. We've become as much a group of friends as anything else. We usually play cards, chat, you know. It's a social thing, regardless of what brought us together. Then he didn't come again last night. He may very well come along next week and everything will be fine, but I think perhaps Margaret got a bit of a spook when you showed up with a similar mark after he's been AWOL for a while."

"It's not similar," Margaret said. "It looks exactly the same!"

George frowned. "That seems unlikely..."

Crowley couldn't help but agree, though he had seen the shock on Margaret's face. Rose stood and turned around, hoisted up the back of her shirt.

A long moment of silence hung in the air, and then George said quietly, "Good grief."

Rose sat down again, eyes narrow with concern. Crowley couldn't bear the haunted look she wore. "What did Danny mean by this *Devil's Bible* being the key to understanding his mark?" he asked.

George shook his head. "No idea. He was always saying strange things like that. Sometimes we'd press him for explanations and he'd clam up. Other times he'd go rambling about all kinds of things I could rarely follow. He wasn't crazy, but he was a bit... left of center, you know? He said there was stuff in this *Devil's Bible* that would give him access to the truth, but he never really clarified what he meant by that."

"Is that why you looked so shocked when you saw my mark?" Rose asked Margaret. "Because it's just like Danny's? Or is there something more?"

Crowley smiled inside. Perceptive girl. He'd wondered the same thing himself.

Margaret frowned. "Partly that. Is your name Rose Black?"

Crowley realized the Wilsons had introduced themselves, but he and Rose hadn't. And the Wilsons hadn't asked. Perhaps they assumed answers would come in their own time, but maybe they had known all along who Rose was. And Crowley himself didn't matter to them, unmarked as he was. The nerves rippled back again. So much unknown, so many possible traps or pitfalls.

"How did you know my name?" Rose tensed, her voice wavering slightly.

"Well, I'm no great shakes with names but that one stuck. I heard it three weeks ago when someone new came to the meeting. Danny wasn't here then either, but we already knew he'd be on a night shift that week, so we weren't expecting him. This new guy had a mark on his arm…"

"But it looked fake," George interrupted.

Margaret nodded. "It did. We were suspicious, but at that time we had no reason to think anything weird was happening. Why would someone fake their way into a group like ours? We're not special people, you know. But this fellow asked if Danny Bedford or Rose Black were in the group."

The nerves in Crowley's gut became a swirl of surety. This place was compromised. His muscles tensed, mind snapped alert. They needed to be away from here quickly, in case the men on Rose's tail were keeping the place under any kind of surveillance.

"How did he know our names?" Rose asked, eyes wide.

"The data breach, I think. When you mentioned it just now it made sense. Danny had been there too. But I think perhaps they were only able to find names among that data, not more personal information, so they've been…"

"Canvassing possible contacts," Crowley said. "They obviously learned of your group and they're trying all they can to find Danny and Rose because of their shared mark. But they must have been gathering more intel, because they found Rose's home last night."

"And Danny is missing," Margaret said, brow furrowing in

concern.

"At the time we asked him how he knew those names," George said. "He told us he'd met you both at another place and was hoping to catch up with you again. He seemed evasive and it made us nervous. We told him we didn't know anyone by those names, just to be cautious, and after the meeting we decided we wouldn't let him in again. But he never came back."

"And neither has Danny," Margaret said. "None of us has heard a word from him since. And we'd never heard of you at all, of course."

"And now you've appeared here at our door," George said.

Crowley's concerns became overwhelming. He caught Rose's eye and stood. "We have to go, I think. Thank you both very much for your help. Can we have a number to reach you on?"

"Of course." George scribbled a mobile number on a Post-It note and handed it over. "If you find Danny, please let us know. We're very worried for him."

Rose stood and they moved into the hall. "This man who came asking after us," Rose said. "What did he look like?"

George gave a rough description of the man and Crowley overlaid the words quite easily onto the man with the gun who had limped from the alley after Rose's kick the night before. He caught Rose's eye and she nodded slightly, that haunted look even more evident in her eyes.

"I'm sorry we couldn't be more help," George said. "But call us if you need anything, or if you think of anything else you might want to ask. We're happy to help if we can. Even if it's just offering some support."

"We are," Margaret agreed. "And I hope you're both okay. I hope all this blows over."

Crowley huffed a soft laugh. Such a thoroughly English attitude, that armed men trying to abduct strangers might be something that would just 'blow over'. "I hope so too," he said anyway. No point trying to convince them of anything else. He did hope they wouldn't get any more visits from the same men though. "Keep up your caution," he said as he shook George's hand. "Keep that chain on your door."

"We will."

Rose's phone rang. She pulled it out, frowned at the screen. "Work," she said. "Excuse me." She tapped to answer, then said, "Hi there. Can I call you back in a min…" She stopped dead, listening. The color drained from her face.

Crowley put a hand to her elbow, concerned.

"Okay, thank you," Rose said, and hung up. "That was my boss from the museum. Apparently someone showed up today looking for me. They got quite angry when they were told I wasn't there."

CHAPTER 11

Crowley stared at his laptop screen, lips pursed, scrolling through reams of search results. Danny Bedford, Dan Bedford and Daniel Bedford had returned a lot of hits, most of them not especially relevant. Eventually he hit upon a news article in one of the London local paper websites. "Here," he said, looking up.

Rose sat on the sofa across the room from him, staring out into the daylight through his front window. The haunted look remained in her eyes. No, he corrected himself. It had morphed. No longer as much haunted as it was hunted. She embodied both vulnerability and strength, and he couldn't blame her for that. He needed to nurture the strength in her, remind her of her agency and power so she didn't fall into despair.

"Here," he said again, a little louder.

She blinked and looked over, his iPad forgotten in one hand. "Sorry, what?"

"I found this article." He turned back to his screen and read. "Daniel Bedford, twenty eight, an orderly from Great Ormond Street Hospital, was reported missing last Thursday." He paused, scrolled back up to check the date. "This is from last week. Anyway, blah blah blah, reports from his workplace, family are appealing for anyone with knowledge and so on. His parents are up in Yorkshire, but according to this they were planning to travel down to London to help police and try to find him."

"Do you think they're going to?" Rose asked in a small voice.

"Find him? No idea." Crowley blew out an exasperated breath. "I wish we knew why these buggers were so interested in birthmarks like yours."

"They're interested in *people like me*," Rose reminded him.

"Yeah, like you." No point in pretending this was anything other than an extremely dangerous situation. But he remembered to appeal to her strength. "But you're tough, and you've got me on your side."

"I'm grateful for that."

"And I'm not going anywhere. I know we've only just met, really, but as far as this thing is concerned we're entangled. I don't plan to leave you on your own until we have this all sorted out."

"Thank you."

"Do you think we should go to the police?" He had been reluctant to ask, but needed to have her input.

"I already put in a call. The guy I spoke to said he'd look into it, but I could tell he was just blowing me off. Couldn't wait to get off the phone. I don't think he even wrote down any of the names or details I gave him." She bit her lip. "It's hard to explain, but I don't think there's time for a police investigation. Twice in such quick succession, coming to my home, armed. These guys are serious. If we sit back and wait, won't that just make me more vulnerable?"

"I agree. Maybe we can approach them if we learn more, but let's stick to learning more and staying hidden for now. And I mean it; I won't leave you on your own until we know what's happening."

He wanted to add, *And I hope I don't have to leave you on your own afterwards either.* But it sounded cheesy and weak in his head and would sound even more so if it came out of his mouth. And it was entirely inappropriate in the circumstances.

"We need to pin down their reasoning," he said instead. "Figure out what they're trying to do, what they want with you. That'll keep us one step ahead of them."

Rose hefted the iPad. "I found this." She turned it to face him and he saw a photo of someone's back bearing a birthmark just like hers.

He had been skeptical when Margaret Wilson had said Danny Bedford had a mark identical to Rose's. He could imagine it was similar enough to spook Margaret, and clearly the connection here, but identical? But this was a photo of a man's back and the mark was indeed identical as far as he could remember from his brief look at Rose's the night before. "That Danny?"

Rose shook her head. "Someone else." She flicked at the screen, tapped. "This is a website where people submit pics of unusual tattoos or body marks. It came up from an image search I threw in for eagle birthmarks. This user's name is BoldGreg79."

Crowley shook his head. "Someone else with the same

mark?"

"What's going on?" Rose's hunted look became frightened again. "How can something as random as a birthmark repeat like a photocopy. Three times now, that we know of. How many more? What am I?"

"That Greg guy got a user profile?" Crowley asked.

Rose blinked, looked back to her screen and tapped. "Yeah. Says Greg Pritchard, location Tiverton."

"That's down in Devon," Crowley mused, wondering if there was any connection beyond the obvious. "Hang on." He went back into a search engine, typed *Greg Pritchard Tiverton*. The first result was a news article from the North Devon Gazette. He drew air in over his teeth, the nerves in his gut roiling again.

"What is it?" Rose came to stand beside him, looked over his shoulder.

"Says here that a Greg Pritchard of Tiverton was killed a month ago in a bungled home invasion."

Rose made a small noise of horror, one hand going up to cover her mouth. "This can't be a coincidence."

"No, it really can't." Crowley took her other hand, squeezed it. "It'll be okay, Rose. We're in front here, staying ahead of the game. We'll figure this out."

"Should we go to the police after all?" Rose asked. "We should just report this, the attack on me, everything. It's all getting out of control."

"I don't know if that's a good idea."

"Jake, Danny Bedford is missing, probably dead. That Greg guy is definitely dead. Surely I'm next! We have to tell someone!"

"Call me paranoid," Crowley said, "but we don't know who to trust." He gestured at the North Devon Gazette story still on the screen. "That's a murder covered up if we're right. How do we know how much reach and power these people have? You said yourself, going to the police will likely make you more vulnerable at this stage."

"So what do we do?"

"I think we need to carry on like we said, gather more information, as much as we can. All the time we're one step ahead, we keep learning and stay one step ahead. We were right not to go back to your place and we definitely can't do that now. You can't go back to work." He paused, thinking. Wondered if he'd been made as Rose's accomplice. What if these guys went back to the Wilsons' place? Had he used his name there? He was fairly certain he hadn't, but maybe it was a chance they shouldn't take. And they'd seen him, maybe they'd snapped a photo, and could make his ID from it.

"What are you thinking?" Rose asked.

"I'm thinking maybe we shouldn't be here either. Let's get some things packed, computer, tablet, chargers, all that. I'll pack some clothes, then we can head to the shops and buy you some clothes to be going on with. Then I think we find a hotel or something and check in while we figure out what to do next."

Rose took a long breath in through her nose, shook her head slightly. But Crowley saw a steely resolve settle into her eyes. "Okay. Drop off the grid, eh?"

He nodded. "Let's go dark, see what we can do. I'm going to call in sick to work, then I'll pack. We leave our phones here and buy new ones with pre-paid credit so we can't be traced by our mobile signal. Then we draw out all the cash we can so we don't have to use ATMs or credit cards any time soon."

Rose smiled crookedly. "You've done this before?"

"No, I just enjoy a lot of crime fiction. We'll be out of here in ten minutes and I suggest we head out of town and set up camp somewhere in the suburbs."

Less than an hour and a half later, armed with all the cash they could pull from their accounts and a bag each with a few changes of clothes, Crowley checked them into a small hotel in Battersea, not far from Clapham Junction train station. The place was run down, cracked walls and peeling paper, but not seedy. Altogether forgettable, usually frequented by traveling businessmen by the look of things.

They had agreed on a double room, Crowley saying they always had a fold out sofa and he'd sleep on that while Rose could have the bed. Better they stay close together all the time they could. They signed in as Mr. and Mrs. Lansing.

"Where did you get a name like that?" Rose asked.

Crowley grinned, remembering the fun-loving goof whose name he had lifted. Melancholy accompanied the recollection. "He was in my unit, great guy. Tim Lansing. Stepped on an IED outside Kabul."

"Killed?"

Crowley nodded. "He used to joke about stepping on an 'IUD'. Goofy sense of humor. I miss him."

"Oh, man, I'm sorry."

"It's okay. All a long time ago, you know. But his name has stayed with me. We were good mates. So I thought I'd use it here."

They went up to their room and Crowley was pleased to see he had been right about the extra fold out bed. It would have been embarrassing had they needed to negotiate other sleeping arrangements. He marveled again at just how bizarre the turn of events over the last twenty four hours had been.

"So what now?" Rose asked, slumping down onto the bed. It creaked and sagged and she made a face. "Comfy!"

Crowley grinned. She seemed to be holding up well. As did he, for that matter. For all his military experience, this situation was entirely new to him. While some of his skillset would be transferable, he wondered how long he could continue to feel in control. He admitted, somewhat reluctantly, that he was enjoying himself, at least in part. Life since active service had been good, but it lacked that edge of adrenaline-charged excitement. While that was generally a good thing, he realized he had missed it a little bit. But he wasn't foolish enough to think this was any kind of game. He would use the excitement to fuel the battle at hand, but not get complacent.

"Danny's interest in the occult sticks out to me," he said.

Rose frowned at him. "What do you mean?"

"Well, he was after this *Devil's Bible* and stuff, acted all weird from time to time. And I remember your lecture at the museum, talking about odd beliefs around birthmarks."

"Oh, so you were listening then. I thought you looked bored."

"I was positively entranced, Miss Black!"

"Sure." She grinned at him and it warmed him somewhere deep inside. "But what's your point?"

He shrugged, not entirely sure where he was going with the train of thought. "I don't know. I'm just wondering if there's anything in that."

Rose pursed her lips, thinking. "Well, I don't know a lot, but some people believe a birthmark can be used to tell the future or even tell who you were in a past life. That sort of thing. There's a common thread in some birthmark mythology about past lives, in fact." Her brow creased again. "I have to be honest, seeing at least three people with a birthmark exactly like mine does make me more inclined to consider supernatural stuff I would have laughed off yesterday!"

"I know what you mean. That's kind of where I was going with this, I think. We ought to consider the possibility that someone out there might be a true believer in some occult birthmark lore. They might be focusing on people with matching birthmarks, or even specifically people with *your* birthmark."

"So what do we do about that?"

Crowley shook his head, raised his hands in defeat. "No idea." He blew out a breath, exasperated. "But Danny apparently said this *Devil's Bible* had the answers. Methods of learning the truth, or something, right? Maybe we need to educate ourselves on any occult connections with birthmarks. See if something useful comes up. Honestly, I'm fishing here, but it could be a connection. And if we learn something more, it might become a future bargaining chip with these thugs who are after you."

"I'll call George Wilson," Rose said, pulling out her newly purchased untraceable pre-paid phone. "He might have an idea of some of that stuff, or direct us where to look."

Crowley nodded and handed over the number.

CHAPTER 12

"Well, this has taken an utterly bizarre turn," Crowley muttered, as he followed Rose into the bright echoing hall and high arches of the Old Bailey's lobby. Light flooded in from skylights in the domed ceiling far above, reflecting off yellow and gold edges, brightly painted frescoes, and shining across the glossy white and black tiles of the floor.

Several people milled around, some clearly tourists and others with the focused intensity of law officials at work.

"Why's it called the Old Bailey anyway?" Rose asked.

"The street outside is called Old Bailey, the courts are named after that."

She gave him a withering glare. "I know that. The most famous law courts in the world, probably, so that much is obvious. I mean, why is the street called Old Bailey. It's a weird name."

Crowley glanced at her, wondering if she was being facetious, but her face was open and without guile as she scanned the impressive interior. "A bailey is a wall. That street follows exactly the old fortified wall that used to enclose the City of London, and these courts were right outside that."

She turned a smile to him. "Ha, there you go. You are a history teacher after all."

"Sometimes, sure. I can tell you more too. The initial location of the courthouse, so close to Newgate Prison, allowed for convenient transfer of prisoners to the courtroom for their trials. Plus, its position between the City and Westminster meant it was a good location for trials involving people from pretty much anywhere in the metropolis. North of the river Thames, at least. Back in the day, crossing from south of the river was a bit more difficult."

Rose laughed and Crowley felt his cheeks color slightly. "You make a text book passage sound interesting. You have a good voice for teaching."

"That wasn't a textbook passage," he protested. "But I have said that or something very like it dozens of times over the years."

She squeezed his hand briefly, then let go. "I wasn't mocking you, I meant it. I think you're probably an excellent teacher."

"Maybe, maybe not. But getting teenagers to listen to anything they don't want to for more than five minutes takes a lot more than knowledge and a good voice."

"You're telling me. Seems like I spend half my day trying to entertain school groups."

A bell rang and the people bustling around seemed to intensify, the crowd thickening.

"That was a piece of luck," Rose said. "I thought we might have to wait a lot longer before a trial turned out."

"I still don't know how likely this is," Crowley said. He looked around the space, spotted the door Margaret Wilson had told them would be there. Security guards milled everywhere, some at stations, others wandering free, roaming in search of ne'er-do-wells.

Rose stepped closer to Crowley's shoulder as the milling crowd thronged the open space. Voices echoed in a rising hubbub of noise, laughter sometimes ringing out. "Margaret said the man doesn't want to be found, so he makes it very difficult."

Crowley shook his head, still almost certain they were being taken for fools. "But the only access to him is via the basement of the Old Bailey? That's a little far-fetched for anyone, right?"

"The only access she knows of," Rose reminded him. "I'm sure this Declan Brown character has many other ways to his…" She petered out, clearly unsure how to describe where they needed to go.

"His secret underground lair?" Crowley finished for her.

They grinned at each other but the weight of the trouble they were in quickly returned.

Rose's brow creased. "We have no other choice at this stage. Margaret assured us this was the man to speak to if we wanted to learn more about Danny's occult ideas."

He returned the squeeze of the hand she had given him moments before, but he didn't let go. He watched the movement of two guards who walked toward each other then paused for a quick chat.

"Here we go!" he said, and gently pulled her along.

They moved quickly through the bustling crowd, Crowley

not taking his eyes off the guards. Another came in through the front doors and started heading in their direction, but his attention was directed elsewhere. Crowley realized they were only going to get one shot at this. Turning his attention to the ornate wooden door in one side of the wide entrance hall, he hoped fervently to find it unlocked. Margaret had assured them it would be, at least during the day when the courts were open. Declan Brown was a man with many suspicions, she had said, and made it so that only the most determined could find him. Margaret had offered to get word to Declan and have the man come to meet them. She seemed fairly confident he would. But Crowley had said there wasn't time when Margaret had said it would probably take a couple of days.

Now, heading for a door marked Private, in plain sight, in the busiest law courts in the land, lying low and waiting for a couple of days didn't seem like such a bad idea after all. Blood rushing, heartbeat loud in his ears, he reached for the door handle. Rose turned, her fingers tightening painfully around his hand.

"The guard's turning around!" she hissed.

But the handle turned and the door swung easily inward. Crowley hauled her through behind him and quickly shut it again. They stood in a narrow wood-paneled corridor, leading away under a series of soft yellow lights. The noise and bustle outside was almost entirely silenced by the thick wood, the stillness sudden and eerie. They stood motionless for several seconds, both doing their best to calm nervous breathing. Crowley realized he still held Rose's hand, firm and warm in his own. He was reluctant to let go, so chose to pretend he hadn't noticed for the time being. They both watched the door like it was about to come alive any moment, but everything remained inert and quiet.

Crowley took a long, deep breath. "Let's go, before someone else does come."

Rose let go of his hand and walked on ahead. Crowley smiled to himself, amused by his disappointment, and followed. Only a few yards along the passage, they came to a door and opened it. No one on the other side, and they hurried on. Another corridor led them to stone steps leading down, all exactly as Margaret had described. She had been brought this way herself, she had told them, by Declan himself. It had been quite the adventure for her, and Crowley could see why. The

Wilsons certainly kept strange company.

They found themselves under the Old Bailey, in a tight passageway of white painted brick. Pipes and air-conditioning ducts ran along the ceiling, barely an inch or two above Crowley's head. Power and Ethernet cables ran along the wall at elbow height, enclosed in a cage-like metal housing. Everything was a strange mix of historical architecture and modern technology.

"How old is this place?" Rose whispered as she hurried along.

"First built in 1673," Crowley told her. "But it's been remodeled lots of times. According to Margaret's description, if we've gone the right way, we should find the Roman wall soon."

"It's here," Rose said, pointing to a section of ancient wall constructed of large stone blocks. "Amazing to think how long this has been here."

Crowley nodded. "The courts are built on the old site of Newgate Prison, which for centuries was the chief holding place for condemned criminals, and not far away is the church of St. Sepulchre."

They paused to look at the old architecture, then scanned around nearby.

"That much is well-documented history," Crowley went on, warming to his subject. "The condemned would be led along Dead Man's Walk up there on street level, between the prison and the court. Quite a few of those, after execution, were buried in the walk itself. But huge crowds would gather, often excited beyond reason, to watch the executions. They would pelt the condemned with rotten fruit and vegetables, or even stones. Sometime in the early eighteen hundreds, I forget when exactly, a massive riot ended in the deaths of twenty-eight people, crushed to death after a pie-seller's stall was overturned. A strange catalyst for such mayhem!"

Rose stifled a laugh. "Oh, that's really not funny, but is it true?"

"It is. People went crazy for the public killings back then. No TV, I guess." They shared a grin. "Anyway, a secret tunnel was subsequently created between the prison and St. Sepulchre's church, to allow chaplains to minister to the condemned man without having to force their way through the crowds, and to move the condemned back and forth as well. Some suggested the tunnel might be used too for the beginning of the journey to

Tyburn gallows, down near Marble Arch. But there's no proof of that, and no proof of other tunnels leading from the one below Dead Man's Walk." Crowley gestured around himself. "Which is where we are now. Carry on and it leads beneath St. Sepulchre's, but Margaret said there was a secret entrance to more tunnels before we get there. All kinds of stories like that have long been conjectured, but to my knowledge, the tunnels have never been found. It's all urban legend."

"But Margaret insists it's not," Rose said. She was smiling, a half-cheeky, half-challenging look.

"What?" Crowley asked.

"While you've been busy lecturing," she held up a hand to stave off his outrage, "which was genuinely interesting, don't worry, I've been looking at Margaret's directions. And I found this." She pointed at the ground beneath their feet.

Crowley looked down, gazed around, but saw only old, well-worn flagstones. "What?" he asked. "I don't see anything."

Rose crouched, brushed her hand over one stone to reveal faint, shallow etched markings. Crowley squatted beside her and squinted in the dim basement lighting. The carving was a crucifix, encircled by a laurel wreath.

"I'll be damned," he whispered.

"Just like Margaret said." Rose traced her finger from the base of the crucifix to the stone block wall, then counted up to the third stone.

Crowley shook his head. "I was convinced this was all a waste of time."

Rose lifted her eyebrows at him once, then pressed her palm against the stone as Margaret had instructed, and pushed. It grated slightly, but moved easily, pressing into the wall a good couple of inches then slowly sliding back into position. Something in the etched flagstone at their feet clicked.

Crowley allowed himself a soft laugh. "Amazing." He pushed down on the flagstone and it sank slowly, then tilted on its central axis, opening up like a car's air-conditioning vent. The gap between the now vertical stone and the next flagstone over was a good couple of feet, plenty of room to slip through, and a metal ladder disappeared down into the gloom. Its rungs were spotted with rust, but it appeared sturdy. Crowley looked up at Rose, met her wide eyes with what he was sure was a matching expression. "Want to go first?" he asked.

She gestured generously with one hand. "I'll follow you."

Chapter 13

Margaret Wilson spooned sugar into the two mugs and then walked to the back door. "Tea, dear!" she called down the immaculately tended garden. The neat, bright green lawn, bordered on both sides by beds of multi-colored flowers, only extended about twenty feet before it ended in George's dark-stained wooden shed. It was a tiny patch of nature in their city street, but it was George's pride and joy.

Margaret frowned when no answering call came. The window of the shed reflected the slightly overcast sky, acting more like a mirror, and she couldn't see any movement inside. The gate in the red brick wall behind the shed, which led out onto their narrow back lane, was closed, so George hadn't stepped out there to the bins.

She shook her head and smiled to herself. Poor old fellow, his hearing was beginning to fail. She'd noticed him regularly nudging the volume up on the television in the evenings, casting sidelong glances at her to see if she noticed. Her nose was usually buried in a book and she pretended to be oblivious.

She picked up the mugs and headed along the flagstone path, like stepping stones through the grass. The shed door was slightly ajar and she nudged it open with one foot, careful not to spill the tea.

"Made you a cuppa, dear," she said. Her scream of horror drowned the crash of the mugs smashing against the concrete footing of the shed. Hot tea splashed over her feet and legs. She ignored the distant pain of the scalding liquid and stared wide-eyed into the barrel of the pistol leveled at her face, not two feet from her nose. Behind it was a hard-faced man, teeth bared in a grimace, and behind him sat George, tied into the chair in front of his wooden desk, black masking tape pressed tightly over his mouth. His eyes were wide and terrified above the gag and he moved his head left and right in impotent denial. Muffled grunts and groans made it through, but no words.

Margaret stood motionless but for the trembling that racked her entire body. She tried to swallow, but her mouth was suddenly too dry to accomplish such a simple task.

The man's grimace turned into a mean smile. "Very good of you to save me a trip up to the house. No need to sneak in now."

"What do you want?" Margaret's voice wavered on the verge of tears. George's wide eyes narrowed in empathetic pain.

The man moved aside from the door and gestured with the gun. "Do come inside."

George shook his head more vigorously, but what choice did she have? If she tried to run the man might shoot her anyway. And he was young and fit, would easily overtake her if she bolted. She wouldn't even make it to the back door, despite the distance across the garden being so small. She stepped inside and the man pointed to a pile of plastic sacks of fertilizer. It was a ridiculous amount for such a small garden.

"It'll take you years to use all that!" she had said the day George brought it all home from the garden center.

"But it was on sale, dear," he had replied. "I simply couldn't ignore a bargain like that. It was less than half price."

Margaret sat and shook her head at the ridiculous train of thought, remembering such pointless minutiae of life. Then again, that *was* real life, wasn't it? All those little things, those seemingly insignificant interactions that actually made up the vast majority of every day lived.

"What do you want?" she asked again. "Money? We don't have much, but you can have it. Please, just don't hurt us."

"I don't need your money. Information is what I'm after."

Margaret nodded slightly. She had assumed that would be the case. Danny's disappearance, then the strange visit from Rose Black and her friend the day before. Something very strange was going on, and she and George had inadvertently stumbled right into the middle of it. Or perhaps it had stumbled right into the middle of them. "Information?" she asked.

"The whereabouts of Rose Black and her friend."

"I'm afraid I don't know…" Margaret's voice choked into silence as the man surged forward and pressed the gun barrel hard into her sternum. It was cold through her light blouse, and he ground it painfully into the bone.

"You see, I think you *do* know, Mrs. Wilson. And I am absolutely certain you will tell me."

Margaret shook her head, adrenaline pulsing up, her heart slamming against her ribs. "But I really don't know…"

"We know she was here yesterday," the man shouted, spittle flying from his lips.

Margaret flinched, clutched her hands together. "Yes, she was here yesterday. But I couldn't help them and I don't know where they went. I don't know where they are!" Her voice rose shrill in panic.

The man leaned closer, his breath stale and redolent with old tobacco and coffee. "I think you do, and I think you'll be telling me. How are you at dealing with pain?" He lowered the gun barrel to press against her kneecap.

Margaret began to cry, muttering, "No, no, no."

George's muffled protestations grew louder, more violent. He rocked the chair he was tied to as he thrashed.

The armed man spun to face him, pressed his gun to George's knee and George suddenly stilled. "Or how are you at watching your loved ones bleed?" he wondered. "Now I'll ask you again. Where is Rose Black?"

CHAPTER 14

Crowley walked slowly, just ahead of Rose. The light from his small flashlight pierced the darkness, swept back and forth across old stone and worn floors. He was mystified, stunned that Margaret's seemingly crazy musings had turned out to be true. How many people had ever walked these secret tunnels? Very few, he was sure of that. Excitement and concern battled each other, made his hand tremble slightly. He hoped Rose didn't notice the wavering of his torch light. He kept it moving left and right just in case.

"We're looking for an Egyptian ankh carved at ground level on a stone that sticks out an inch or so further than the others," Rose said, using her own small penlight torch to read her notes. "That's like a crucifix with a looped top, right?"

"That's right." Crowley paused, squinted ahead. "There." He steadied his light on one stone protruding slightly from the wall.

They approached it cautiously. Rose watched up and down the tunnel while Crowley felt around for the edges of the door Margaret had described. The ladder down was lost now in the gloom behind them and the tunnel continued on. He wondered where it might lead. The historian in him was alive with glee at the thought. Once all this was over, he was definitely coming back here and he planned to explore every inch of the place. He paused. When all this was over. When might that be? What might the outcome be? He mentally shook himself. *Keep your mind on the battle at hand, soldier.*

His fingers found the deep groove above the stone carved with the ankh and he got a good grip with eight fingertips and pulled. The door moved more easily than he had expected and he almost stumbled back. The stones were cut thin, made a simple façade over a thick wooden panel hinged deep in the wall. An ancient, crumbling set of stairs led down into darkness.

Secret tunnels within secret tunnels. How far did all this go? "Here we are then," he said, and started down.

Rose followed. He heard the soft scrape as she pulled the

door closed again. "It's cold down here!" she said.

Goosebumps ran along Crowley's exposed forearms, the chill old and permanent. "Yeah. I don't think this place has ever been warm, no matter how hot the days might get. We're too deep now."

They emerged into an open space, pale stone walls and flagstone flooring. Three deep pits took up the majority of the floor space in the long room, arched recesses along one side. A wide, arched doorway led out the far end, a wide mouth onto complete darkness.

"What is this place?" Rose whispered.

Crowley shook his head, smiled. "I've seen lots like it. It's an old Roman bathhouse. Loads have been found in various places over the years. Whatever might have been above this, some dignitary's villa or whatever, has long since fallen to ruins and London has grown over it like an ever-thickening mold. There are many who think things like this exist all over the place, buried in numerous lost underground parts of the city. I've never really given it much credence before, but maybe I should reconsider that."

Crowley shone his light into the wide doorway at the other end, picked out a passage leading away. "This way, I guess."

They moved forward and had only covered a few yards when Crowley's soldier sense prickled. Was that the scrape of a shoe he heard? Before he could turn to locate the source, a soft, warm voice came from his left.

"Don't move. What do you want here?"

Crowley took a deep breath, quelled the sudden spike of adrenaline. "Are you Declan Brown?"

"Who's asking?"

"My name is Jake Crowley, and this is Rose Black. We were given directions to find you by Margaret Wilson."

"Ol' Maggie, eh?" Shadows moved in one of the alcoves and a man stepped out into Crowley's light. He was short, but muscular, his skin a deep shade of chestnut brown. Tightly curled black hair was cut fairly close to his head. His eyes were large and friendly in the gloom, his smile wide. "Well, if Maggs sent you then you must be okay. You'd better come in."

He turned and went back into the shadows of the arch. Crowley looked back to Rose, gave her a grin and a shrug, and followed. Beyond the arch was a small anteroom, maybe a changing room for the baths, Crowley speculated. At the back of that space was a wooden door pushed wide. Light flickered and flared as Brown lit a glass oil lamp inside, revealing a comfortable-looking room with threadbare couch and armchairs. Brown turned up the light, chasing the shadows out of the large room to reveal a wooden table surrounded by four dining chairs, several bookcases bowing under the weight of books. A small gas camping cooker stood to one side, on another table loaded with canned food, bread, cutlery and other cooking tools in one corner.

Brown hung the lantern from a hook in the low, brick ceiling and turned to face them. "Have a seat. You want a cup of tea?"

As Brown made three mugs of tea, Rose gave him a fairly good, though abridged, version of what had been happening. "And so we decided we needed to learn more about what Danny Bedford believed," she finished. "And Margaret told us you were the man to talk to about that stuff. You and Danny studied occult things together, she told me."

When he turned back with the mugs, Brown seemed unsurprised. "I brought her here to visit once. She thought it was tremendous fun. I knew she'd remember the way, you see. I'd divined that someone would need my help, and find it through her. And here you are. The wheel turns, eh?"

Crowley sipped tea, kept his mouth closed and his ears open, trying to get the measure of the man. He seemed entirely comfortable in his subterranean solitary confinement, unfazed by a lack of modern conveniences. And, Crowley reluctantly admitted, he appeared to be completely sane, contrary to everything Crowley had expected. Then again, madness often presented in strange and subtle ways, so Crowley wasn't about to make any firm assumptions yet.

"So that's why Margaret sent you to see me?" Brown said, sitting down. "Something with Danny? I'm worried. I haven't been able to reach him for too long."

Over Brown's shoulder, Crowley read the spines of books on the shelves. Most titles covered subjects of occultism, history, Nazi Germany, ancient cultures, geography. For such a small collection, it covered a surprisingly extensive range of subject matter. Brown, it seemed, was an educated man. "You haven't been able to divine what happened to him?" Crowley tried to keep the skepticism from his voice, but failed rather spectacularly.

Brown smiled softly, shook his head. "It doesn't work like that."

"Margaret seemed to think you might have more answers for us," Rose said, her voice a little weak. Perhaps she doubted the likelihood of help from such a strange quarter, but Crowley thought maybe this was the closest they might have got to an answer yet. If there was an answer to be found. Just because they had lots of questions, it didn't automatically follow that there were answers to them all. "You believe," she paused, lost in thought for a moment. "You know," she went on, "a lot more of the lore and history of this stuff than we do, Margaret said."

Brown smiled. "And I do believe too. I have reason to believe. You told me about your mark, and I have seen Danny's. These are powerful things. The influence of history to make itself heard through the marks on generation after generation of people is well-documented."

Crowley wanted to roll his eyes, but kept the urge in check. Not least because of Brown's relaxed, easy delivery. He didn't sound evangelical in any way, showed no signs of zealotry despite his bizarre choice of abode.

"Some people believe that a birthmark can be read like a tarot card," Brown said, sitting forward. He kept his mug clasped between his palms, almost as if praying to it, and Crowley wondered if he should reassess his thoughts on the man's fanaticism. But Brown continued on, as casually as if he were talking about the price of milk. "In that way, it's believed a person's future can be told. But you know what? I don't buy that."

Crowley hid his smile behind his mug as he sipped.

"Birthmarks, I believe, are windows to *past* lives." Brown downed his remaining tea in one long draught. "This is a more common belief and one I do share."

Crowley winced at the thought of the tea scalding Brown's throat, but he just smiled and put his mug on the ground. "How does that work?" Crowley asked. "Does a person have the same birthmark as someone in the past, is that it? We know at least three people now have a mark the same as Rose's. Does that mark travel back through history? In their family line or something?" He couldn't believe the questions he was asking, but the investigation had led them this far and it was pointless to shy away from its continued progression, no matter how unnatural that might seem. "Should we be searching for a historical figure who had the same mark as Rose?"

Brown shook his head. "Not so literal. The birthmark tells you the way someone died. The markings match the death wound. Imagine some birthmarks you've seen and then think of sword wounds, spears, bullets."

"There are lots of birthmarks that don't make sense that way," Rose said. "I mean, a small mark on an arm isn't going to be an echo of some ancestral death, is it?"

"Maybe not. Or maybe that tiny wound got infected and did lead to the death of someone." Brown smiled again. His grin was wide and easy, gave him an open, friendly expression it was hard to ignore.

This guy could sell snowplows to the Bedouin, Crowley thought to himself.

"I'm not suggesting all birthmarks are necessarily death marks," Brown went on. "Just that some deaths are significant enough that they echo down through the ages, through generations, as marks permanently on the skin from birth."

Rose frowned, shook her head slowly. "But neither my mother nor father have a mark like mine."

Brown raised his palms. "So I guess their lives are not intrinsically tied to the life of their ancestor like yours appears to be. Your mark may well connect you with the death of someone back in your genetic history and there's something here, now, that ties you together."

Crowley turned to Rose, skepticism rising again despite his attempts to take all this seriously. "So we're looking for someone who was ambushed by an eagle?"

Brown left half a smile on one side of his mouth, but his brow wrinkled in a frown, puzzled.

Rose shot Crowley a glare, and he looked away, let the joke die. "What do you know about the *Devil's Bible*?" Rose asked.

Brown's eyebrows popped up. "Now, there's an interesting artifact, and an even more interesting story accompanies it, especially with regard to past lives. If the *truth* is known."

Crowley stiffened, and shot one finger up to silence them both. Brown and Rose watched him with wide eyes, alert. "Footsteps," Crowley whispered. A soft tap and scuff in the distance drifted along the stone chambers, drawing nearer. Crowley had noticed them, but the strange acoustics made it impossible for him to determine the direction.

Brown nodded, gestured out the door and right, across the

Roman baths.

"We need to go," Crowley said. "But that's the only way I know. Is another way out of here?"

CHAPTER 15

Subterranean London

Brown moved quickly, unhooked the lantern, and pointed to one of his bookcases. "Help me here. Rose, close that door, there's a lock inside."

Crowley didn't question. He slipped his fingers behind the wood where Brown indicated, and pulled. The thing moved far more easily than he had anticipated, and completely silently, as if it ran on oiled runners.

"Rubber wheels underneath." Brown grinned.

Behind the shelving stood a low wooden door, like a trapdoor in the wall. As Rose locked them in, Brown pressed a hidden trigger in the wood and the trapdoor popped open. "Mind your head," he said, and ducked inside.

Crowley waved Rose ahead of him and dropped to his knees to crawl in after her as the door behind them rattled. The noise became a vigorous shake. Presumably whoever was on the other side realized they had lost the element of surprise. Booms echoed in the small room as heavy kicks thudded into the wood.

"That won't hold them for long," Brown called back. "Hurry."

They moved single file on hands and knees for several meters and, as Crowley was beginning to wonder how far they could carry on like this, Brown's lantern illuminated a larger space. He and his light dropped from sight, then the brightness bobbed around somewhere below them.

"The drop's only a few feet, but don't twist an ankle," the hermit called up, waving his light to guide them. As Rose and Crowley joined him on an uneven flagstone floor, he turned and pointed. Two wide tunnels led away from the opposite side of the room. Old pipes and wooden boxes, long since broken down and dilapidated, hung off the walls.

"This is an old maintenance room," Brown said. "I made my escape tunnel through to here years ago. It's saved me a few times."

"Maintenance for what?" Crowley asked.

Brown grinned. "The London Underground. You guys

have to go in the dark now." He pointed to the tunnel on the left. "I'll go that way, try to draw them away. Then I can lose them in a maze of old, uncharted catacombs. I know my way around, so I'll have the advantage over them. You take the other passage."

"We have torches," Crowley said. "Or I can use the light on my phone."

Brown shook his head. "It'll shine back and give you away. That way goes for about a hundred feet, then you'll hit a door. Feel for the handle, it's unlocked. Close it behind you, then use your light. You'll be in a side tunnel of the Central Line. Go right, follow your nose, you'll pass through another disused maintenance room. Go right through and follow the tunnel again and you'll find the tracks. Keep your ears open for trains, eh? Don't get hit. You'll come out at St. Paul's station."

Crowley reached out, shook Brown's hand. "Thank you. I wish we'd had more time."

"You're welcome. Now watch out for the homeless people down there. Be nice to them if you can. They're broken, not evil."

"We will. Thanks."

The sound of splintering wood echoed along to them.

Brown winced. "That's my front door. Go! Oh, and based on everything you told me, I suggest you find the *Devil's Bible*. It won't be easy, and don't be confused by urban myths and old legends. Find the *real* one."

Without another word he ran across the maintenance room and into the left hand tunnel. His light glowed back in a pale, watery sheen. Rose shot for the other passage and Crowley followed, voices and cursing floating into the room behind them.

Once out of the glow of Brown's lantern, the darkness was absolute. Crowley caught up to Rose, made them both stumble.

"Sorry, can't see a thing."

"Let's hope they can't either." She grunted as Crowley heard her bump into something. "Here's the door." The handle creaked and the door scraped as she pushed it open. Crowley crowded through behind, pulled the door closed, and flicked up the flashlight app on his phone. The new corridor was red brick. Old, but far more recent than the large sandstone blocks of the lost Roman rooms. And Brown had mentioned a warren of catacombs. Crowley ached to come back and have time to explore the area. The historian in him was lost in wonder at the possibilities. What might he find? Perhaps he would visit Declan Brown again and request the man's assistance.

They heard muffled shouting and a crash, then an echoing report.

"That was a gunshot," Crowley said, no doubt in his mind that he was correct.

Rose bit her lower lip. "Declan?"

"We have to assume he's okay, given that we can't know anything else." He hoped hard that it was true. For all his strange ways, Declan seemed like a decent guy and Crowley would hate to have brought death or injury down upon him. "Come on." Not pausing to further consider the situation, Crowley turned right as instructed and hurried away, Rose on his heels.

The passage angled left and right, dusty old electrical boxes on the walls to show they were moving into more recent architecture. Crowley slowed as a soft orange glow appeared ahead. He killed his flashlight app and stalked forward slowly. Murmuring voices drifted to them, guttural and cracked, the conversations of derelicts and winos.

Crowley nodded ahead. "Declan warned us about this. Let's just go right through, try not to make eye contact, so we can avoid delays."

The glow emitted from an old steel barrel, crackling with fire. Rags and bits of construction timber were crammed into it, burning merrily. Sparks leapt and danced like fireflies. Dark smoke roiled up and cascaded over the low ceiling like an inverted ocean. The acrid air made Crowley's eyes water, his breath catch in his throat. Several people lounged or sat around, their body odor filling the space more than their physical presence, despite the smell of smoke and burning wood. Combined with the filthy fire it made Crowley both disgusted and saddened. Poor lost souls.

"Ey, darlin'!"

Rose yelped as one toothless, stick-thin man in a dirty, ragged coat and oily jeans stepped out of the gloom to paw at her.

"I think you're in the wrong place, darlin'!"

Crowley stepped up. "We're just passing through. We don't want any trouble."

The man leered, wet lips splitting in a black grin. "Lot more of us than there are of you, mister. Maybe we'll take a toll from you, eh?"

Laughter and grunts of agreement echoed out, movement sudden and all around as several others moved to join the man and back up his case for a cost of passage.

"You look like you got a lot of money."

"Any cigarettes?"

"Pleasures of the flesh, I think!"

"Take their phones, worth a mint these days!"

Crowley squinted left and right, taking a moment to assess the situation, but Rose decided to act. She cursed, loud and vibrant, and swung a heavy kick up into the man's groin. He howled and folded to the floor, gasping huge sobs of pain.

"Anyone else?" Rose yelled. "I have had enough today!"

But Crowley was already moving. He grabbed her arm and towed her through the room, making the most of the stunned moment of shock. Bright, wide eyes in grubby faces followed them, but the people remained where they stood. A short passage led from the other side of the hobo home and he ducked into it. A bright light filled the space ahead, a loud, vibrating noise coming with it. Then air punched into the tunnel in a strong wind, whipped at their hair and clothes as a tube train hurtled past, windows a flicker play of bored commuters and garish tourists. It passed as suddenly as it had come and silence descended in its wake. The murmuring and angry voices behind them rose to fill the quiet, and Crowley and Rose moved quickly on.

They emerged into the train tunnel, the tracks glistening as Crowley tapped on his white torchlight again. Red bricks arched away over their heads, dripping here and there with echoing drops. A smell of electric metal and dampness pervaded their senses, gravel crunched underfoot with a variety of old litter, wrappers and plastic bottles mostly, peppering the dark, sooty stones.

Crowley looked up and down the track. "Which way?"

Rose, eyes wide, breath fast, shrugged. "Brown said it was the Central line. Doesn't really matter, there'll be a station either…" She jerked backwards and screamed as an arm appeared around her neck and hauled.

Crowley bit down on the adrenaline that flooded his system and leapt forward, expecting the homeless population from behind them. Hopefully too weak and untrained to be a real threat if he was fast. Rose was already moving to defend herself when a loud clear voice said, "Hold still and no one gets hurt."

Crowley had a moment to realize this was no hobo before Rose twisted and drove one elbow back into her attacker's ribs. It was a powerful blow, elicited a bark of pain and surprise, but not enough to make him lose his grip. Though she had made space and she stamped down and back, grinding her heel along his shinbone and down onto the fragile bones on top of his foot.

He swore effusively, hopping back. He tried desperately to keep his hold, but Rose was too quick and too strong. In the face of his various pains, he had to let her go. He had a gun in the other hand and that came up swiftly. "You bloody people," he said, and Crowley kicked out, his shin connecting under the man's forearm. The gun went off, deafening in the enclosed space, the muzzle flash a blinding glare, but the bullet whined harmlessly off the brick somewhere above and behind them.

Fury masked Rose's face in the dancing light of Crowley's phone as she lifted one knee and drove a front kick into the attacker's chest. He huffed out his breath again, then his back and head hit the wall behind him and he yelped, staggering slightly as the impact stunned him.

Crowley grabbed for the gun arm before the man could gather himself to shoot again and, as he slammed that arm against the wall, Rose stepped in and dropped a brutal elbow strike into the attacker's temple. He folded up like dirty laundry and collapsed silent to the filthy ground. Rose threw one more kick in for good measure, panting rapidly, fury still etched on her features.

"I. Have. Had. Enough!"

Crowley looked at her, grinned. "You're hardcore!"

She looked up, the veil of panic and self-defense lifting. She managed a shaky smile. "We make a good team."

Crowley crouched, picked up the man's gun and pocketed it. "Just in case. Come on, there's probably more coming and we weren't exactly quiet just then. Not to mention everyone back in that room."

They ran side by side along the tracks, listening hard for approaching trains. It was only a few hundred meters before a bright light glowed up ahead. They emerged into a crowded Underground station, St. Paul's according to the sign, as Brown had said they would. Dozens of people on the platform looked at them in surprise, two filthy and wild-eyed strangers emerging from the darkness. Crowley nodded like it was no big thing, threw smiles to anyone looking too long. They clambered up onto the platform and he took Rose's hand and led her through the people.

"Don't talk to anyone and keep your head down," he whispered.

They took advantage of the English default position of politeness, sure no one would challenge them, especially if they made no eye contact. Crowley hurried up the stairs and headed for an escalator, desperate for the fresh air and daylight of the city. He'd had enough too, especially of being subterranean.

CHAPTER 16

"It was a good idea to get out of London," Crowley said as they walked across well-manicured green lawns. "Not only to learn more, but I feel better with some distance between us and those goons."

Rose nodded, eyes scanning the impressive pale building before them. "As long as they didn't track us and follow. I've always wanted to visit Sweden, but didn't really expect to do it under circumstances like this. You're not going to lose your job, are you?"

"No, I pulled the sudden death of a family member card to make sure I wasn't expected back any time soon. As far as work knows I've taken a red-eye to New York."

"Thank you."

Crowley put a hand on her shoulder. "I told you I wouldn't leave you alone in this. Whatever it takes. What about you and work? Didn't you call in sick? How long can that last?"

Rose twisted a contrite expression. "Actually, I called Dr. Phelps before we left London. He's my boss at the museum. I told him that the virus I claimed to have was a little white lie and I'm actually going through some really difficult personal stuff right now. I didn't want to tell him everything, but said I needed to get away for a week or two, have some space."

"And he didn't push you for details?"

"No, Charles is a decent guy. He told me he'd put through the form to give me two weeks' vacation leave. Told me to actually take a holiday, look after myself."

Crowley nodded. "He does sound like a decent guy."

"There's a few of you about."

The National Library of Sweden loomed over them, bright in the sunlight. Two stories of pale yellow frontage, regular, intricately framed rectangular leadlight windows filled the majority of the flat façade, with the central section set slightly forward of the rest. An extra level stood above the two stories of the central block, *KONGL. BIBLIOTEKET* carved into an orange-hued panel of stone between two large gray coats of arms.

Crowley frowned. "Kongle..?"

Rose laughed. "It's short for *Kungliga Biblioteket*. Means the Royal Library. But it's known as the National Library as it houses everything of importance to Sweden."

"Impressive building."

Rose pulled out her phone, tapped up a page she'd found earlier. "Royal book collections had been held at *Tre Konor*, the castle of the Three Crowns, since around the 1660s. There was a fire in 1697 and stuff was stored in various places until Gustaf Dahl was commissioned to build this place. It was started in 1871 and completed seven years later. It's a cast iron construction if you can believe that. The two wings were added in 1926 and 1927."

"I wonder why Declan and Danny were both talking about finding the *Devil's Bible* when it's common knowledge that the thing is kept here?" Crowley pointed at the huge building. "Hardly secret."

Rose shrugged, put her phone away. "Declan also said something about not believing in myths and fakes. About finding the real one, whatever that means. Let's find out."

Inside, the building was breathtaking. Two stories high outside, it was one massively tall room inside, regular columns supporting the roof with three deep levels of bookshelves. The ground floor held numerous reading desks and the next two levels of books could be accessed via mezzanine walkways skirting the wide open space, brightly lit by countless windows. Crowley paused and breathed in the calm magic that always accompanied libraries, especially ones as old and huge as this. Passage to other rooms led off the main space and he walked alongside Rose, marveling at every detail, as they made their way to the library's most famous acquisition, The *Devil's Bible*.

The huge book was contained in a sealed glass cabinet in a side room and Crowley's mouth dropped open at the sight of it. He thought he had known what to expect, but the manuscript in all its glory was mesmerizing.

Rose spoke again, voice low and respectful. "*The Devil's Bible* or *Codex Gigas*. It's also been known as the *Codex Giganteus*, meaning the giant book, and the *Gigas Librorum*, which means the 'book giant'. Also called *Old Nick's Bible*, and *The Black Book*. Whatever you call it, it's pretty impressive."

The massive manuscript on the stand behind the glass was

nearly a meter long and half a meter wide. It had thick board covers with scrolled metalwork corners, and heavy, uneven pages.

"It's the largest medieval manuscript still in existence," Rose said, reciting from memory. Crowley had quietly watched her studying up on the book while on the plane into Stockholm, glad she had found a focus to distract from her predicament. Anything was good, any movement forward to feel like they were tackling the problem. He desperately hoped they would learn something here that might put them ahead of whoever was after Rose, give them some clue to what they were being hunted for.

"It's made from over one hundred and sixty animal skins," Rose went on. "Takes two people to lift it. Written in Latin around 1210 AD, it's reported to have brought disaster and pain to any and all who have possessed it. And to many others around them, apparently. Plague, mental illness, fire and destruction." She glanced at Crowley and grinned. "However much of a skeptic a person might be, there's history attached to this thing that's pretty chilling. Its story is packed with mystery, misfortune and evil. It supposedly originally had three hundred and twenty pages, but seven have been removed, lost. No one has any idea why or where they are. Some people think they contained highly secretive magic or rituals. More likely they contained the monastic rules of the Benedictine monks, which needed to be kept private."

"Maybe that's what Declan meant by the real one. Those missing pages?" Crowley leaned forward, looking closely at the beautifully neat script, the even lines of handwritten Latin in pictures mounted around the display case. The book itself was open to the full page drawing of the Devil that gave the book its name. "Must have taken a long time to write this. I wonder how many people worked on it."

Rose chuckled. "Right there we have some of its darkest history. Legend has it that it was completed in one single night, by just one monk."

Crowley gave Rose a look of disdain. "Really?"

"That's what I read. The monk was condemned to inclusion for his sins. That means he was to be bricked up alive and left to starve. He tried to avoid his fate by selling his soul to the Devil who helped guide his hand to perform the impossible task of making this. Anyway, the book contains both New and

Old Testaments, as well as a number of historical works and medical writings, and that portrait of the Devil. People say that's evidence of the pact made."

Crowley looked closely at the famous portrait. It was quite horrible, depicting the Devil as an ugly, squatting creature with clawed hands and feet, fire snorting from nostrils in his blue, grinning face. "But we don't actually believe all that 'written in a night' stuff, do we?"

"Most likely it was produced in a Bohemian monastery in the early thirteenth century, transcribed by a single scribe whose identity remains a mystery. And it probably took a long time."

"Your memory for this stuff is impressive!"

"Museum brain! And it's all speculation, really. But we shouldn't discount any possibility until we know a thing for certain. I'm not an especially superstitious person, but I know for sure that I don't know everything, so I try to remain open-minded."

Crowley nodded, accepting the wisdom of that. "Sure, but who was it who said, 'Don't be so open-minded that your brain falls out'?"

A curator wandered toward them, smiling politely. "Wonderful, isn't it?" she said in English.

"Are we that obviously tourists?" Crowley asked.

"I overheard your conversation. You've done a lot of homework, eh?"

"We're fascinated by it," Rose said. "We'd love to know more of the truth."

The curator nodded. "Its true origin is unknown, but a note in the manuscript says it was created in the year twelve ninety-five in the Benedictine monastery of Podlažice in Bohemia, known as the Czech Republic today. Shortly after that the manuscript went to another monastery, in Brevnov near Prague."

"How did it end up in Sweden?" Crowley asked.

"That's not the most honorable of stories. In 1594, Rudolf II, the Holy Roman Emperor, King of Bohemia, and King of Hungary, Croatia and Slavonia, took it to his castle."

"Quite a string of titles."

"Isn't it! Anyway, the bible was kept at Rudolf's castle until it was stolen by the Swedish army during the Thirty Years War and became a part of Queen Christina of Sweden's personal collection. Now we keep it here."

"Stolen goods!"

The curator inclined her head, but changed the subject. "You were talking about the Devil's portrait. You know it also contains a magic formula on how to overcome evil, misfortune and disease."

"Isn't it supposed to have caused those things?" Rose said.

The curator laughed. "Indeed. Inside is also a calendar containing a list of saints and local Bohemians, used to keep track of the feast days of the Church. All the indications are that it was the life's work of one person, as you said, but of course, we doubt the one night legend. Historians estimate the scribe may have conceivably spent as many as twenty years on such a monumental work."

Crowley walked slowly around the display, still in awe of the scale of the book. "How is the deal with the Devil supposed to have helped the monk atone for his sins anyway?"

"The story goes that the monk had committed terrible sins, though it's unclear exactly what. In an attempt to avoid being walled up alive for those sins, he promised to write, in one night, the biggest holy book ever conceived, to make the monastery famous. He quickly realized the task was well beyond him and, in desperation, turned to the Devil for assistance. The Devil demanded his soul as payment and the monk included the full page portrait of the Devil as thanks. It's said that his achievement did indeed spare him from inclusion, but he lost all peace of mind and his life became a living hell. The church, rather than condemning the evil book, has actually studied it in great depth."

"That's a sad and awful story," Rose said quietly.

"I'd love to have a closer look," Crowley said. "What are the chances of us getting a proper look, seeing the other pages?"

The curator smiled politely but shook her head. "No chance at all, I'm afraid."

"What if we offered…"

She silenced him with a finger. "You can't offer anything. But I'm more than happy to chat with you all about it. It's my specialty here."

Crowley had to respect her professionalism but was a little disappointed she had shut him down so quickly. His charm usually worked a bit better than that, especially with women. He chose to pick her brains anyway. "There's a story that some pages are missing?"

"Yes, seven pages at best guess. Removed by persons unknown and now lost. Whether they've been destroyed or are kept in secret somewhere we may never know."

"*May* never know? You think there's a possibility they could be found?"

"Well, the only way to read them would be to find the original bible." She gave him a conspiratorial smile.

Crowley and Rose exchanged a look. "So this is maybe what Declan meant," Rose said.

Crowley nodded, turned his attention back to the curator. He gestured at the glass cabinet beside them. "This isn't the original?"

"This one's a fake. It's not modern, it's an ancient manuscript, but it's not the original, and it's said the text has been changed. And those pages you mentioned may not be missing in the original, of course."

"Why would someone fake it and change things?" Rose asked.

The curator shrugged. "Those who believe in the power of the text may have any number of reasons to alter, replace, or simply remove certain sections. The history of this thing is drenched in death and many would have it destroyed entirely if they had the chance. We're lucky this copy is as complete as it is, really."

"But it's still a copy?" Crowley pressed.

"Yes. We don't make that especially public knowledge, of course. But you two are clearly serious scholars in this regard. Maybe not just tourists after all?"

Crowley shrugged. "Maybe not. Where might we find the real one?"

"You must understand, people who know the real history have been searching for hundreds of years. I'd love to have the time and money to search myself one day. If I *did* have the time and money, I'd start in the Czech Republic, where I could retrace the history of the bible from its original creation. Others have done so, of course, but all it takes is the right seeker. Someone smart and determined enough."

"Looks like we have a lot more research to do," Crowley said. "I might have some contacts I can pull in for some favors."

The curator raised her eyebrows. "Please, if you learn anything, will you let me know?" She handed him a business card. "Use the email address on there? I'd love any information you get."

Crowley took the card and shook her hand. "Absolutely, and thanks for your help."

He was a little surprised when she smiled briefly before turning back to Rose and handing over another card. "You too. Please contact me with *anything* you think I might like to know."

They strolled back through the library's main room, heading for the warm day outside.

"I must be losing my touch," Crowley said wistfully. "That curator showed no interest in me at all. I was hoping to charm a little more information out of her than that."

Rose laughed loudly, causing a few heads to turn in the still building. She controlled herself and leaned close to whisper. "You really are a man."

He looked at her in confusion. "What's that supposed to mean?"

"I don't think any man has enough charm for her. Didn't you notice? She was looking at me the whole time. Why do you think I got her card, too?"

CHAPTER 17

Stockholm

Their hotel room in the center of Stockholm was a little like something from a fairy tale. White walls and a high, crenellated roof over a dozen stories of tall windows, each with a bright orange awning over a small balcony. The room inside featured opulent twins beds, high-windowed views over the city, but all the modern features anyone could hope for.

"This is a beautiful place," Rose said wistfully, leaning into the bay window to stare out. "I wish I could be here under less stressful circumstances."

Crowley watched her for a moment, enjoying the curves of her hips and butt while stifling his feelings of concern. He knew he could walk away from this situation any time if he wanted to, but Rose couldn't. That must feel pretty terrible. Then again, how deeply embroiled was he now? He had been seen with her by the attackers on at least a couple of occasions. Maybe he was fooling himself and he was as entangled as she was. Probably best to assume that was the case and use the motivation to work harder to get it all figured out.

"Maybe we should come back when this is all over," he said with a smile. "Have a little holiday to celebrate."

She glanced back over one shoulder and he was pleased to see she was smiling. "Planning our future?"

He shrugged, raised his hands theatrically. "Just, you know, speculating."

She said nothing more, turned back to stare out into the night. Lights sparkled across Stockholm, glittered off a river right outside. Stars above seemed to be a strange reflection of the urban landscape below, the sky cloudless.

Crowley sighed. "I'll see if my old army intel buddy is available."

"I sent a message to Charles Phelps," Rose said, without turning back from the window.

"Your boss at the museum, right?"

"Yeah. I asked him for some help, but was deliberately oblique about it."

"Cool. Best to stay as far under the radar as possible," Crowley agreed. "But it'll be good if he does provide a connection. And I can trust Cameron, so let me see what he can do." He dialed and it rang several times. He was expecting voicemail any second when a groggy voice answered.

"Y'ello?"

Crowley smiled. "Did I catch you napping?"

"Who's this?"

"You don't recognize my dulcet tones? It's Jake Crowley."

Cameron laughed at the other end. "Crowley pronounced like holy, sir! How are you, man?"

Crowley laughed with him, remembering the drill sergeant yelling in his face about how the man didn't care for pronunciation and Crowley could drop and give him fifty pushups and think about what was more important than a name. "Old Sergeant Hopkins! Such a ball-breaker."

"Saved both our lives in Afghanistan, though," Cameron said. "More than once."

"He did that. I hope he's enjoying his retirement."

Cameron yawned expansively. "I *was* napping for what it's worth. I'm working night shift now."

"Ah, sorry to disturb you then. What are you doing?"

"Security stuff. We're not all smart enough to get teaching jobs."

Crowley laughed again. "Bulldust, my friend! I don't believe a word of it. You're still hooked up, right."

The smile was evident in Cameron's voice. "Of course I am. What do you need?"

Crowley explained what they had learned of the *Devil's Bible*, its supposed history and the facts about the possibility of an original somewhere out in the world. "I'm guessing the general public aren't privy to the kind of history files you might have through military intel," he said. "Any chance you might be able to find me a lead?"

"Sounds like quite the history lesson you're planning," Cameron said, becoming serious. "You okay?"

"I'm in an interesting situation."

"That why you're calling from an unregistered phone?"

Crowley smiled crookedly. "Yeah, that's part of it."

"And you're safe there in Stockholm?"

Crowley had to laugh. "You're good, I'll give you that. I didn't tell you I was in Stockholm."

"No, but you did tell me you'd been to that library. Besides, my trace has got close enough that I know what hotel you're calling from. Haven't narrowed it down to which room yet. Or how many hookers you've hired."

"Don't bother. You've got this number now and you can call me back on it. We'll be leaving here in the morning, so keep it all to yourself, okay?"

"Sure. I'll see what I can learn."

"Thanks, mate. I owe you."

"No, you really don't," Cameron said. "I've a debt to you I'll never repay."

"I was just doing my job, same as Sergeant Hopkins."

"You came back for me. That's going above and beyond. I'll get you whatever I can. And be careful, okay? It sounds like you're in something deep."

Crowley nodded, even though Cameron couldn't see. "Yeah, it's pretty messy. But we'll be okay."

"We?" Cameron said. "I knew you had hookers in there!"

"I'll talk to you soon, Cam. Thanks again."

"You got it."

Crowley hung up and turned to see Rose sitting on the edge of the opposite bed, watching him with serious eyes. "You sure you can trust him?"

Crowley nodded. "There are few people in this world who I trust more. We have a long history, Cameron and I."

"It's nice to know there are people you can really lean on in a bind."

"It is. Really good friends are few and far between, but they matter. Regardless of how much time or distance falls between, they'll always be there."

"You're doing a good job of acting like that for me right now. I can't tell you how much I appreciate it."

"You don't need to keep thanking me. I'm here for you."

"And I can lean on you?" Her eyes twinkled, something cheeky in her half-smile. Or was that just wishful thinking?"

"Absolutely. You can lie on me if you like." Crowley's cheeks flooded and burned the moment the words were out of his mouth. He'd had no idea he was going to say anything like it and cursed his motormouth. He knew he was a little off-center with how to talk to Rose knowing she liked girls. "Of course, that doesn't mean I… What I mean to say is…"

Rose laughed, a vibrant, rich sound. "You know, Jake, I do

enjoy lying on a good man if the mood is right."

Crowley opened his mouth once or twice to reply and quickly felt as though he was gasping like a landed fish. "That's good to know," he managed at last and his cheeks burned even hotter. For a guy who prided himself on being a fairly accomplished ladies' man, Rose certainly had him flipped inside out. And she seemed to know that and be enjoying the hell out of it.

"I'm going to get changed and go to bed," she said. "It's been a long day and I'm exhausted."

Crowley nodded and decided against saying anything else in case he sounded like even more of a fool. She slipped into the bathroom and Crowley sighed, more confused than ever.

CHAPTER 18

Natural History Museum, London

Doctor Charles Phelps looked from one printout to the other and frowned. The data all seemed to be in order but the two studies directly contradicted one another. The beauty of science, he thought to himself with a wry smile. They would need to commission more tests and that would require further funds applications, taking more time away from the direct pursuit of research and cataloging. But no matter, that was the job and he couldn't expect to enjoy every aspect of it.

He tapped his desk intercom, waited for Jaini to respond. When she did, he said, "Can you find me a funding form, please?"

"More paperwork, eh?"

Phelps sighed. "Isn't it always?"

"I'll bring you one in a moment... Oh." Her voice changed, clearly addressing someone else. "Can I help you?"

Phelps heard a man's voice, but couldn't make out the words. Then the connection cut as Jaini took her finger off the intercom. She could be easily distracted sometimes, must have forgotten entirely that she had been talking with him.

He rose and went to his office door. In the reception area outside a man stood clutching nervously at a flat cap. Jaini stared up at him from her desk, face a mask of concern.

"...and we can't find her," the man was saying. "It's really very important and now we're worried about her safety too."

"Who?" Phelps asked.

Jaini jumped, twisting in her seat to look back at him. The man with the hat moved forward, limping on one clearly injured leg.

"It's Rose Black," the man said. "She's gone missing and we really need to reach her."

"Missing?" Phelps frowned. That didn't make a lot of sense, unless Rose simply hadn't mentioned to this person that she was taking an unplanned break. "Who are you?" he asked the stranger.

"My name's Yardley, sir, Pete Yardley. I'm Rose's cousin

on her father's side."

"And Rose has gone missing you say?"

"Yes, sir, we can't reach her. She's not answering her home phone, or her mobile. We went by her place and there's no one home. Now your secretary here tells me she's not been into work lately. We're very worried and we have news she needs to know."

Phelps looked the man over. He seemed earnest enough, appeared guileless and genuinely concerned. But another man, one far less pleasant, had also come looking for Rose not long ago. Things were awry here, but perhaps this man was telling the truth. Phelps had a duty of care to his employees and was bound by certain confidentialities, but it wasn't like he was a doctor or therapist. "News she needs to know?" He wondered if it might be to do with the 'personal stuff' Rose had been so reluctant to talk about.

"Her grandmother..." The man frowned. "*Our* grandmother has fallen very sick. She's had a completely unexpected stroke and she's really not well at all. I don't think she's going to make it, you see, and I know Rose would be so upset if she missed out on that."

"They're close are they?"

"Oh, thick as thieves those two, yes."

Phelps nodded softly, almost to himself. "Well, I'm not at liberty to divulge too much information about employees, Mr. Yardley. But I can tell you that I've heard from Rose in the last twenty four hours. Last night, in fact. She's quite well."

Visible relief washed over Yardley. "Oh, it makes me so happy to hear that, sir. I can't understand why she's not reached out to her family, or why she's not contactable."

"Well, Rose rang me and said she needed some time off and she's taken a short, unplanned holiday, that's all. I'm sure it didn't really occur to her to let everyone know. And as for her phone, she might be somewhere without reception, or have roaming turned off to save money."

Yardley nodded vigorously. "Yes, yes, of course, that all makes sense. Do you have any idea where she is? I really need to let her know about her nan."

Phelps shook his head. "I can't tell you where she is right now, but I did help her out by making an introduction for her to an archivist at Prague Castle. She messaged me that she was planning to visit and did I know anyone she could chat to."

Phelps laughed a little ruefully. "Even when she's supposed to be on vacation, she's still working. Perhaps you can leave a message for her there?" That didn't seem to be giving too much away of Rose's private life, and if this man really did need to get that news to her, he could maybe do it that way.

Yardley smiled broadly. "That's wonderful, sir, thank you very much. I'll do exactly that. And when she turns up at that Castle, they can get her to call me right away. I just hope she gets the message soon enough."

"So do I. Best of luck."

Yardley nodded his thanks and scurried awkwardly from the office on his injured leg.

Phelps sighed and shook his head. People's lives were complicated and thankless so often. "Let's hope she doesn't miss her grandmother's passing, eh?" he said to Jaini.

The secretary nodded and handed him a sheet of paper. "Let's hope. Here's the funds application you asked for."

"Ah, you're a brick. Thank you!"

Patterson limped from the Natural History Museum cursing Rose Black under his breath. He couldn't wait for an opportunity to pay her back for the injury to his knee. Might never work quite the same again, the doctor had told him. She would pay for that.

As he hobbled down the front steps he pulled out his phone and tapped a name in the Recent Calls list. It was picked up after only two rings.

"Anything?"

Dean grinned. "Pack an overnight bag, Jeffries. Tell Mr. Landvik we're going to Prague."

CHAPTER 19

Crowley walked beside Rose along Golden Lane, on the outer edge of Prague Castle. Cobblestones lay damp beneath their feet after a light rain, the sky still occluded by low, pale gray clouds. But that did nothing to dull the brightly colored small houses along the lane, duck egg blue and salmon pink, corn yellow and moss green. Low tiled roofs and squat chimneys topped the buildings, almost like a model village. It made Crowley feel like some kind of strange giant. On the opposite side of the narrow street, the castle walls rose, imposing sandy colored bulwarks dotted with patches of tall windows and black guttering.

"Hardly feels real," Crowley said. "Like a purpose-built tourist attraction."

Rose laughed. "That could be said for a lot of old Europe, I think. But it's been around a long time. In the sixteenth century alchemists lived here, trying to turn base metals into gold. That's where the name comes from, Golden Lane." She pointed. "And that house there, apparently, is where Franz Kafka lived from 1916 to 1917."

"Really?"

She flapped a pamphlet at him. "I picked this up at the hotel on the way out. That's what it says."

"Well, there you go. But this part isn't particularly relevant to us, is it?"

"No." Rose pointed to an access path to the main castle. "The *Devil's Bible* came to Sweden from inside there. That much was confirmed by the librarian in Stockholm. So if what they have is a copy, the original must have been here first but then replaced with the one the Swedes took."

Crowley pursed his lips. "Unless the one here at Prague was a copy all along and that's what was taken?"

"Sure, but then we need to know more about how it got here from wherever King Rudolf lifted it. If we learn that we might get one step closer to the original."

"And that's assuming the whole original or copy thing isn't just a myth." Crowley held up a hand to stave off any protestations. "I know. We can't know anything for sure without following it up. Let's go inside. Your contact there now?"

Rose checked her phone for the time. "He should be. The number Charles gave me was a mobile, so I texted rather than called. But he messaged back that he was starting at ten today and it's ten thirty now."

They made their way to the entrance to the castle, walked under an intricate golden archway over the gate. Either side, statues of battle stood imposing over the gateposts. On the left, one muscled warrior killed a man with a wickedly long pointed knife. On the right, a cloaked fighter smashed his opponent with a massive club.

"Amazing sculpting," Crowley said.

Rose twisted her mouth in distaste. "Bit violent for my liking. They're the Fighting Giants, apparently."

The castle before them was four main stories of pale stone, then a roof story under red-brown tiles. They entered and made their way through high and impressive spaces, vaulted ceilings with floral stonework, bright religious iconography, tall windows, both clear and stained glass.

"Another place I'd love to visit with more time and less bad guys trying to kidnap me," Rose said.

Crowley nodded. He had to agree, the place was breathtaking. "Add it to the list."

Rose checked her notes again and then sent a text message to the contact Phelps had given her. He texted back almost immediately. "Damek says he's coming to meet us. He'll escort us to the archives."

"Excellent. You've got useful contacts."

"Anything come of your army friend? Cameron was it?"

Crowley shrugged. "Not yet. But he's the kind of guy who'll get a bit between his teeth and keep running with it. I imagine I'll hear from him in another day or two with everything anyone in the world knows about this thing!"

"You are Rose?"

They turned toward the voice and saw a young man, maybe mid-twenties, tall and slim. He had long brown hair pulled back into a ponytail and wore thick-framed glasses, tight jeans and a denim shirt with mother-of-pearl press studs holding the pockets closed.

Crowley frowned. He'd been expecting a stuffy old professor type, not some young hipster. Then again, Rose was a contemporary of this guy and she was no stuffy professor either. Stereotypes rarely proved accurate, he reflected.

"That's me." Rose extended a hand to shake. Crowley didn't miss Damek's gaze traveling all the way down and back up her body in a way the young man probably thought was subtle. Or maybe he just didn't care for subtlety. "This is my colleague, Jake Crowley."

"Your colleague?" Damek smiled, a little too smugly for Crowley's liking.

He shook anyway, reminded himself not to judge too quickly. "Good to meet you. Thanks for seeing us."

"It's not a problem," Damek said, his English excellent despite a fairly strong Czech accent. "I studied with Professor Phelps for one year on university exchange before he took the job at the museum. You work with him now?"

Rose laughed. "A little presumptuous to say I work with him, but yes I work for him."

Damek shook his head, smiling. "You do yourself a disservice, Miss Black. The Professor himself described you as working together."

"Well, that's very generous of him. And please, call me Rose."

Damek led them from the public galleries through a couple of cool, quiet stone corridors, then into his offices. Crowley was irritated to realize he was quite lost, no idea which way to run if trouble started. He also realized he'd started thinking like a cat again, always clocking the exits from any room, watching faces, twitchy around sudden movements. It was war training kicking back in and he had to welcome it, though it raised some uncomfortable memories. *Focus on the task at hand, Jake,* he told himself.

Damek's offices were large but low-ceilinged, with modern fittings among old stone. Several filing cabinets and glass-fronted display cases lined the walls, and row upon row of shoulder high bookshelves filled one end of the room. At the other end were several desks, many with papers or volumes strewn across them. Despite the signs of work, no one else occupied the archives as Damek led them to the biggest desk in one corner and offered them seats. He turned to a cabinet behind him bearing a kettle and multi-colored, mismatched mugs, and began to make tea. "I asked Phelps what you needed to know and he was a little vague. You have a particular point of interest?"

Rose flicked a look at Crowley and he shrugged, nodded encouragingly.

"*The Devil's Bible,*" Rose said. "*The Codex Gigas.*"

Damek set mugs of tea before each of them and sat on his side of the desk with a cup of his own. "Quite the artifact, that one. Have you seen it?"

"We've seen the one in Stockholm…" Rose trailed off, one eyebrow raised.

Damek chuckled. "Ah! You don't believe the book in Stockholm is the genuine article?"

"Do you?"

"It's surely a conspiracy theory," Damek said, and sipped his tea.

Rose's face fell, but Crowley saw something in the young man's eyes. Amusement, mostly. "You don't believe it's a conspiracy theory."

Damek looked at him, eyebrows raised. "I don't?"

"No. And the librarian tasked with curating it in the National Library of Sweden made no secret that she believes theirs is a copy."

"Honestly, I'm not sure what I believe. The history is messy and there are many conflicting stories. It's very hard to pin down any real facts and I do try to only believe in the things I can confirm, things I can corroborate."

"Have others asked you about it?" Rose asked.

"No, it's really only something a few conspiracy theorists believe, but no one I know takes it seriously. No one with any authority, at least. But of course, we know without a doubt that we don't know everything. Anything is possible." He sipped tea, brow furrowed in thought. "In truth, very little is known about the bible. Its history is tied in very closely with Rudolf II, whose seat was this very castle for a long time, but Rudolf was an… interesting man. He's often credited as being a rather useless leader. It's said that he was responsible for starting the Thirty Years War, but the truth is he was a real Renaissance man.

"Rudolf had little interest in politics and ruling, but a great interest in the arts and sciences. He was a great patron of the arts, a true art lover, and gathered a significant collection. He was a devotee of occult sciences and learning. He was instrumental in seeding the scientific revolution, the age of reason. Without his efforts, things in Europe today, even throughout the world, might be very different. But he has been largely vilified by history."

Damek was in full lecture mode, suddenly not a young hipster any more but a knowledgeable academic, comfortable in his field of expertise. "Rudolf collected all manner of art and curiosities. He developed an entire wing of the castle here to house his collection. You know, the adjective Rudolfine, as in 'Rudolfine Mannerism', is often used in art history to describe the style of art he patronized.

"But more interesting, to my mind at least, were his occult studies, particularly his interest in astrology and alchemy. Those things were considered mainstream scientific fields in Renaissance Prague. Rudolf's lifelong quest was to find the Philosopher's Stone and he spared no expense to bring Europe's premier alchemists to his court. He performed his own experiments in a private laboratory. He was even rumored, at one point, to own a copy of the Voynich Manuscript."

"Really? Was he respected for these things?" Crowley asked. "Or ridiculed?"

"Depends on who you're talking about. It was a very different time, of course. He was supposed to be ruling across several kingdoms, and was chastised for failing in that pursuit, but others greatly respected his interests. Nostradamus, for example, prepared a horoscope dedicated to 'Rudolf, Prince and King'. That's a fairly strong endorsement of the man."

"Are there any stories that connect Rudolf with the *Devil's Bible*?" Crowley asked.

Damek sipped his tea. "It's well known that Rudolf possessed it, but I'm not aware of any particular stories about that." He frowned and scratched at his chin.

Crowley chose not to interrupt, Rose clearly feeling the same way. They exchanged a quick glance, part amusement, part frustration.

Damek sniffed and nodded, as if to himself. "Yes, of course. You know, you should investigate the story of the Golem of Prague. That's the only other relevant reference I can think of."

"Should we?" Rose leaned forward, put her elbows on his desk, charm turned up to eleven. "Can you show us?"

Damek smiled at her, like he was not in the least bit surprised that this beautiful woman was besotted with him. Crowley made sure his eyes didn't roll so far that only the whites showed. The precociousness of youth. Then again, this archivist was almost certainly less than ten years younger than Crowley. Perhaps he shouldn't deride the young guy's self-confidence so easily. It might be jealousy surfacing, but it was clear, at least to Crowley, that Rose was playing the Czech archivist like a prize fiddle.

"For you, of course I can." Damek went off among the many shelves while Crowley and Rose shared a quiet laugh. She winked as Damek returned with a large, leather bound volume. "Here it is."

CHAPTER 20

"**The thing is,**" Damek said, clearly pleased with himself, "we have more of the story than most. Do you know anything of the legends surrounding the Golem of Prague?"

"Nothing," Crowley said.

"I have vague recollections about it being made to protect the local Jews or something." Rose frowned, shook her head. "Let's assume we know nothing and you tell us everything."

Damek nodded, leafing through the large tome on his desk. "Okay, I'll summarize for you from here." He cleared his throat, affected the air of a lecturer again. Crowley preferred him this way. It seemed more natural. "So we have the rabbi of Prague at the time of Rudolf's reign, a man named Judah Loew ben Bezale. He was also known as the Maharal. According to the legends, he created a golem to defend the Prague ghetto from anti-Semitic attacks and pogroms." Damek smiled up at Rose. "Your memory is very good, after all."

"Yes, but I have no idea what else went on."

"Well, that's where it gets particularly interesting. Depending on which version of the legend you read, as there are several slightly varying accounts, Rudolf II was to either expel or execute the Jews in Prague. Either way, things were not looking good for them. So to protect the Jewish community, the rabbi took clay from the banks of the Vltava River and used it to construct the golem. He then used a variety of rituals and Hebrew incantations to create the *shem* which would give the golem life."

"*Shem?*" Crowley asked.

"A golem receives its life and powers from a powerful… spell, if you like, written on paper and put into the golem's mouth. The more powerful the practitioner, the stronger the *shem*, therefore the more capable the golem, you see?"

Crowley nodded. "Right, okay. So this rabbi, this Maharal, he was powerful?"

"By all accounts, almost divinely so. He is the hero of the piece, after all."

"Right. Go on."

"So the Maharal's golem was called Josef, but more commonly called Yossele. The legends say that Yossele was able to make himself invisible, and that he could summon spirits from the dead to act out his will. A powerful golem, you see, from a powerful rabbi. The only care Yossele required from Rabbi Loew, the Maharal, was to ensure he wasn't active on the day of Sabbath."

"That's Saturday, right?" Crowley asked.

Damek nodded. "The golem had to rest on the Sabbath so that it would do nothing to desecrate the holy day. Rabbi Loew would remove the *shem* from Yossele's mouth on Friday evening and return it on Sunday morning." Damek looked up from his book and smiled. "Now, here's where it gets particularly good. One Friday evening, Rabbi Loew forgot to remove the *shem*, and the golem Yossele did indeed desecrate the Sabbath. There is one version of the story where Yossele fell in love, and when rejected, became a violent monster. Other accounts have the golem finally free on the Sabbath to act out a murderous rampage against those who would persecute the Jews. The popular accounts go that the rabbi finally managed to pull the *shem* from Yossele's mouth and immobilize him in front of the Old New Synagogue, whereupon the golem fell in pieces. The body parts were stored in the attic *genizah*, a secret hiding place, from where it could be restored to life again if needed. Some legends say the body of Rabbi Loew's golem still lies in the synagogue's attic, but when it was renovated in 1883, no evidence was found. Other versions of the myth state that the golem was stolen from the *genizah* and entombed in a graveyard in Prague's Žižkov district, where the Žižkov Television Tower stands now. A more recent legend tells of a Nazi agent finding the golem in the synagogue attic during World War II. He tried to stab Yossele, but he died instead." Damek grinned at them.

"Good stories," Crowley said. "But you're holding something back."

Damek's grin became a laugh. He pointed to the page again. "A film was made in the attic in 1984, but that crew found no evidence either. And besides, the attic is not open to the general public, so we can't corroborate any of this."

Crowley grew impatient. He felt as though the archivist was toying with them. "So this is all very fascinating, but what does it have to do with Rudolf or the *Devil's Bible*?"

Damek raised one forefinger dramatically. "You asked for the whole story as if you knew nothing. So that's most of it. But remember, I said we know something of the legend that others don't?"

"We remember," Rose said, sounding a lot more patient than Crowley had. "So what's the special angle you have?"

"Well, the suppressed part of the legend is that when the Rabbi forgot to remove the *shem* that Friday night, the golem took its opportunity to come after Rudolf. Remember, Yossele was charged with protecting the Jews in Prague, so what better way than by destroying the Holy Roman Emperor himself, the man in charge of that persecution? And here's where it connects back to the *Devil's Bible*.

"That Sabbath day, the golem came after Rudolf, who, fearing for his life, took shelter in a secret place where he kept his most secret possessions. The parts of his private collection that he wanted to keep the *most* private. Among them, the *Devil's Bible*."

"I thought it was common knowledge that he possessed it," Crowley said.

The archivist shrugged. "It's just a story and this makes it more exciting, no? Just because people knew Rudolf had the *Codex*, that doesn't mean they knew where he kept it." He looked back down to the pages of his book. "Anyway, the golem found Rudolf's hiding place easily. It says here Yossele 'discovered Rudolf along the pathway to hell'. When it also found the *Devil's Bible* there it decided it had also discovered the source of Rudolf's evil. So the golem, rather than simply killing the King, consumed the *Devil's Bible*, thus purging the evil from Rudolf's heart and ensuring the ongoing safety of the Jews. However, the act cost the golem its life and it was never seen again."

Damek closed the book with a smile. "Only we have that particular legend, and it is fanciful, I know. But it's the only story of which I'm aware that connects Rudolf to the disappearance of the original *Codex Gigas*. And perhaps that's why any existing version, such as the one in Sweden, is a copy."

Crowley took a deep breath, determined not to let his annoyance show. It was fanciful indeed and he wasn't sure all this journeying and time had been worthwhile. Had they hit a dead end?

Rose stood and reached a hand across the desk. "Thank

you so much for your time, Damek. It's been truly enlightening."

Damek shook but looked a little crestfallen. "You're leaving so soon?"

"We have a lot to see and do."

Damek frowned. "Well, you should look around some more here first. Much of Rudolf's artwork is preserved."

Rose pursed her lips, quite convincingly feigning a real interest. She smiled at Damek and leaned on the desk. "Are there any works of art or literature from Rudolf's collection that aren't on public display? Perhaps because they were too controversial or something. Maybe the Voynich Manuscript?" She winked and the archivist flushed.

"There are, in fact, a number of paintings that haven't been on display in decades, but not because of their content or subject matter. Simply because their quality is not up to snuff. The displays are kept to those items that are best preserved."

"You think we could have a look?" Rose asked. "I like things other people don't get to see."

Damek laughed and stood. "It's really not very interesting, but for you, of course."

He led them from the office along a stone corridor and then to a heavy metal door with an electronic keypad beside it. He tapped in a code.

There was a soft hiss as the door opened. "Climate-controlled storage," Damek said back over his shoulder as he led them inside and closed the door behind them.

The room was large and cool, dancing in halogen light as Damek flicked a switch and several overhead bulbs flickered into life. Row upon row of shelving held all manner of treasures. The shelves were differing in size, small ones holding books and scrolls and piles of paper. Larger ones with boxes and bags. Larger still had paintings that stood facing out.

Rose and Crowley strolled back and forth among the shelves making appreciative noises, Damek proudly following, but sticking most closely to Rose. Crowley wasn't sure what they were looking for, if there was even anything of interest to be found, when one dark and faded painting caught his attention. He grimaced, the image eliciting a deep and visceral reaction inside him, simply from observing it. He didn't like it at all, but couldn't take his eyes off it. The work was fine and intricate, showing a round tower, with a staircase beneath descending past people in torment. The stairs led down to a flame shrouded figure that looked vaguely like an ape. Inside the belly of the figure squatted a horned, clawed figure that Crowley recognized immediately as the devil from the *Codex Gigas*, the very drawing that gave the *Devil's Bible* its name.

Noting that Rose and Damek had their backs to him, Crowley quickly snapped a photo with his phone, then called the archivist's name. "What's this tower here?" he asked. "Is it a real place?"

"Most definitely. That's Daliborka, or Dalibor Tower. It stands at the eastern end of Golden Lane. Dating back to 1496, it served as a prison until 1781. It's named after its first inmate, Dalibor of Kozojedy."

"What a grim looking place," Rose said. She leaned close and Crowley knew she had spotted the tiny image of the devil inside the ape-like creature at the bottom. She didn't say anything.

"A prison, eh?" Crowley said. "Cells and dungeons and things?"

"Oh, yes. There's a dungeon with monumental vaults, and a circular opening in the floor through which offenders were lowered into the oubliette via a pulley."

"From the French *oublier*," Rose breathed. "To forget."

"Indeed. Just a dark hole in the ground with only one way in or out, through that hole at the top. Where people were left and forgotten."

"Horrible," Rose said, and shook herself.

Damek smiled. "The Dalibor Tower is included in the castle tour. You should take the tour before you leave."

"Thanks so much," Crowley said. "We've certainly enjoyed this private tour." He headed for the door, Rose in step beside him, and Damek hurried ahead to open up.

"Nothing else I can do for you?" Damek asked, though the question was directed to Rose.

"No, we've taken up enough of your time," she said diplomatically, bestowing a warm and friendly smile on the man.

Damek's features fell. "Well. I'll walk you out then."

CHAPTER 21

Dalibor Tower, Prague Castle

The tour of Dalibor Tower left less than an hour after Crowley and Rose had emerged from the Prague Castle archives. They'd had time for a coffee and a chat in a small café near Golden Lane to discuss where they might turn next.

"Not much help, really, that Damek," Crowley had said.

Rose shrugged. "But those paintings in storage were more interesting, having heard the story of the golem. Let me see that picture again."

Crowley tapped it up on his phone and Rose nodded.

"That image is definitely the devil in the *Codex Gigas*," Rose agreed. "And the ape-like outline could be intended to represent a golem."

"I'd say so."

"But you do realize golems aren't real, yes?"

Crowley slipped the phone away again with a smile. "Legends and stories often have factual origins, though, so we can't discount anything."

Rose gave him a mock-withering look. "I am a historian, remember?"

They had quickly finished their drinks and joined a group of twelve or fifteen others for the Dalibor Tower tour. From the outside, it was a pale stone, rounded artillery tower, with a squat, pointed red tile conical roof. Small, square windows marched in a spiral up the sides, following the stairways inside. The interior was the same pale stonework, with heavy, dark wooden beams overhead.

The tour guide was an animated young woman with short, platinum blonde hair and bright red lips. She spoke with barely any accent, if anything sounding more American than European. "Daliborka, better known internationally as Dalibor Tower, is a cannon tower built into the slope above the Deer Moat of Prague Castle. It was constructed by Benedikt Ried in 1496. Originally it was higher, but only five stories have survived until today. Of course, it is most famous as a prison, named after Dalibor of Kozojedy, the first prisoner in 1498. He was imprisoned for his part in a nearby serfs' uprising, and for harboring rebels on his land. Legend says he learned to play violin to earn his living in the tower. Daliborka was used as a prison until 1781."

They were led down into the cool basement, the guide's words trailing back to them. "Of course, everyone is most interested in the dungeons. There are four cells around this room, the walls over two and a half meters thick.'

The floor of the dungeon was a circular pattern of orange brick, rough stone walls rising to a high vault above. The center of the floor drew everyone's eye, dominated by a raised stone circular opening like a well, with a metal grid over the top to prevent an accidental fall. And, presumably, to keep prisoners in assuming they ever managed to get that high after being lowered several meters into a dark hole in the ground. Above the opening hung a disturbing array of metalwork, chains and manacles.

"This is the famous oubliette," the guide said with a wide smile. "The round hole you see is the only access to a large circular space beneath. Around the edges of the space are several smaller cells, where up to four prisoners would be imprisoned at a time and… left. After all, the name oubliette comes from the French word 'to forget', and that's exactly what happened. Who knows what might have become of those people once they were thrown inside." She leaned forward, eyes wide. "Or what they might have done to *each other*!"

The tour group made dutiful noises of amusement and disgust and Crowley zoned out the guide's talk as he stared around. The whole room gave him the chills, not only because it was actually cold inside. The idea of the suffering endured here, especially down in the darkness of the oubliette below, made his insides churn. He had suffered some dark and seemingly inescapable internment himself in the Middle East and any kind of prison brought back painful recollections. Especially ones as medieval and horrendous as this one. He shook off the thoughts and shuffled closer to the oubliette.

The tour began to move on from the dungeon and Crowley snagged Rose's sleeve. "You go on. I'll meet you at the far end of the Golden Lane in an hour."

Rose shook her head, and glanced nervously at the group moving away. "No way, I'm not leaving you."

"It'll rouse too much suspicion if we both disappear. This

way, if someone notices I'm gone, you can say I wasn't feeling well and went back the way we came. You can carry on with the tour and cover for me if necessary, so no one comes back looking."

"I suppose that makes sense." Rose looked from Crowley to the tour group and back again. "Okay, but be careful. And good luck!"

She hurried to catch up with the group and Crowley slipped to one side for a moment, ensuring no one could see him loitering if they glanced back. Once he was sure they were all gone and he was alone, he snuck back to the oubliette. If the place had given him the creeps before, it was magnified ten-fold now that he was alone.

He checked the large bolts holding the metal grid over the top of the oubliette and tested them with a finger. They seemed pretty solid. Frowning, he took out a pocket tool, opened it up, and started working at the fastenings. It took a while, and made some noise, but slowly he managed to loosen the two main bolts holding the grill in place on either side. With a smile, glancing nervously around, sure someone would appear to discover him any moment, he carefully lifted it aside.

On the way from the café back to the tour, they had passed an unoccupied work site. The tradesmen had presumably been on a coffee break of their own. Crowley had surreptitiously snagged a strong-looking nylon rope from a pile of tools and stuffed it into his jacket. He was glad of the find now as he unfurled the rope and tied it off to a sturdy metal stanchion nearby.

Crowley took a deep breath, scanned quickly around once more, then slid down the rope into the dark hole.

CHAPTER 22

Beneath Dalibor Tower

Crowley's feet touched the flagstone floor and he stood in a narrow pool of light from the entrance high above. The oubliette was deep, the ceiling curving away from the hole and disappearing into darkness. The walls of the prison were lost in inky shadow. Looking up at the entrance, Crowley frowned. A person would have to be a spider or a cockroach to escape, clinging to the roof upside down just to reach the hole, let alone have the skills to undo the grill from the inside if it were closed up again. He shuddered at the thought. The sooner he got back out of this place, the better.

The air was a damp chill in his lungs, dust and age penetrating his pores. He slipped a flashlight from his pocket and its beam pierced the darkness. The flagstones went flat to the walls, which curved all around to make a circular room some fifteen or so paces across. Then the stone walls rose, large blocks pressed close together. Four openings, like the cardinal points on a compass, marked the four individual cells. The room was otherwise featureless and austere. Crowley imagined multiple prisoners, colluding to escape. But even if one tall man stood on another's shoulders, they still wouldn't be able to reach the access hole high above. It would take three men standing atop one another to manage that, and only the best acrobats were likely to succeed. Certainly not starving, beaten, weakened prisoners.

He went to each individual cell and looked in. Four empty spaces, no taller than a man, only a few paces square. After the last one, Crowley stood back, exasperated. What now? The place was empty, as bare and cold as a desert at night. Frustrated, he went back into one of the cells and looked more closely, playing his torchlight slowly over the stone blocks of the walls. Marks and writing became clear when he took time to notice them, scratched into the rock presumably with small stones. Some were simply tally marks, maybe counting off days spent interred, though how anyone might measure the passing of days in the basement of a basement was a mystery. Perhaps they weren't days, but something less innocent.

Other marks were words in an unpracticed hand, the language unintelligible to Crowley. All the cells had marks of some kind, some more than others. In the third cell he paused, heart rate fluttering slightly faster. Ever so faint, almost obscured by more recent carvings, was the outline of a devil. And not just any devil, but the strange, squatting creature from the *Codex Gigas*, crudely rendered but recognizable. Crowley pulled out his pocket folding tool and scraped at the image, and the surrounding stone. Sandy mortar rained down from a section softer than elsewhere. Frowning with concentration, Crowley carved deeper and revealed a kind of dip in the top of the brick beneath the mortar he had removed. A dip just big enough to slip in his fingertips and give some grip. Was it a handhold?

He pulled, but it was stuck fast, not budging even fractionally. Crowley brushed at the block, blew dust away, then held the flashlight in his teeth as he worked more at the surface. Either side of the devil carving were two circles, only about half an inch in diameter. They looked to be a slightly different shade to the rest of the block. He dug into them with his knife point and the same sandy mortar drifted down.

Crowley switched from the knife to a small screwdriver tool and dug into the circles, quickly revealing a deep hole in the stone. He worked his way in and the screwdriver tip slipped through and there was a sound like a popping cork. Crowley grinned and quickly cleared the second hole. He'd read about this kind of method and discussed it while teaching his ancient history classes. The Egyptians used similar techniques in the pyramids. The stone had been set in place, the holes used to suction air out of the space beyond until the block was set tight, hermetically sealed, and then the holes plugged with mortar. Now that he had broken through, the pressure equalized and the block shifted in its seat.

Crowley put his tools away, held the flashlight in one hand and used the fingertips of his other hand in the groove atop the block. He pulled and the block slid easily free. The one below it moved against the first and Crowley pulled that aside too. Each block was heavy, hard to manhandle, but he was strong enough to lift each free and put them on the floor. The opening he had made was just big enough for him to crawl through.

He shone his light inside first, but it was difficult to lean in and see. *Gonna have to simply go in and see where this goes*, he told himself, steeling his jittering nerves. Excitement and fear in roughly equal measure made his blood run fast. He wriggled into the opening, torch in his teeth again, until his hands found the cold hard stone of the floor on the other side. He walked his hands forwards, pulling his body through, until his legs were in and he dropped his feet to the ground. He sat back in a crouch and took his flashlight from his teeth to pan it around.

The space was much bigger than the cell he had come from, easily twenty paces or more square with a high stone ceiling. Old wooden cupboards and a rickety desk occupied one wall. On the desk was a book stand, big enough to hold a large tome, and candles had burned down to trickling, lumpy stubs. A human skull and a dusty dagger sat next to the book rest. Marks on the floor seemed to depict strange sigils, angular characters and the point of at least part of a pentacle.

Crowley slowly twisted, playing the light around the walls and gasped, his heart slamming into his ribs, when the beam of brightness revealed a hideous face, looking right back at him.

CHAPTER 23

Crowley sat back hard on the cold stone but took deep, steadying breaths. The face was huge, and ugly, but made of stone. Or some kind of pressed clay maybe. Moving in for a closer look, Crowley grinned at the revelation. This giant was clearly the golem of the stories they had heard. Or at the very least, a copy of it. The thing had been broken in two, the stomach section smashed open. Just the upper torso, from somewhere around the sternum up, was big enough that as it sat on the floor, it was eye-level with Crowley, and he was not a short man. The face had wide-set eyes, deep and almost thoughtful. Its nose was short and slightly flattened, above a wide, lipless mouth that seemed set in a grimace of anger or pain. Or maybe frustration.

Large chunks of the midsection lay scattered around the room, angular and irregular, the result of some cataclysmic shattering strike. The legs, still joined together by large, ragged sections of pelvis, were each at least as long as Crowley was tall. When this thing was whole it would have been terrifyingly massive. Crowley ran a hand over the smooth, brown stony shoulder, wondering if it really was the golem of the legend, hundreds of years old. Once animate, now broken and inert, could this thing really have walked with a magical *shem* in its mouth?

But it didn't answer the biggest and most pressing question in his mind, which was the location of the original *Devil's Bible*, or what might have happened to it. Crowley stalked around the room, looking more closely at the cupboards, all annoyingly empty. The desk was equally unforthcoming, but he pocketed the dagger for later. It had a leather-wrapped hilt, shiny and smooth with age and use, and a slightly curved blade about six inches long. The metal of the blade bore pit marks and some chinks in its sharpened edge, but was in surprisingly good condition. The hermetic sealing of the chamber had preserved it against time well.

Crowley looked at the skull for a moment, wondering who

it might have been. What unfortunate soul had their head interred in this creepy occult cave, sealed in presumably forever until Crowley had arrived to disturb its rest? But he couldn't bring himself to touch it.

He looked once more around the room, once again frustrated. To have found a secret chamber, but have it tell him nothing was perhaps more galling than having never found it in the first place.

He returned to the golem, staring at its agonized face. His brows knitted as it occurred to him that the *Codex Gigas* could easily have been hidden inside the monster, with ample room to spare. It was more than big enough.

He shone his light into the bottom half, kneeling to look down each leg, but saw nothing. Returning to the top half, he carefully tipped it over onto its side, grunting with the effort of managing the enormous weight. When he shone his torch inside the capacious torso, it revealed a kind of shelf set into the creature's back. The shelf had a lip along the front and some half a meter above it, a leather strap hung limp. A node of clay in line with the strap seemed perfectly set to anchor the leather in place. It was all too convenient to ignore. The size and placement was perfect for the *Devil's Bible* to sit on the shelf and be held in tight by the leather strap secured across it about halfway up.

"The golem didn't consume the bible," Crowley said to himself in a whisper. "It housed it."

The smile of discovery fell off his face at the sudden emergence of hushed voices, drifting to him from far away. But not that far. Had some tour guide or other employee discovered the grill he had removed, his rope hanging down into the oubliette?

The sound of feet slapping gently on the floor caused his already racing heart to double-time. Whoever it was had used his rope and descended into the lower dungeon. He quickly doused his light and peered out through the opening, into the tiny cell and the oubliette beyond.

A man stood beside Crowley's rope, illuminated by the light falling from above. In one hand, he held a gun, light glinting off the gray metal of its barrel as he pointed it around the empty space. In the man's other hand was a flashlight, which he lifted and flicked on. It had a red filter and light like spilled blood danced around the pale stones.

The man looked slowly about himself, pausing at each of

the four cells to shine his light in. His face was shadowed, but Crowley easily saw his focus and concentration. This was not a castle employee.

There was no way Crowley could worm his way through the small opening from the secret room and into the cell to jump the armed man. He'd be trapped like a lobster in a pot. As he sat back, wondering how on earth he would avoid the man's attention, the red light spilled into the small cell outside his hiding place. The man saw the dark square of the removed bricks and grunted in satisfaction.

"Found something," he called up into the light, and moved forward.

Crowley stood beside the gap, mind racing with possibilities. If the man looked inside before he came through and Crowley was close enough to jump him, the man would easily shoot at point blank range. If Crowley waited across the room, the man was sure to see him and get a shot off before Crowley had a chance to cover the distance. In an enclosed space with nowhere to run, the man with the automatic pistol had all the advantages.

As the gunman hurried toward the opening, Crowley looked frantically around. His time was almost up.

CHAPTER 24

Beneath Dalibor Tower

Rob Jeffries crouched outside the small cell and shone his red light on the two large stones, sat beside the hole they had been removed from. He frowned. Landvik sure had him do some unsavory things, and crawling around creepy dungeons was definitely high on that list. He should have sent Dean Patterson down after all, but the guy was constantly complaining about his injured knee. Jeffries wondered again if the loser was overplaying the hurt to get out of the tough jobs. Surely that Rose Black woman hadn't kicked him hard enough to do the kind of damage Patterson complained about. Then again, Jeffries had to respect her skill if she had. Tough woman.

He moved into the small cell and shined his flashlight into the space beyond the removed blocks. The room was large, but seemed empty. He considered firing a round or two into the room ahead of himself, but thought better of it when he considered the noise and the potential ricochets.

Instead, he put his arm with the light through the hole, then the other hand with the gun, and played both around inside, looking over the top as best he could. Nothing. And no one made a grab for him. He leaned his head in, groaning with the tightness of the fit, and checked again. Nothing. A desk, a cupboard. He looked to his left and saw a massive statue, broken and lying around all over one side of the room.

With a grunt of effort he wriggled and pushed his way through, fell unceremoniously onto the cold flagstones, and quickly gained his feet. He turned in a full circle, light and gun aligned as he tracked every inch of the room. No one. He looked closely at the floor looking for trapdoors, scanned the ceiling for other openings, the wall for ladders. Nothing. He kicked at the large statue and a couple of pieces lying around. "Ugly damn thing," he muttered.

It looked as though someone had been here before them, no doubt Rose Black and the man she had dragged along with her, but they appeared to have missed them. So close, it was infuriating.

He crawled back out through the tight access gap and went back into the pool of light and the rope. "There's no one down here," he called up to Patterson.

"The girl's not there?"

Jeffries rolled his eyes, ground his teeth. "What do you think 'no one' means?"

"You checked thoroughly."

"Yes, I did! If the girl and her friend were here, they've gone now."

"Why did they leave the rope? Leave evidence they were here?"

Jeffries shook his head, bit down on an abusive response and said instead, "I guess they were in a hurry. Or maybe they just didn't care."

"What are we gonna tell Landvik?" Patterson called down.

Jeffries barked a derisive laugh. "Landvik? Nothing right now. We'll have to decide what's next before we tell him anything. Now, either come down here and check for yourself or pull me up. It's creepy as hell in this hole."

"All right, all right, keep your hair on."

Jeffries pocketed the gun and flashlight, wrapped the end of the rope around one ankle, and gripped on. "Pull!" he called as he began to climb and he heard Patterson's grunts of effort as the man finally started doing something useful.

Crowley kicked away a large slab of clay and scooted out of the golem's large torso. The hiding place he had crawled into was cramped and uncomfortable, and the two chunks of broken golem pelvis he'd used to conceal himself had been a sloppy effort, but the man with the gun hadn't looked very hard, despite what Crowley had heard him calling up to his friend.

Crowley stood and dusted himself off, taking deep breaths to settle his racing nerves. That had been way too close for comfort and only the fact that the gunman hadn't realized the golem was hollow had saved him from a dangerous, almost certainly deadly confrontation.

Urgency pressed at Crowley's heart and mind as he mentally kicked himself for leaving Rose alone. He'd gotten so caught up in the search for the bible that he hadn't considered the people who were after Rose might have caught up with them already. Or at all, for that matter. He had become sloppy thinking their flight from the country had bought them all the time they would need. His mind flickered to the archivist, to the introduction Rose's boss at the museum had made for them, and realization washed over him in a cold flood. Their pursuers had obviously been to Rose's workplace and got the information from Professor Phelps. Crowley desperately hoped that man was okay. He needed to get back to Rose, get on the move again, and put some new distance between them and their pursuers.

Cautiously, he made his way back through the tight gap, out of the small cell and into the oubliette. He couldn't get out of this miserable place soon enough. A chill shot up his spine as he emerged into the larger space and looked to the pool of light falling from the access hole high above. Light was all that fell down.

His rope was gone.

CHAPTER 25

Dalibor Tower

Crowley stood, fingers linked together atop his head, staring into the column of wan light from above. Trapped in an oubliette. His heart hammered, ice washed through his gut. It was a nightmare made real. The opening high above, designed specifically to thwart escape, mocked him with its brightness.

He took a deep breath. He wouldn't rot down here. At worst he would have to yell for help like a recalcitrant child and keep yelling until he was hoarse. Eventually some official employee would hear, they would come and help him out. But he would be in a lot of trouble, maybe even arrested. And then where would that leave Rose. He couldn't allow that to happen.

He turned to the walls, curving slowly up to the exit. Maybe he was fit and strong enough, his military regime of fitness maintained, at least to some degree. He certainly wasn't the wasted prisoner who might have been thrown into this dungeon in days past. He found a wall with what appeared to be the widest trails of mortar and began to scratch it out, make a hand hold. He got a toe into one mortar course, reached up and wedged his fingers into the highest he could reach, and hauled. The stone was hard, sharp edges scraping at the skin of his fingers, dragging against his nails. His muscles strained as he pulled and managed to get a meter or so off the ground. He reached up again, scraped a patch of sandy mortar free and pulled again. Teeth gritted, grunting with the effort, he gained another meter. He allowed himself a moment's congratulation, ignored the nagging thought of how he might get across the ceiling even if he scaled the wall, and slipped.

He yelped, skin barking off one knee and each fingertip as he slid down. He gouged his hands in and managed to arrest the fall. Two meters up, one back. This would take a while.

He glanced down, the flagstone floor still insultingly close, and began to climb again. He made it up another couple of meters, then craned his neck to see back over his shoulder. Could he get high enough, then brace his legs against the wall and push back, leap across the space to grab the edge of the hole high above?

His brow creased in concentration, and despair. Who did he think he was? Spider-Man? Regardless, he pushed on, reached up for another handhold, and fell.

For a moment he seemed weightless, then air rushed past, whipping at his hair and jacket, and the hard stone floor slammed into his back. The breath was hammered from his lungs, his bones flexed and flesh howled as he curled into a fetal ball and groaned. He dragged air into his battered body, squinted against the hurt and dragged air in again. He let his panic settle as he mentally searched for any specific pain, any broken bones.

Bloody idiot, he thought to himself. *Could have smashed your stupid skull.*

He might be less use to Rose if he were arrested, but he'd be no use to her at all if he was dead. He climbed slowly to his feet, testing every limb, thankful he wasn't more than bruised. Lucky. Frowning, he scoured the dungeon, looking for anything else. A trapdoor, a bricked up entrance to some other tunnel that he could maybe clear with enough time and some improvised tools. Anything. But there was nothing to be found.

Accepting his fate, he walked back to the middle of the space and looked up through the light to the hole high above. He would have to call for help after all. Maybe he could tell them that he'd been intrigued by the grill covering the oubliette and had leaned on it for a better look inside and it had given way. But that was clearly not the case, given its position from where he had removed it earlier. So maybe he should tell them he had lifted it aside for a better look, but fallen in like a clumsy fool. Then how would he explain his lack of injuries from a fall that far onto stone? But there was no rope in evidence after all, nothing to show his premeditation in accessing the dungeon. Perhaps they would believe he had been both uncommonly foolish and lucky.

He jumped as a shadow appeared above, a human shape in silhouette blocking out most of the light. "Hey," a voice called down. "Need a lift?"

CHAPTER 26

A grin broke out across Crowley's face. "Rose!"

"You appear to be in a bind."

She busied herself for a moment, then Crowley's rope dropped back down into the oubliette. He'd never been more glad to see an inanimate object in his life. He climbed up hand over hand, quicker than a monkey up a fresh banana tree. Once back out into the tower, they worked quickly, removing the rope, replacing the grill over the dungeon entrance, then hurried from the dungeons. Checking for any guards, thankful to see none, they jogged away and were soon strolling back along Golden Lane.

Crowley kept alert, scanning constantly for the bad guys. His body ached all over like he'd not only been hit by a bus, but that it had reversed and had a second go to make sure. "How did you know to come for me?" he asked, finally relaxed enough in their safety to talk again.

"Not long after we left the tower, I spotted those guys." She winced. "I recognized them, of course. I'll never forget those faces since they attacked me." She flashed him a grin. "One of them is limping pretty badly though. Looks like I got him good with that kick."

"Good for you! It's the least they deserve."

"I knew I had to follow them, but I also knew I couldn't get too close. If they saw me, they wouldn't bother with you and I'd be in trouble. So I followed them, but at a safe distance."

"You shouldn't have done that."

Rose smirked. "Then you'd still be in that hole."

"I know, but that's my look out. They're after you, they mean you harm."

Rose shrugged. "We're in this together. I wasn't going to leave you. Anyway, I kept out of sight. When they went into the tower, I was scared for you, but had no idea how I could follow them in without being seen. And if they had gone down after you and I followed down the rope, I'd be a piñata for them."

Crowley chuckled. "Yeah, that would have been bad. One

waited at the top, so you'd never have got down probably." He winked. "The one with the bum knee."

"So maybe I could have taken him, after all. Anyway, not knowing what else to do, I waited outside. It wasn't long before they came back out. I waited until I was certain they were long gone, then came back for you. Your rope was still there, just piled up on the floor by the opening." She lifted his hand and looked with concerned eyes at his scraped fingers. "Glad I did." She bit her lip, hesitated, then, "I have to admit, I was afraid they'd done you in."

"I'm not that easily finished off." Crowley gave her a wink. "I thought you looked awfully glad to see me alive and well." He couldn't keep the hint of flirtation from his voice.

"Only because it meant I didn't have to climb down and haul out a corpse!"

Crowley laughed. "Fair comment." Before he could say more, his phone vibrated. He looked at the screen before answering and smiled. "Cameron, my army intel pal." He stepped into the shadow of a building, away from the bustling people, to answer.

"How are you, man?" Cameron asked.

Crowley grinned crookedly. There was an awful lot to tell there. Instead he said, "Still alive thankfully. You?"

"Yeah, I'm well. Might have found something for you on the *Codex Gigas*."

"I hope it isn't anything to do with Prague Castle," Crowley said. "If it is, we're already ahead of you."

"Funny you should mention Prague Castle," Cameron said. "It definitely *was* there once upon a time. But I think it might have been stolen."

Crowley felt a mild surge of hope. Maybe this excursion wouldn't turn out to be the end of their quest after all. "Stolen, you say? By who?"

Cameron chuckled. "That's the funny part. You'll like this."

CHAPTER 27

"I still can't believe you're descended from Aleister Crowley," Rose said.

From the cluster of white buildings with terracotta-colored roofs, and the beautiful sandy beach with crystal clear water, Crowley and Rose had climbed into the hills behind Cefalu. The contrast was stark, from the quiet, pleasant town to the scrubby, overgrown ground near the infamous Abbey of Thelema.

"Not exactly descended from," Crowley said. "Distantly related to. It's not quite the same."

Rose gave him a studied look, raised one eyebrow. "You're really going to draw that distinction?"

Crowley laughed. "Yeah, well. It is kinda cool, in a creepy sort of way. Which is, of course, the best sort of cool. I just don't bring it up on a first date."

The small city of Cefalu sat behind them in the curve of its beach, the Tyrrhenian Sea glittering beyond. The huge Norman Cathedral dominated the eastern side of the town, its exterior well preserved, largely decorated with interlacing pointed arches and pointed windows. On each side of the façade, a massive four story tower rose into the bright sunny day.

Through the trees and scrub, they could just make out the Abbey of Thelema, their target, with the large flat expanse of the Cefalu Stadium overshadowing it from above, perched atop the hills. The Abbey building itself, nothing more than an old house despite its grandiose name, was nonetheless forbidding, almost foreboding.

Crowley was secretly proud of his connections to Aleister Crowley, the English occultist, ceremonial magician, poet, painter, novelist, and mountaineer who founded the religion and philosophy of Thelema. The man's own mother had called him "the Great Beast" and he was denounced in the popular press of the time as "the wickedest man in the world", and a Satanist. None of which the man denied, identifying himself as the prophet entrusted with guiding humanity into the Aeon of Horus in the early 20th century. Though he had died in 1947, his influence was still strong throughout modern occultism. Crowley's own study of the man for personal and historical reasons had left him keen to know more, only lack of time had prevented deeper study. The mysteries around the strange fellow were legion.

Maybe none more so than this building, which Aleister had called the Abbey of Thelema. Though only a small house, it had been used as a temple and spiritual center founded by Crowley and Leah Hirsig in 1920. One of the primary tenets of Thelema was the law, "Do what thou will shall be the whole of the law". The Abbey was named in accordance with the concept, the name borrowed from François Rabelais's satire *Gargantua and Pantagruel*, where an Abbaye de Thélème was described as an "anti-monastery" where the peoples' lives were "spent not in laws, statutes, or rules, but according to their own free will and pleasure." Rather fitting, Crowley thought now as they approached, that the building was run-down and dilapidated, as broken down as the man himself had become in later life. He had always wanted to see the place, since his earliest studies into the Great Beast. Now he was distinctly underwhelmed.

Modern day followers of Thelema no doubt visited the site often, but Aleister Crowley himself had been kicked out of Sicily by Mussolini after the Great Beast's reputation for wickedness became too much for even that dictator to bear, and the man's Abbey had been degrading ever since. Crowley had told all this and more to Rose as they traveled to Sicily, yet he was still underwhelmed to finally see the place for real.

"Did your friend say where we should look for the bible?" Rose asked, breaking his train of thought.

"Just that he found a number of references to indicate the *Codex Gigas* was here," Crowley said, staring up at the grubby white walls of the building. "And that Crowley paid a visit to Prague Castle shortly beforehand. They have Intel that Aleister Crowley boasted of some great and secret discovery at Dalibor. We have good reason to believe the *Codex* had been stored in the golem there, but it's gone now."

"So your mate thinks Aleister Crowley stole it?"

"Aleister Crowley definitely read the book, or at least some of it. Passages from it are quoted in the Holy Books of Thelema, including some apocryphal lines that might be from the real codex, if perhaps he did have it rather than studying a copy. There's no way we can know that unless we see the real *Devil's*

Bible, of course, but hopefully we'll find it here. Probably too much to hope, but you never know."

"I feel like we're running from one amazing discovery to another, but always one step behind seekers who came before us."

"We are, but the people hunting us are yet another step behind. Hopefully we'll catch up with all this and learn something useful before they catch up with us."

Rose grimaced. "Even if we do learn something, it might not help us."

"Any other ideas?"

She sighed. "Still no. Oh well, ever onwards!"

"It's a pretty exciting adventure all the same, isn't it?" Crowley couldn't keep the enthusiasm form his voice. "I mean, purely from both our interests as historians?"

Rose's face brightened. "Yeah, that's true. Once this is all over I have enough stuff to go back and investigate to fill three more careers!"

The building had a tiled roof, an old TV aerial mounted on the short porch over the front door, but the doorway itself was blocked and boarded up. An open window to one side, a red *666* and Star of David spray-painted on the white stucco beneath, looked like it might provide the only access.

Crowley glanced around, ensured no one was nearby, then pushed himself up onto the sill. "Come on then." He dropped inside and Rose quickly followed.

Inside was dim and cool but not dark, plenty of sunlight penetrating through gaps in the roof and open windows. Inside was more dilapidated than the exterior, the roof fallen in in many places, paper and plaster peeling and falling from the walls. Broken furniture remained in places; tiles were missing from bathroom and kitchen walls. The place smelled of damp and rot, with an over tang of sharp ammonia, no doubt from the droppings of animals or even, maybe, people.

"We need to find the main room, I guess," Crowley said. "*La Chambre des Cauchemars.*"

Rose wrinkled her brow, probably drawing on school French lessons. "The Chamber of Nightmares?" she asked.

"That's what Aleister Crowley called it. He and Jane Wolfe decorated the entire room with mystical murals, but apparently only some of the paintings remain. Cameron said they have records of Crowley consulting the *Codex Gigas* in there. Who knows where it might lead, but it's all we have."

They stepped into the next room and knew instantly it was the one they sought. Large areas of green painted plaster contained images of trees and portraits, symbols and animals. Uneven text ran in crooked lines around the images, all of it with an almost child-like bearing. Crowley and Wolfe had not been great realist painters, it appeared, but their work was evocative and powerful nonetheless.

"So if clues are to be found, they'll be found in here," Crowley said. "At least, let's search here carefully before we start poking around in the rest of this garbage dump."

They walked opposite ways around the room, peering closely at the murals. Crowley remembered some of the names from the top-up research he had done on the journey here. *La Nature Malade*, the *Mural of Heaven*, the portraits of the *Degenerates*. He paused to look more closely at one detail of the *Mural of Heaven*, a shape almost like a keyhole, with sharp points to either side, rendered in red paint. Words and numbers in white in Thelemic script were contained inside. Rose joined Crowley as he crouched and stared.

"I can't find anything," she said, voice heavy with disappointment. "What's that?"

"'Aiwass gave Will as a Law to Mankind through the mind of The Beast 666'," Crowley quoted from memory. He sat back on his heels. "You see, Aleister Crowley never claimed to have thought up the religion of Thelema himself. Rather it was dictated to him via Aiwass. By his account, a possibly non-corporeal being that called itself Aiwass contacted him and dictated the text that became known as Liber AL vel Legis, or The Book of the Law, which outlined all the principles of Thelema."

"Fascinating," Rose said. "But that's not what I meant." She leaned forward to point past him, to a tiny depiction not far from the red keyhole design. "What's *that*?"

Crowley shuffled sideways and squinted to see more clearly. "Well spotted!" he said. The painting showed a dark gray man of short, wide proportions, almost exactly like those of the giant golem he had recently seen below Dalibor Tower. The depiction of the golem was separated in the center, its upper half hovering above an even smaller depiction that was nevertheless undoubtedly the squatting Devil from the *Codex Gigas*. Below the recreation of the Devil were the golem's wide legs, and below the legs a series of small vertical lines.

Rose moved closer, pressing against Crowley as she leaned in for a better look. He enjoyed the proximity of her, the warmth of her body. He also enjoyed the unselfconscious way she leaned against him.

"They're arrows," she breathed.

"Hmm?" Crowley jumped slightly, felt his cheeks redden as she looked at him with a crooked smile.

"Keep your mind on the job at hand, soldier."

He laughed. "Sorry, slightly distracted there." He looked to where she pointed, secretly ecstatic that she made no move away from him, their hips and shoulders still touching. And she was right. The small vertical lines were arrows pointing downwards.

Crowley looked to their feet and the detritus they squatted on. Reluctantly he made the move away from Rose's warmth and picked up a broken roof tile to scrape at the floor, dragging dirt and broken wood aside. Under the filth was nothing but a floor tile. Crowley frowned, pulled a penknife from his pocket. As he dug the tip of the blade under the tile, it lifted easily.

"Not fixed down," he muttered, almost to himself, and slipped his fingers underneath to lift it. It came up to reveal plain cement beneath, but written on the cement were several tiny letters and numbers, with strange symbols at the start of each line.

"They look like coordinates," Rose said. "But they're too short to be actual map coordinates, I think."

Crowley nodded, lips pursed in thought. "They are. I've done more than enough orienteering and stuff in the military to recognize any kind of map notation. That's not what this is. But maybe it's something similar." He stood and looked around the room. "Hmm, maybe…"

Rose stayed crouching, quietly watching, as he paced back and forth a couple of times. After a moment he returned to the revealed notes and placed his hands on the floor. He put one hand against the wall, placed his other hand in line with it, then moved on his knees marking out the width of four fingers at a time, hand by hand, doing a strange crab-walk as he counted. After a few feet, he stopped. "What's the second line say?" he asked.

Rose looked down, brow creased in confusion. "Well, there's a strange symbol like the first line, then W, and hash marks totaling nine."

"Right." Crowley turned ninety degrees to his left and measured out nine sets of his fingers.

"Next?"

Rose read out the next line and Crowley moved again. After a couple of minutes and Crowley zig-zagging across the room, hands and knees filthy now, she said, "That's the last one."

Crowley was across the room from her, smiling. He dug around under where his hands had last been and his smile widened. He lifted a floor tile out of the way and then pulled against something. A leather strap emerged from the dirt. He pulled harder and a section of tiled floor lifted as one like a trapdoor.

"Wow," Rose said. "What did you just do?"

"History in effect!" Crowley said. "The symbol at the start of each line is a *shesep*, an old Egyptian unit of measurement. It's based on hands. The *shesep* is four fingers wide. I remember teaching this earlier in the year. So those notes are a unit of measurement, then a compass direction, then the number of units in hash marks. They're like a code to find this strap that was concealed under a tile. The strap released the mechanism of this trapdoor."

"Well, look at you, genius history teacher." Rose moved over to kneel beside him. "What's down there?"

Wooden steps led down into darkness. Crowley pulled a small flashlight from his pocket and flicked it on. "Only one way to find out."

They descended the steps and immediately came to a solid-looking wooden door. It had two iron hasps-- one high, one low. Each hasp was secured with a padlock, each padlock the kind with rolling wheels and numbers.

"Well, that's annoying," Rose said. "Any guesses at the combinations?"

"One has three numbers, the other four," Crowley said, looking more closely.

"666 might be a little too obvious," Rose said doubtfully.

"But Aleister Crowley did attach significance to it," Crowley said and turned the tumblers. The three wheel lock popped open. "That was easy!"

He crouched to the lower lock, with four rollers. "Now what? Maybe dates?"

"When was Aleister Crowley born?" Rose asked.

"1875." He put that in, but the lock remained closed.

Crowley pulled out his phone and tapped up the browser to look up some more dates. They tried the birth dates of several of Aleister Crowley's partners and lovers, the date the house in which they stood had been purchased, but quickly ran out of ideas and the lock remained stubbornly closed.

"This is infuriating!" Crowley said. "Maybe I should just kick it down."

"Looks pretty solid," Rose said. She flicked him a grin. "Not that I doubt your strength and manliness, of course."

He couldn't help smiling, despite the frustration, but he turned back to the door, seriously considering violence against it.

"Hey, wait," Rose said. "When was this Thelema thing founded? Like, did it have a particular date of inception?"

Crowley lifted an index finger. "Good call! Aleister Crowley's great spiritual moment came when he and his wife of the time, Edith, were in Egypt. That's when he claims the being, Aiwass, dictated the Book of the Law to him. That was in 1904, if I remember correctly."

Rose smiled and nodded at the lock.

Crowley turned the tumblers to 1-9-0-4 and the lock popped open. "Ha!" He turned to Rose, close beside him in the confines of the basement stairwell, and kissed her cheek. "Well done!"

She grinned, seemingly not offended at all by his enthusiasm. He stepped back, gestured for her to open the door.

She shook her head. "I'd rather you went first."

"Fair enough!"

Crowley pushed the door open and shined his torch around inside. The room was small, plastered walls battered and broken, old stone showing through. All around the space were the remains of smashed statues. Crowley recognized several pagan deities, and assumed the others were similar creatures he didn't recognize. In the center of the room stood a pedestal, and upon it an old carved book holder, like a lectern without the stand. The wood of the thing was dark and highly polished, the edges an intricately carved curling serpent's body. It was wide and broad, easily big enough to have held the *Codex Gigas*. A beautiful thing to behold, but Crowley found it rather disturbing too. And no giant book rested on it.

"It feels different down here," Rose said quietly, as if too loud a voice might disturb more than the dust. "Older... more real, maybe." She pointed to the wooden stand. "You think it was there?"

"I think it might have been. But it's not now. I guess someone else figured out all this stuff before us. Again!" Crowley moved closer to inspect the stone pedestal on which the book rest sat. Where carvings on the sides had been chipped away, he saw a depiction of horns and a faint TAVRB.

He turned to Rose, his eyebrows high. "This was a *taurobolium*."

"Now that I do know from the museum," Rose said. "Something to do with Roman bull sacrifice, right?"

"Right."

"So what does that tell us?"

Crowley sighed. "Nothing really."

"So if the book was here, what happened to it?" Rose asked, but the question wasn't directed to him. More to the world at large.

"It would suck if we've got this far to hit a dead end," Crowley said. "Then again, I've thought we'd met a dead end before now and we found another way forward." He made a slow circuit of the small room and found nothing but broken statuary. Desolate, he returned to Rose, still beside the *taurobolium*.

His attention became suddenly focused and he leaned forward.

Rose moved closer. "What is it?"

Crowley brushed dust off the top of the stone to reveal two words in Latin, not faint and worn like the rest of the pedestal, but sharp and recent. The carving deep, stamped across the surface like a curse, or perhaps a cleansing. *SEDES SACRORUM*.

Crowley read it aloud, dark certainty filling his mind. He turned to Rose. "I know who took the book."

CHAPTER 28

Cefalu, Sicily

The walk back down the hill into Cefalu was pleasant under blue skies with a soft, warm breeze. The scent of the ocean was strong, fresh and briny, a perfect antidote to the rot and fungal spoors of the Abbey of Thelema.

Rose drew in long deep breaths, striding purposefully away. "I'm glad to put that place at my back. Creepy as hell."

Crowley nodded. "You're not wrong. It's all kind of weird overlain with something unpleasant, don't you think? I mean, something besides the age and neglect."

"Yeah, it gives me the creeps just thinking about it. Let's forget we were ever there now we've got something to go on."

"Good plan."

She glanced back at him, slowed her pace to let him catch up and fall into stride next to her. "So what *have* we got to go on?" she asked. "What was that inscription again?"

"Sedes Sacrorum. You'd know it as the Holy See."

She stopped, stared hard at him. "The Vatican? Come on, Crowley, that's going a bit far, isn't it? The Vatican took the book?"

Crowley gestured forward, enjoying her shock. There was melodrama to everything occurring that he couldn't help revel in just a little bit. It served to remind him just how boring his life had become as a history teacher. Despite the fact that their lives were in danger, Rose's especially, he hadn't experienced thrills like these since active service and he realized how much he missed them. "The Vatican has a secret army, if you believe the rumors and conspiracy theories."

Rose barked a laugh, falling into step with him again. "Well, I'm not sure I do."

Crowley couldn't blame her for that. "Hear me out. There are lots of rumors about secret societies, legends about occult connections, all kinds of stories, and it's not something you can simply write off wholesale."

"You really believe in that sort of thing?" Rose asked, but her incredulity had waned.

Crowley raised his hands, a gesture of uncertainty. "Honestly, I think most of it is complete bollocks, but there is one thing of which I am absolutely certain." He trailed off, memories coming at him like enemy fire, stirring emotions deep in his gut that he would rather stayed quiet.

Rose must have seen his face blanch. She put one hand on his shoulder as they walked. "You okay?"

"Yeah, sorry. I have a little army baggage, that's all. Anyone who served is haunted at least a little bit."

"And it's relevant to all this stuff?" Her voice was soft, kind.

"Very relevant. One thing I know for certain... at least, as certain as I can be, is that there's a powerful group called the Knights of the Sedes Sacrorum."

"The SS?" Rose interrupted.

Crowley shook his head. "That was the name the SS went by, but this is a different group. These guys are the Knights of the Holy See. I crossed paths with them once in Iraq. We were fighting the Republican Guard, Saddam Hussein's elite branch. The firefight was going down around some museum, I forget which. Things were complicated over there and I don't remember one event separate from another most of the time. But while I don't remember exactly where this happened, I'll never forget *what* happened.

"We were pinned down across a square from the museum, trying to take out the Republican Guard because we thought they had prisoners in a tower block on the other side. The block was already mostly rubble, but still had loads of places to imprison people. Then these guys swept in from the other side and wiped the Iraqis out like they were kids playing at war. Whoever these guys were, they went through the Republican Guard like smoke and straight into the museum. We took a moment to mobilize, shocked, you know? Not sure what to do. But these guys were in and out before we knew what was going on."

"They stormed the museum?"

"Yep. But there was no resistance inside there and they were out again in no time, laden down with stuff they'd... looted, I guess. When we got inside, the place had been stripped bare. No artifacts, nothing. Everyone with me figured the Iraqis had cleared out the valuables, well ahead of the invasion, but I saw those guys leaving with boxes and sacks they didn't enter with. And I've always wondered."

Rose frowned. "What makes you think these guys were associated with the Vatican though?"

"One of them was wounded when they swept through the Republican Guard. He was the only one I saw who took a bullet. I was at the back of my squad heading in after they'd gone into the museum and I stopped, dragged him behind cover. They'd taken out our enemy, after all. Were they on our side? I didn't know, but I couldn't leave him there writhing in pain. While my guys went in, I tore open his shirt to try and staunch the bleeding, and I saw a small tattoo over his heart. KOSS, with a strange kind of logo, or sigil, you know? Years later I looked it up, and found it was the same as this group, the Knights of the Sedes Sacrorum."

"Interesting, but not definite," Rose said.

"No, but I believe it. Almost as soon as I applied the bandage, two of his men came barreling in and hauled him off. That's when I saw the others carrying all that loot. One of the two told me to forget I'd ever seen them."

"Heavy," Rose said. "So assuming this group is real, who are they? Vatican relic hunters?"

Crowley laughed. "Yeah, maybe. All I could find in my research were conspiracy sites alleging they're the personal army of the Vatican, answering only to the Pope. They're culled from the best of the Swiss Guard and other devoted followers."

They reached their hire car, parked on a grassy verge on the edge of Cefalu, and slumped into the seats. Crowley started the engine, looked at Rose before he pulled away. "Regardless, that inscription up in the Abbey of Thelema indicates the book was taken by these Knights. So that means the Vatican Secret Archives. And *that* means we have to go to the Secret Archives next, but the problem now is how the hell do we get in? That's where the trail leads, but it's not like we can just walk in. I don't know much about it, but I do know you have to apply well in advance and hope to receive permission to conduct research there." He raised his eyebrow at Rose, wondering how far her museum contacts might stretch, how many favors she might have left to call in.

Rose smiled at him and nodded to the road ahead. "Let's get going. I think I might know a way."

CHAPTER 29

The Vatican

Crowley and Rose walked the busy streets of Rome heading for the Vatican. Sunshine filtered brightly through a soft cloud cover, the day warm without much breeze to move the air. Crowley found himself increasingly comfortable in Rose's presence and felt that she was also relaxing with him. Of course, the tension of the situation, the pressures of pursuit, still weighed heavily on them both, but Crowley thought maybe they were both also enjoying the thrill of the hunt. And there was no doubt they made a good team. He desperately wanted Rose to be safe from her pursuers, but part of him would be disappointed when all this was over. He hoped she'd still be a part of his life even then.

Eventually they battled heaving crowds along the Via di Porta Angelica and came to the Porta Sant'Anna. Like so much of Rome, the road and the sidewalk were dark gray cobblestones, square and slightly uneven. Pale double columns, topped by impressive stone eagles, flanked the gate before them. Curlicued iron bridged the span between the columns and the cobblestone road continued up a slight rise. Crowley and Rose walked past Swiss Guards in their almost clown-like uniforms and continued between yellow stone buildings with tall arched windows.

Ahead of them stood the impressive bulk of the Cortile del Belvedere, the Belvedere Courtyard, designed by Donato Bramante in 1506. Crowley marveled at the High Renaissance architecture, the density of design and imposing stonework.

"Really quite the place, huh?"

Rose smiled at him. "You've never been before?"

"No. Always been on my list of places to see, but I hadn't got around to it yet. It's kind of weird to come under these circumstances."

"Yeah, can't argue with that. But this is somewhere I have been before. Though I wish we were on vacation, taking in the sights at our leisure."

Crowley threw her a cheeky grin. "I'd like to go on vacation with you too. Maybe once this is all over we can come back?"

Rose shook her head, but her eyes were alive with amusement. "I think I might prefer white sandy beaches and crystal clear seas for a while once all this is over."

"I know just the place," Crowley said. "Jervis Bay in Australia. I went there a few years ago. Amazing place. I could show you. And the places I could rub lotion onto you."

"Let's keep our focus on this business for now, shall we?"

Crowley grinned. "For now? Sure."

Rose let that one pass and led the way to an entrance, adjacent to the Vatican Library, guarded by another Swiss Guard in his yellow, red and blue puffy uniform. "Here we are," she said.

Crowley looked around, the open buildings, the milling crowds. "Not quite what I expected. I thought the Secret Archives would be more... secret."

Rose laughed. "Don't let that word confuse you. In Latin this place is called Archivum Secretum Apostolicum Vaticanum, or in Italian it's Archivio Segreto Vaticano. But in both cases, the translation of secret is misleading. A better word, according to the official word from the Vatican, would be 'personal'. Apparently in reference to the private letters and historical records of past Popes. The archives were created by Pope Paul V in 1612, and while it's true that outside researchers can't just enter at will, there is a designated reading room. More than a thousand researchers request access annually, and they're usually granted it. The archives used to be closed up tight, but in 1881 Pope Leo XIII opened them to researchers."

"So we're just going to go in and ask them for the *Codex Gigas* and they'll bring it out to us?" Crowley asked. "I'm not buying that!"

Rose laughed. "No, of course not. But don't you have more faith in me than that yet?"

They approached the entrance together and Rose smiled warmly to the Swiss Guard on duty. His face was stern, giving nothing away. "We have an appointment at the reading room," she said.

He gestured for them to step inside and Crowley threw the guy a wink, more to annoy him than anything else. He understood guard duty, but the guy didn't have to be so dour. Then again, if Crowley had to dress like that every day he reckoned he might lose his sense of humor pretty quickly, too.

Inside the reading room, they were met by a middle-aged man with thinning blond hair and a paunch stretching the front of his collared white shirt. "Your entry card please?" His voice was heavily accented Italian, but clear enough.

"I'm afraid we don't have one," Rose said, and Crowley's stomach lurched at the smirk the man gave them.

"Then you will have to leave immediately." He raised a hand to attract the attention of the Swiss Guard outside, but Rose put a hand on his forearm and flashed a wide smile.

Crowley took his turn to smirk. No one could ignore that look when she put it on and this Vatican official was no exception. He paused, reddening slightly at her touch, one eyebrow raised.

Rose left her hand in place on the man's arm and pulled a letter from her pocket with her free hand. Crowley could see it was a printout of an email, but the type too small for him to read. She had clearly been busy on their journey here.

The man read slowly, then frowned. "A moment, please."

They waited quietly while the man disappeared through another door. Crowley watched all around, as casually as he could manage, sure the Swiss Guard would descend on them any second and drag them away.

Rose smiled at him. "Trust me, Jake. Honestly, you're skittish as a cat."

Eventually the man returned, looking more harried than when he had left. "Please, follow me."

They were led through a door and into a long marble hallway, high domed ceilings with intricate frescoes impressive overhead. Another man, tall and thin with thick black hair and suspicious eyes nodded once in greeting. He held out two laminated badges on green lanyards. "Sorry for the delay, we had to make these especially for your visit and we weren't quite ready."

"Thank you so much," Rose said, the embodiment of politeness and gratitude.

But something nagged at Crowley, tickled his hindbrain and put him on edge. He took the badge and the linen gloves the tall archivist offered, still uncertain. But so far so good. Maybe he should chill out and trust Rose, but he had long since learned to trust his nerves and instincts. He didn't think he would be relaxing too much all the time they were here.

"Please," the archivist said. "You must exercise great care

with all the items inside. Anything you choose to look at must be treated with great reverence. I will suffer the wrath of His Eminence a thousand times over before I will allow documents in my care to be damaged."

"Of course," Rose said. "We won't give you any cause for concern, I promise."

"My thanks. Then this way please."

The archivist turned and escorted them inside.

Chapter 30

The Vatican Secret Archives

Crowley and Rose were led through into a long room redolent with the scents of ink and parchment. Crowley reveled in the smell, like the big library in Sweden or the best secondhand bookshop, a smell that had said *magic* to him since childhood. Though he wondered what kind of magic might be present in this particular library.

"This is the reading room," the archivist said. "You want to start here?"

A long table dominated the room with high-backed wooden chairs along either side. Shelves jam-packed with volumes and files covered every wall. A second, mezzanine level of shelving circled the room above them.

The archivist indicated a doorway at the end, lit with a hard fluorescent strip. "Through there to the lofts and other areas." He looked pained. "Your clearance is fairly generous. Would you like me to accompany you?" His tone of voice clearly implied that he desperately wanted to accompany them and be rid of them as soon as possible.

Rose lit up her irresistible smile again. "Thank you, but no. We'll be fine."

The archivist winced, but nodded and withdrew. No other researchers were present in the reading room and Crowley suddenly had the sensation of being a kid locked in school overnight, somewhere he shouldn't be with a wild run of the place.

"So really, how did you pull this off?" he asked.

Rose grinned. "I have my ways."

"There's got to be something serious to this, though," he pressed. "Being left to our own devices in here?"

Rose drew in a long breath. "I'll tell you, but it's a secret you share with no one!" When he nodded his assurance, she went on. "I have a contact at the Vatican museum who was once an altar boy, and he had a... special relationship with a man a couple of decades ago. That man is now a cardinal, right here in Vatican City. And no, I'm not giving you any names."

"A special relationship, eh?" Crowley said. "I think I know what you mean."

Rose nodded, twisted a wry smile. "My contact has undeniable proof of the relationship, and needless to say the Cardinal is happy to do the occasional favor for him these days. This time, he passed one of those favors on to me."

"You're amazing," Crowley said, genuinely impressed. "I mean it, you have hidden depths, incredible friends, you kick butt when you need to."

Rose laughed. "Calm down, Jake. I don't need a fan club!"

"Well, you've got one, president and lifetime member, me!"

Rose put a hand on his shoulder, her palm warm. "Well, thanks. And you're pretty fan-worthy yourself."

There was a moment of silence that Crowley was reluctant to break, but Rose did it for him. "All these shelves are far too small to hold anything close to the size of the *Codex Gigas*," she said. "And besides, it would hardly be in the public reading room. Let's go deeper."

They went through the brightly lit doorway and passed through an area with official Papal correspondence in shelf upon shelf of bound volumes.

"Not likely to be here either," Crowley said, feeling the weight of the documents and the weight of history pressing down on him. "This is a monumental task, looking through something of this size. It's huge. Where's our best bet?"

Rose shrugged. "No idea. I guess we start exploring. I know there are massive archives in the lofts above the west wing of the Cortile del Belvedere. That would be this way."

She moved on and Crowley followed, eventually climbing up steep stairs into a seemingly endless room with tightly packed metal shelves laden with boxes and files, all filled with documents. The place was dim, soft strip lighting spread far apart above the narrow passages between the shelves. Their shoes rang out on the polished cement floor as they walked. Crowley scanned the spines of manuscripts, neatly handwritten in fading ink marking histories of centuries past, featuring names like Borgheses, Avignon, and Napoleoni.

"This place is mesmerizing," he said quietly. "So much information…"

Rose paused, looked back the way they had come. "I read that the total length of the shelves in this section is over thirteen kilometers."

"We can never hope to cover all that in anything less than several weeks of careful study," Crowley said, feeling lost. "But then, this doesn't look like the place either. All the shelving is too small to house anything like the *Codex Gigas*."

"Let's try the bunkers," Rose said. "They're the most recent addition, commissioned by Pope Paul VI, in the sixties, I think."

They made their way back down, through more corridors, then down again to the first of the two underground floors.

"Even more shelves here," Rose said. "Forty-three kilometers of them this time."

Crowley groaned. "Holy crap." He laughed at the unintentional joke. "Literally!"

Rose laughed along. "Well, we need to check anyway. Documents pertaining to royal families are kept here, among other things, so maybe there's info on Rudolf's family."

"Maybe," Crowley agreed. "But that's going backwards. We already know he had it and lost it."

They walked along more shelves, thousands upon thousands of pages of information, the sheer volume of it all starting to become a little overwhelming. But still, nowhere that looked even vaguely likely to house something the size of the *Codex*.

"I don't think we'll find anything here," Rose said. "But according to my earlier reading, the most special items are kept in a climate-controlled area adjacent to this level. I wonder if our clearance extends that far?"

Crowley shrugged. "Let's find out."

CHAPTER 31

After a couple of false turns, Crowley and Rose found their way to a large red double door.

"This way?" Crowley asked.

Rose shrugged. "My research only revealed so much. We'll have to try it and see."

Crowley pushed the brushed aluminum door handle down and the door swung easily open. "So far so good."

They entered a room with a set of short steps to their right leading up toward a second mezzanine level. To their left was a white wall with a heavy metal door front and center. Straight-backed wooden chairs stood either side of the door and a huge circular mural in grays and whites, a dozen feet in diameter, hung suspended above it.

"Now that looks promising," Rose said.

"May I help you?"

Crowley jumped like a naughty schoolboy, then hardened his face, annoyed he'd been spooked. A man in robes descended the short flight of steps to their right.

"You shouldn't be here," the man said.

Crowley gathered every bit of his teaching experience to put authority in his voice, determined to reverse the situation and make the man in robes feel like the recalcitrant one. "We're personal guests of His Eminence." He thrust the quickly made badge under the man's nose.

Crowley smirked inside as the man quailed at Crowley's assertive tone. He glanced at the badges and frowned, but nodded reluctantly. "Ah, yes. You wish to access the climate controlled archives."

"Yes, thank you," Rose said, her tone entirely opposite to Crowley's. She flicked him a look as the man in robes stepped toward the doors.

Crowley grinned and raised his hands, mouthed, *What?*

Rose couldn't keep the amusement from her face, but she shook her head in exasperation. The door popped and brushed the pale floor as it swung open. Inside were numerous pale blue filing units with thin shelves, rows of compactor shelving, with three-handled wheels on the ends to move them left and right for access. The air was still and dry, a sense of importance heavy in the atmosphere. As soon as they were inside, the man in robes shut the door behind them and turned to face them, wringing his hands slightly. He was clearly uncomfortable with interlopers in his sacred space. Crowley really couldn't blame him for that.

"What's your name?" Rose asked him, still the embodiment of politeness.

"Lorenzo."

"Hi Lorenzo. I'm Rose. We're so sorry to disturb you, but we're on very important business."

Crowley looked at the hundreds of wide, shallow drawers. None of them looked even close to big enough to hold the *Codex*. He made a slow circuit of the room, wondering if any of the compactors might have deep enough shelves to hold it. Lorenzo followed him like a shadow, the man's nerves grating and beginning to feed into Crowley's own agitation. But Crowley did his best to ignore the man, kept up his slow tour while Rose went in the opposite direction. After a few moments they shared a hopeless glance, both obviously thinking that it was unlikely the *Codex* Gigas was anywhere in this sterile, neutral space. Crowley looked into the space between a couple of open compactors and decided he would have to wind the wheels and peer into each one to be sure when Lorenzo spoke again.

"What can I do for you? What are you hoping to find?" Impatience was evident in the man's voice.

Crowley and Rose exchanged another glance and the truth passed silently between them. They weren't going to find it on their own. Crowley decided to take a chance.

"We're looking for a very old book. A large one." He spread his hands as he spoke to indicate the approximate size. "Lots of fancy artwork on the inside."

A look of alarm passed over Lorenzo's face, but he quickly recovered. "We don't have anything like that in here. As you can see, we don't have the space to store something of that size." He visibly relaxed as he gestured at the storage drawers. "We primarily have individual documents here that require special care. I'm sorry I can't help you." He forced a smile that didn't quite reach his eyes.

"What about in these?" Crowley asked, pointing to the wall of compactors. "You could easily store a body in there, let alone a large book."

Lorenzo frowned, not amused by Crowley's snide dig. "Well, you're welcome to look in each one, but you'll see they all have shelving that could not accommodate anything of the size you indicated."

Crowley pursed his lips. Despite the man's chagrin and nervousness, those words had the ring of truth. It seemed they wouldn't be finding the *Codex* in this room, and Lorenzo was quite comfortable in his certainty of that fact. But Crowley hadn't missed the man's look a moment before.

"Where *should* we look for a book like my friend described?" Rose asked.

Again a flash of alarm crossed Lorenzo's face, that look again, then a smile broke out. "I'm afraid I don't know. I'm very sorry I can't help you. If that will be all?" He turned in the direction of a desk in one corner and took a couple of steps toward it.

"Say, what time do you get off work?" Crowley asked casually.

Lorenzo turned back, frowned. "Why do you ask?"

"In case you and I need to have a conversation about the call you're about to make."

The color drained from Lorenzo's face, his cheeks going paler than the storage cabinets all around.

Rose stepped between them, flicked a quick look of caution at Crowley, then said, "Don't mind him. He's a bit eccentric. May I know your family name? I'd like to tell His Excellency how you tried to help us."

"Caballo," the man stammered. "Lorenzo Caballo. And really, I'm sorry I don't know where to find the item you seek." He went to the door and held it open, his face a mask of discomfort.

Rose nodded to him and went out, headed for the red doors back to the corridor. Crowley followed, giving Lorenzo a sarcastic smile as he left. This whole process was beginning to grate on his patience. Unrestricted access to the Vatican's most private places, and they kept hitting dead ends. But it wasn't over yet. Lorenzo had maybe revealed more than he intended to.

"That was another pointless excursion," Rose said once Lorenzo had shut himself back inside.

"Maybe not." Crowley gestured back the way they had just come. "Let's find out what's directly above that room."

CHAPTER 32

Vatican Archives, Diplomatic floor

After some careful back and forth, eventually finding the right set of stairs and a helpful corridor, Crowley and Rose emerged into a large set of rooms with high white ceilings and polished wooden floors. Bas relief friezes in multiple colors hung over each doorway between rooms and each room was packed with ostentatious cabinets, carved wood with brass handles. Every size and shape of storage filled the space, the aroma of old wood and incense heavy in the air.

"Blimey," Crowley said, looking around himself and peering through a door at the far end into another, similar large space, equally full of varied cabinets.

"I recognize this from my research," Rose said. "This is what they call the Diplomatic Floor." She frowned as she searched her memories. "Constructed by Pope Alexander VII in 1660," she said eventually. "It houses documents from the fifteenth century to the Napoleonic era."

Crowley looked at her with raised eyebrows, genuinely impressed. "That's some recall you have there."

Rose laughed. "I told you before. We call it 'museum brain'. You develop a skill for data retention when you work long enough in research. Besides, I only read about it this morning." She looked around and shook her head. "But I can't see the *Devil's Bible* being here."

"Let's at least spend a little time checking it out. It's not like we've made any real progress elsewhere." Crowley began opening cupboards, scanning the piles of documents and manuscripts in each one. "Besides, I have a hunch…"

Rose followed him, dutifully opening a few doors here and there. "What makes you think it's up here?"

Crowley smiled. "I'm a teacher. That means I spend a lot of time around teenagers telling tales, trying to cover up their wrongdoings! I was watching that guy's face while we were in his sealed archive. Each time we mentioned the book, his eyes flitted directly upward for a split second. If he were being deceptive, he'd have glanced to the side. Let's just say that if that guy has much money, I'd love to play poker with him. He'd be broke in no time."

They continued to wander through the maze of cabinets. Crowley checked each one thoroughly, sure that he wasn't mistaken about Lorenzo's tell downstairs. After half an hour he began to think that maybe he was seeing things where nothing existed, so desperate was he to find the *Codex*. Were they chasing ghosts, stumbling around like idiots after something that might not even exist?

Two men in red robes walked toward them, both with stern expressions. Crowley stood, faced them boldly. Rose moved from behind a cabinet she had been investigating and made a small noise of surprise. She came to stand beside him as the men approached.

Crowley smiled broadly. "Bongiorno." He wasn't entirely sure that was the correct greeting, but it was about the sum total of his knowledge of Italian.

The men slowed, still frowning, but didn't stop. Once they had walked past and left the room, Crowley let out a breath he had been holding. "This is so frustrating," he said.

Rose nodded, hands on hips. She turned in a slow circle. "It's the proverbial needle in a haystack."

"If it's even here."

Rose stopped, suddenly still and focused. She leaned forward, peering between two tall cupboards designed like elaborate wardrobes. Beyond them was a smaller, squarer cabinet of dark wood with a deep grain.

"What is it?" Crowley asked.

Rose walked forward, pointing. "Look at the design on the front of that. Kinda stands out a bit, don't you think. Are they fish?"

Crowley followed and the motif certainly did stand out. And it threw a flood of memory at him from his research years ago after his run in with the KOSS troops in Iraq. "Not fish," he said. "Priests dressed as fish. I know something about this." The design showed two men face to face either side of a stylized tree. The men wore entire fish bodies, the fish heads pointing up from their heads like huge hats, the open mouths not unlike a papal miter. The scaled bodies of the fish cascaded down behind the heads, lying tight to the men's backs like form-fitting capes. The fish tails fanned out behind the men's heels, almost brushing the ground. The two each held a bucket of some kind in one hand, their other hand raised as if in a benediction. Atop the tree motif was a large oval object, looking an awful lot like a pinecone.

Rose crouched beside Crowley to get a closer look. "Priests dressed as fish?"

Crowley chuckled, nodded. "Remember how I said I looked into all this conspiracy stuff after that weird experience in Iraq? This matches a lot of it. You see, thousands of years ago, a couple of thousand years BCE at least, there was a group of folk called the priests of Dagon. Now you're going to have to bear with me here, because this gets a little crazy. Dagon was the fish-god of the Philistines and Babylonians and he wore a fish head hat, supposedly the origin of the Pope's headwear today. See the open fish mouth? Looks like a mitre? In Chaldean times, the head of the church was the representative of Dagon and was considered to be infallible, was addressed as 'Your Holiness', and his subjects had to kiss his ring." Crowley grinned. "This god-king sound familiar?"

Rose made a wry face. "Very papal."

"Right. The tree there is a representation of the tree of life, or maybe the tree of knowledge. The pine cone represents the pineal gland, which is a tiny pine cone shaped endocrine gland in the brain, deep where the two halves of the thalamus join. I mean, you can take this stuff all the way down the rabbit hole. Some folk think that whole region of the brain is where the design of the Eye of Horus comes from with the ancient Egyptians. And I have to be honest, the resemblance is uncanny. Others think the god Dagon in his fish suit was actually an interstellar traveler in a space suit and so on."

Rose blew out a derisive breath. "And this is where we start to put on our tin foil hats, is it?"

"Oh, we've needed to have those on for a while already. Anyway, the point is, lots of conspiracy theorists think the modern Catholic church is actually built on the cult of Dagon and all that stuff that went along with it. That's why you so often see the pinecone shape in Catholic icons, the mitre hat and so on. So this cabinet here, with this design carved on it, is a pretty interesting find. Especially as, while I was researching the Knights of the Sedes Sacrorum, I discovered that their coat of arms bears a symbol very much like this, two fish priests face to face over a tree of life. That guy whose wound I patched up, with the KOSS tattoo? Those letters were written below a design very much like this."

Rose swallowed, looked from Crowley to the cabinet's strange carving and back again. "So we open this up and we find the book?"

Crowley shrugged, smiled. "It's about the right size to have the *Codex* Gigas standing up inside."

Rose took a deep breath and tried the cabinet handle. It clicked and the door swung open. Inside were shallow shelves with row upon row of small leather-bound volumes. Rose let her breath out in a rush of disappointment. "Damn it!"

Crowley narrowed his eyes, leaned past the side of the cabinet and back. "Not so fast. The depth of these shelves is all wrong."

He began pulling the small tomes out in twos and threes, handing them to Rose to stack neatly to one side. Glancing around regularly in case anyone came, working as quickly as he could, Crowley soon had all the books out. He tugged at the now bare shelves and something shifted. He moved for a better grip, took hold of the uppermost and lowest shelves, and pulled. The back of the cabinet slid forward with a slight protest of grinding wood, bringing all the shelves with it. Crowley worked the cumbersome arrangement back and forth a few times and eventually it slipped free of the cabinet.

Standing in the revealed secret compartment was a tall book, its cover pale tan with borders of intricate pressed designs around a central plate of narrow diamond lines. In the center was an eight-pointed rosette of metal, with bright blue inlays and a raised central, flat-topped cone. Each corner of the thick embossed leather cover had brass quarter plates, similar in design to the central rosette, with Celtic-styled winged horses facing each other under raised knobs like the cover's center.

Crowley and Rose sat on their haunches for several heavily silent seconds, staring. Eventually Crowley turned to face Rose and a moment later she met his gaze.

"This is it!" He pounded his fist into his palm. "We bloody found it!"

CHAPTER 33

Crowley reached for the book, then paused. He dug in his pocket and pulled out the linen gloves the archivist had given him earlier, then carefully removed the tome from its hiding place. He grunted under the weight of it, then Rose, her hands similarly covered, helped him maneuver it free.

The weight of it was almost overwhelming, as was the scent of its leather bindings and thick pages. It was three feet tall and nearly two feet across. The pages made the covers flare at bit at the edges, the book as thick as Crowley's hand was long from the heel of his palm to the tip of his middle finger. He ran his hand over the cover, amazed to be in the presence of it at last. Something so old, supposedly so powerful. And not the fake in Sweden that everyone knew about, but had they discovered the unsullied original?

"Hey look." Rose pointed into the cabinet.

Removing the book had revealed other items that had been secreted behind it. Small statues of stone and wood, documents, tablets. "Man, I wish we had time to look at all this stuff!" Crowley said. He pulled his phone out and took a series of quick photos into the cabinet, his flash a stark beacon with each one.

"We need to be careful," Rose said. She rose on her knees to look over the strange cupboard, scanned quickly left and right. "Someone could come any minute. It's weird the book is hidden here on the diplomatic floor."

"I don't know," Crowley said. "It makes a certain sense to hide it somewhere people wouldn't think to look. Better than putting it behind a door with a sign reading 'Seriously evil stuff hidden here'. And it's just as well that guy down in the sealed archives knew it was here, because only his nervousness tipped me off. If he was a better poker player we might never have looked up here as closely as we did."

"All true enough," Rose agreed. "But now what? We certainly can't take it with us. We need to focus on any bits that differ from the known copy."

Crowley pointed across the room. "There's a quiet corner

over there. Come on."

He quickly slipped the false shelving back into place and put the books back in. Between them, they each took one end of the *Codex* and shuffled across the room, behind a large double-doored cabinet into a shadowed, dusty corner.

"I've spent hours while we've been traveling studying images of the *Codex* from the Swedish files," Rose said. "Let me see if I can spot any differences."

"Museum brain at work again, eh?"

She grinned at Crowley. "That should be my superhero name."

He laughed softly. "The Mighty Museum Brain comes to save the day."

Rose began riffling through the pages as carefully as she could. Several times she made some noise of discovery, assured Crowley she hadn't seen that particular page before, and they both took snaps with their phones.

Several times, when Rose pointed out a particular page or passage that she was sure she hadn't seen before, Crowley felt uneasy. Though he couldn't read the words, something about their very shape on the page seemed to ooze evil, as if the ink itself had a malevolent personality and the words only emboldened that.

There were numerous drawings not present in the Swedish copy of the Bible, and one section of five pages in a row that were entirely new. Some of the pages bore cryptic designs that reminded Crowley of Satanic and occult rituals he had seen in his previous researching. A lot of it seemed almost clichéd, as though someone were playing at occultism, then a page would be turned to reveal something heavy with such a foreboding presence that Crowley had to resist the urge to physically step away from the thing, to turn and run and never look back.

As they both photographed everything they could, they repeatedly shared looks of concern, almost pain, clearly finding some relief in the fact that it wasn't only one or the other who felt disturbed, but that they both were discomforted by what they had found.

They finally reached the end and Rose said, "This end paper is different. Look, the design is not unlike the squatting Devil that we're used to, but what's this weird script beneath it?" She snapped a photo and Crowley leaned in to look, took a photo of his own.

"Another one I don't even like to look at," he said. "It feels almost…" He looked up quickly, head tilted to one side. "We need to get out of here."

Rose looked up at him, then back over her shoulder. "What is it?"

"Someone's coming. In fact, several someones."

They pocketed their phones and grabbed up the book between them, hurrying low between cabinets back to the cupboard emblazoned with the strange fish priests. Footsteps rang out through the large room, coming from at least one room away, but getting closer.

"Do we have time for this?" Rose hissed.

"We have to hide it again, in case we need to come back for another look. If they know we've found it, they might move it somewhere else and we'll never see it again." Crowley pulled the shelving forward, books and all, and jiggled it incautiously to get it free. The footsteps drew nearer, now accompanied by voices. One voice was deep and serious, angry, another wheedling and obsequious. A third voice joined it, all speaking in quick Italian.

"Come on," Crowley growled and the shelves popped forward, scattering the books at his feet.

They slid the *Codex Gigas* back into place and Crowley pushed the shelving back in to conceal it. The footsteps and voices sounded terrifyingly close, surely inside the room now. Crowley and Rose grabbed handfuls of books, crammed them onto the shelves willy-nilly, with no concern for the welfare of their covers or pages. Voices almost on top of them, Crowley pushed the cabinet doors closed, but they sprang back, meeting resistance. Eyes wild, he shuffled the books on the shelves, tried to get them to sit in neat alignment. He tried again and the cabinet door clicked closed.

The voices stopped, then started again quickly, moving directly toward them. Crowley stayed low and scrambled around the cupboard to crouch behind it. Rose pushed in beside him, her breath shallow and fast. Footsteps stomped up to the other side and the voices started in again, rapid and annoyed. They were so close that Crowley could smell the cloying cologne of one, the clinging incense on another. He nodded toward a tall cabinet directly across from them, winced and dove for it. He quickly made room and Rose slid in beside him, quiet as a shadow.

He grinned and pointed. There was a way between two more tall cupboards, then a row of smaller ones that led close to a far wall. Beyond the small cupboards was a door into the next room and he knew from memory that they could go from that room down stairs to the corridor and make good their escape.

He heard the doors of the cabinet with the fish priest motif click open and a voice raised to a new level of fury. He winced in annoyance. Whoever was there had seen their haphazard stacking of the books. Their desire to conceal the *Codex Gigas* again seemed to have been a waste of time. A sense of loss clawed at Crowley's gut.

"Go!" he whispered, and ran in a low crouch between the tall cupboards and down behind the low row. Rose on his heels, they shot from the room into the next and made a beeline for the exit. In moments they were running down echoing stairs, laughing like fools, heading for the sunshine outside, with no sounds of pursuit behind them.

CHAPTER 34

Hotel Contilia, Rome

"I think I'm making some headway here." Rose sat back, let out a deep sigh, and ran her fingers through her hair.

"Not for lack of effort. You've been at it for a while."

On their return to the hotel room, Rose had sat studying the photographed pages of the *Codex Gigas*, especially the strange script beneath the newly discovered sketch of the squatting devil. With help online and a couple of phone calls and emails to colleagues, she had established that it was a version of old Akkadian, an extinct East Semitic language that was apparently spoken in ancient Mesopotamia. Akkadian names were first found in Sumerian texts from around the late 29th century BCE, she told him, and around 2500 BCE texts fully written in Akkadian began to appear. Rose was bright-eyed as she described the thousands of texts that had been excavated over the years, conveying everything from mythological narrative to legal texts, scientific works to political reporting, and more. By the second millennium BCE, two forms of the Akkadian language were used in the region, Assyrian and Babylonian.

"The passage we found, it's got a, I don't know, malevolent vibe to it. It's dark, portentous even. I get the chills just reading it, but it's also kind of exciting." Her museum brain was hard at work, fascinated by the subject matter.

Crowley tried to ignore the sense of foreboding that crept up his spine. "What's it all about?"

"It's very old, it pre-dates Assyrian or Babylonian." She bit her lip. "It describes a ritual for extracting past lives."

"You mean exploring so-called past-life memories?" Crowley asked. "I don't think anything like that is real. Isn't it just nonsense that crystal healers and psychic mediums use to pull a few more quid from hopeful clients?"

Rose shook her head, eyes glittering, lost in the joy of research and discovery. "Well, not according to this. If I'm right, it not only extracts memories, but causes a person to actually revisit past lives. To somehow psychically re-live them. Of course, I'm almost certainly not getting it all right and these things are always laden with allegory and hyperbole, but that's the thrust of it."

"But isn't that even more hocus-pocus nonsense? Bad enough that a two-bit psychic would try to make up past life stuff for someone. But to actually claim they could do a ritual to have someone experience those lives?"

"That's what this suggests. And it's not for two-bit psychics. This is real old-world occult magic."

"That's just two-bit psychics from longer ago, isn't it?"

Rose laughed. "Maybe. Or maybe not. We can't really know, but this is very old and very well protected stuff. There might be more to it."

Crowley stood and stretched. "I'm going to take a shower." The day was beginning to wear on him and, though the historian in him was almost as excited as Rose about what they might have discovered, his brain needed a rest.

He stood under steaming water in the hotel room shower, enjoying the hot sear of it over his skin. The head-clearing steam in the small cubicle refreshed his thoughts, and they soon turned to the beautiful woman with whom he shared this adventure. He and Rose had been sharing twin rooms, too paranoid to have separate rooms, but beyond that everything had been the very model of proprietary behavior. Rose always locked any bathroom door when she went for a shower, taking her clothes in with her. Crowley took his clothes too, to dress in private and not embarrass her, but he always left the door unlocked when he showered. Just in case. He was probably being a fool, but there was no point in literally locking any chances away. Hope sprang eternal, after all.

It wasn't long before that faint hope evaporated and his mind drifted back toward the strange passage from the *Codex*. What if Rose was right? What if they had discovered ancient rituals and occult practices? Even if the actual substance of the texts was complete nonsense, the historical significance *was* intimidating. And the discovery of the real *Codex Gigas*, surely that was something they needed to make public.

He frowned and tipped his face up into the hot water. They had put those books back in such a hurry that whoever had come looking for them would be in no doubt that the *Codex* had been discovered. Which meant it would already have been moved. Either in its strange cabinet or in an entirely new receptacle. One thing was certain: wherever it was now, it would be harder than ever to find and searching again would almost certainly prove fruitless. But they had found it, they had touched it. The thing did exist. And they had photographic records of pages the church had tried to keep hidden from the world. That had to account for something.

But was it any help with their current predicament? Had they learned anything that might help Rose to be free of these thugs chasing them all over Europe? For all they had learned, they still had no idea what significance Rose and her birthmark had to those people. At least they might have some information now with which to bargain.

Something crashed in the room outside the bathroom door. Crowley opened his mouth to call out to Rose, ask if she was okay, but some instinct stayed his tongue. As he bit the words back there was a muffled cry and something else crashed over. Crowley's adrenaline spiked.

A man's voice shouted, "This is her. Take her."

Ice rushed through Crowley's veins despite the still cascading hot water. He left the shower running to mask the sound of his movement and slipped over to the door. Butt naked and burning with rage, he flung the door open and strode into the room. There was no sign of Rose, but two men jumped, startled from their hurried search of the luggage at the foot of the beds.

Their shock turned quickly to amusement at the sight of Crowley, dripping wet, package swinging free, and that bought him the moment he needed to get the better of them. By the time they realized he planned to attack them, his foot was already driving into one man's stomach in a powerful kick. That one folded over with a whoosh of forced breath and Crowley turned to the other just as that man raised a gun, a snub-nosed revolver only inches from Crowley's bare chest.

Crowley twisted sideways, batting the man's arm in the other direction as the gun kicked and barked. Crowley grabbed the gunman's wrist, pulled it hard across his chest and drove out the elbow of his other arm. His strike cracked directly into the gunman's jaw and the attacker fell like a sack of rocks, out cold.

The one he'd winded was staggering backwards, still half bent over, clutching his gut with one hand and scrabbling in a pocket with the other. No doubt he was belatedly going for his own gun. Crowley took two quick strides and brought his knee up under the man's chin. There was a bony clack as the thugs teeth snapped together and his head came up. Crowley tucked in a fast right hook and that one dropped unconscious, too.

Panting with the exertion, Crowley rushed to the hotel room door, but the hall outside was empty. He couldn't very well start running naked through the building and he was sure Rose would be long gone by now anyway, spirited away by whoever had taken her. The fight had been quick, but it had surely given the abductors more than enough time to get outside. They wouldn't hang around and he had next to no chance of finding Rose in a crowded city like Rome. His best bet lay with the men on the floor behind him.

He quickly wrenched russet-colored curtain ropes from one window and set about binding the thugs up as they groggily regained their senses. He bound their wrists together, sat them back to back and tied another rope tightly around their chests. He ran to the other side of the room as the men began to groan and protest, pulled down ropes from the window on that side and bound each of their ankles tightly together. One of them tried to kick out, but a solid slap to his cheek quieted him again and Crowley had them trussed up in no time, back to back, their immobilized feet out to either side.

"Where's Rose?" he yelled into the face of the man who had tried to kick him.

That one clenched his teeth and stared daggers at Crowley. The one on the other side was no more forthcoming.

"Who the hell are you people?" Crowley shouted, shaking them both, repeating himself over and over.

They both remained close-mouthed, not even taking the opportunity to curse him out or tell him they weren't going to talk. Tough cookies, the pair of them. But Crowley was tougher.

He tore open their shirts, ignoring their rage-filled eyes, checking for tattoos. He had expected to see something similar to the crest and KOSS tattoo he had seen on the soldier in Iraq, but found no ink.

Though they were both marked, in the same spot on the high left side of their chest. Not with a tattoo, but with the scarred welts of a brand, made by a red hot iron. It was a symbol Crowley recognized but couldn't place, an even-armed cross, each of the four limbs having three tails at ninety degrees to give the design the impression of spinning. At the center of the cross was a double circle. Underneath was a kind of looping set of lines that looked like it might say something, but Crowley couldn't make it out.

"What's this mean?" he asked. "Your special little club?"

Again, they remained tight-lipped.

"*Where's Rose?*"

The men sneered, beginning to enjoy Crowley's impotent rage. He ground his teeth, found his phone and snapped a photo of one man's brand. He sent the image to Cameron, his army intel buddy, with a message asking what it meant, especially if it was a known brand of any gang or organization. What the hell might he do if Cameron found nothing? Intel, even the depths and vast variety the army had access to, could only go so far. A stray thought inserted itself into Crowley's mind, flashing across his consciousness like a car's headlights on a dark night. A name. He had heard a name somewhere, thought it might be useful, then forgotten about it. Only now, thinking about Cameron again, did he remember. Where had he been? The voices had been muffled, as if from far away…

The oubliette! That was it. When he had been hiding out in the broken golem, those idiot thugs who had come looking for him had mentioned a name. He racked his memory, and slowly recalled the bones of the conversation.

Why did they leave the rope? Leave evidence they were here?

I guess they were in a hurry. Or maybe they just didn't care.

What are we gonna tell Landvik?

Landvik? Nothing right now. We'll have to decide what's next before we tell him anything.

Crowley smiled. The old brain wasn't entirely spent yet, even if it did take a while to throw back vital information. He sent Cameron a follow-up text.

Cross check with the name Landvik (sp?)

The phone pinged back almost immediately.

Leave it with me.

Crowley nodded to himself. Good old Cameron. Meanwhile, he would see what these thugs might tell him, whatever it took. He returned to the men tied together on the floor.

"You will tell me what I need to know," he said, his voice calm and measured now. He had skills of which he was not proud, and had vowed to never use again since his discharge from the armed forces. But for Rose's sake, he knew he would do pretty much anything.

"I've done this before," he said quietly. "Many times, to my shame. Now tell me. Where. Is. Rose?"

His calmness and threat had no greater effect on the men than his rage, so Crowley stood up straight, nodded as he drew in a long breath. "Right. Let me put on some pants and then we'll get started."

CHAPTER 35

Waves rocked beneath the boat and Rose trailed a hand in crystal clear water almost as warm as her blood. Silver bullets of fish shot past in glittering shoals, changing direction in an instant. Bright coral rose and banked as her boat drifted, many-branched sculptures in orange and blue, yellow and red. Busy white and red banded shrimp danced and worked across the reef, industrious and focused. Alongside them, parrotfish pecked and plucked as they fed.

A dark shadow swept over the idyllic blue and Rose lay back in the boat to look up. Into a cerulean sky rode a deep, roiling black cloud, lightning arcing and flashing inside. As Rose's brow creased in confusion, drenching rains dropped from the clouds, stirring the calm surface of the ocean, soaking her to the skin in moments. The rain felt like a million tiny darts, spiking her flesh, battering her face. Rose thrashed and tried to turn over, tried to shield her head with her arms, but her body wouldn't respond. Something hard and sharp bit into her wrists, ground against her ankles as she kicked. A deep buzzing drilled into her ears and the rain faded as her eyes flickered open. Fluorescent strip lights high above, fastened to a sheet metal ceiling, flickered and hummed.

Rose couldn't hold in a sob as real life flooded back, men attacking, punches and crushing hands, then a needle, then blackness. She passed out again.

When she next came around, her hands were numb where the bindings restricted her wrists against the arms of what seemed to be some kind of dentist's chair. She lay reclined almost flat, her ankles tied to the end of the long seat. She wriggled her fingers, pins and needles dancing up her forearms as she forced the blood to move. The memory of the needle came back to her, harsh-faced, angry-voiced men holding her down, the stinging strike of it and then a hot, painful swelling in her shoulder. Her vision swam almost immediately, like she tried to see through frosted glass, then blackness. She frowned, tears tumbling over her cheeks, as she tried to remember more. A rushing, tiny squares of light… No, tiny windows. A plane? Yes, she had been flown somewhere. In a small plane, a private jet with beige leather seats. She struggled, twisting and hauling against her bonds, but they wouldn't budge. Her head pounded, her stomach swam, like she'd been drinking far too much and just needed to sleep… She closed her eyes and darkness took her again.

Rose woke to the sound of a door sliding open, metal grinding on metal. She had no idea where she was except that it appeared to be a large warehouse or workshop of some kind. She craned her neck to see back behind her, ignoring the sickening thump of her headache, and caught the movement of someone large and blond moving into the room, closing the door behind himself.

The man was tall and well-built, muscles pushing against the fabric of a dark suit and white shirt but he wore no tie. His shoes were shiny, though soft-soled and silent on the cement floor. He approached Rose with a neutral expression on his square-jawed face. His blond hair was cut short, his eyes piercing blue. Rose began gasping, panic washing over her, and she struggled again against the ropes that wouldn't give an inch.

"Please, remain calm," the man said, though his face gained a hard edge that frightened her further.

"Remain calm? When I've been kidnapped and held captive? You'll excuse me if I don't take your advice!" Her tongue was large and dry in her mouth, her words slurred. Just how much had they drugged her? How long had she been out?

"Well, I'm sorry for your discomfort, I really am. But you have information that we absolutely must retrieve. And we simply can't take any chances on you slipping away again. You have proven most elusive."

Rose frowned, trying to pinpoint the singsong nature of the man's voice. Her head was stuffed and muggy, thoughts dragging through it like they weighed a ton each. "If it's the stuff about the *Codex Gigas* you want, the *Devil's Bible*, it's all on my phone. I'll give you the passcode. We found all kinds of stuff…"

The man tipped his head to one side, his face apologetic. "We've already cracked your phone, thank you. And we've taken everything that was there. You know, you really did us a favor." Scandinavian, Rose suddenly realized. His accent was Swedish or Finnish or something like that. He smiled. "We must thank you for finding that particular artefact. There really is some very helpful stuff there."

Rose swallowed, her face twisted in discomfort and confusion. What the hell did this man want then? And how many were with him? Were they the same people who had been trying to capture her in London and Prague? They must be, though she hadn't seen this particular guy before. Maybe it was another group, a rival group. She just wanted to be rid of the whole ridiculous situation.

"We also enjoyed the photos that were presumably for your boyfriend. Or girlfriend? We'll definitely be keeping copies of those."

Rose scowled but was too frightened and confused to really care. The photos he referred to had been part of a short-lived but very enjoyable relationship that involved a lot of sexting. That particular affair had burned bright and short, and she really should have deleted those pictures, but it never really occurred to her that some kind of international gang would be abducting her and cracking her phone. It was all too surreal to even get mad about.

"So since you already have everything you want, and some bonus photos too, what do you want now? Just let me go!"

"I'm sorry, but I'm afraid we simply can't do that."

Tears breached Rose's lids again, trembling made her knees and shoulders shiver. "I have no interest in whatever it is you're doing. I only started this search for the *Codex* because it seemed you were after me and there might be a connection. That it might have shown me a way out, or given me something to give you, to get you off my back. You have everything now. I just want to be left alone." Despite the tears, her voice was strong, defiant. She knew her eyes flashed furious anger at the man and she saw a level of respect reflected in the gaze he gave back to her.

"It's not that simple." He offered her a weak smile. "There's something else we need."

"Fine! No problem. Whatever it is, I'll tell you. Just tell me what you want!"

The man shook his head. He seemed genuinely contrite. "You don't understand. What we need is *inside* you. And we have to take it."

CHAPTER 36

Crowley stood over the two unconscious men, fury raging through every fiber of his being. He was angry that Rose had been abducted, angry that he had been so close by and let them take her, and angry that he had been reduced to these measures to learn more. He certainly wasn't proud of the fact that he knew torture techniques, and he absolutely hated having to employ them.

An old sergeant he had served under once said, "When we torture, we're barely a single step away from being wild beasts. But sometimes, especially in war, being a wild beast is the only way to survive."

"A single step away?" Crowley had asked. "What's the last step?"

"Actually eating your enemy," the sergeant had said. Then he grinned crookedly, but his eyes were pained. "And don't write off that possibility either, just in case."

And what had Crowley learned this time? Not a whole lot, as was often the case with torture. If you pushed too hard, people would tell you anything, just to make you stop. They'd tell you what they thought you wanted to hear, to make sure you didn't hurt them any more. One of these two had been something of a buttercup and started out that way, blabbing all kinds of contradictory stuff. Some people couldn't be tortured because they were too scared of pain and poured out everything and anything, and right away it was uncertain how much was good info and how much was desperate shots in the dark. In many ways, it was the best defense against torture, but too hard to fake. But the other one, he'd been something of a hard man.

The second guy had tried to hold out. He'd stared Crowley in the eyes and gritted his teeth and refused to say anything. So Crowley amped up the pain. Still the guy held out. So Crowley went back to work on the weak one, knowing he wouldn't last long. Sure enough, that man passed out in no time. Crowley returned to the tough guy, more rattled now than before, and he upped the ante again. Hiding his own disgust at what he was doing, acting like he enjoyed it and had all day to spare. One of those things was true, after all. Without a lead, Crowley had nothing to go on, no way to find out where Rose might have been taken. The stress of that threatened to unhinge him, after all he had managed so far. And slowly, the tough guy cracked, just a little bit.

"You'll never get there in time," the thug finally said through swollen lips, his head lolling, half-conscious. His words were almost lost among sobs.

"Get where?" Crowley cajoled. "Where can I never get?"

"It's too far, you're too late." The man's voice was almost singsong as he surfed consciousness, blacking out and swimming back briefly.

"Where's too far?"

"It's too far. Berk's too far."

"Berk?" Crowley said.

The man's eyes snapped open as he forced himself into a moment of strength despite his myriad hurts. He cursed Crowley out quite elaborately. Then, "You'll never break a soldier of the esserar..." Then he sneered and gave in to Crowley's ministrations, his head falling forward. His chin rested against his chest and a dribble of blood and saliva ran into the thick blond hair there.

Crowley frowned. Berk and a soldier of the esserar? He must have not heard those things correctly. That was another problem with torture. If they finally told you something useful but it was a word you didn't know or a language you didn't speak, it was easy to miss. Especially through busted lips, missing teeth, restricted throats and whatever else might have been inflicted on them.

Crowley's eyes tracked the rivulets of scarlet blood on the man's chest and he winced, again horrified by his actions. Then his eye fell on the strange brand again, raised welts of shiny scar a little pinker than the man's skin. He crouched, looked more closely. It was entirely possible that the little swirl of writing under the circular design could be letters, an acronym. Capital letters. He moved to check the other thug and smiled, the truth of it confirmed in this man's slightly clearer brand. Not esserar. It was three capital letters: SOR.

He stood, looked around the room. It was dangerous to stay here much longer, especially in case whoever had taken Rose sent others to find the men who hadn't returned. They'd booked into the hotel under a false name, so perhaps Crowley should just slip away. He gathered his things and packed Rose's few possessions too. Carrying two backpacks, he hurried out of the room, locking it behind himself. The cleaner would have a shock in the morning when she came in to find those two tied up and bleeding on the floor. But they'd get help, no doubt be sent to the hospital, and they would hardly come clean to the police about what had happened.

Crowley went cautiously down the back stairs, doing his best to keep his face down from the many security cameras. There would already be footage, from when they had arrived, but his identity here in Rome was the least of his concerns right now. And he had a feeling he would be leaving the country soon. He just needed to figure out where to go.

Out on the street, in the warmth and bustle of a normal Rome day, he walked two blocks, then hailed a cab. Once the driver was well under way to the airport, Crowley called Cameron.

"Yo, not much yet, I'm afraid."

Crowley nodded to himself, not surprised. "I might have more though. Perhaps it'll help you?"

"I hope so. I've got all kinds of bits and pieces here, but nothing concrete. I can't tie it all together."

"What about the acronym SOR?" Crowley said. "And a place. Berk. Or something like that. Maybe with an 'e' or 'u'? Could even be an 'i', I suppose. I don't know. The guy wasn't talking very clearly."

Cameron chuckled down the line. "You been up to some old tricks, Crowley?"

"Not particularly willingly, but yes."

"Must be a bit of a thrill for a history teacher."

Crowley grinned, despite his anxiety for Rose. "You know what? It kind of is. It's exciting to be back out in the world, taking some risks and cracking heads. I always said I didn't want to be shot at any more, though, and that still stands. Too many idiots pointing guns at me lately."

"I hear ya," Cameron said. "I don't miss that." His voice was a little distracted.

"What have you found?" Crowley asked, trying not to get excited that there just might be a lead.

"How about Birka?" Cameron asked, and spelled it out.

"Yep, sure could be."

"Because that fits with Landvik, the name you messaged before." Cameron made a sound of satisfaction. "Ah! And SOR. That's what it says under those brands in the photos you sent me."

"I think so, yeah. One guy called himself a soldier of the SOR."

"Then I've got something. Okay, it's messy, I'll have to dig more, but here's the general shape of it. SOR is short for the Sons of Ragnar. That's a reference to Ragnar Lodbrok, a Viking hero."

"I've seen that show, *Vikings*," Crowley said. "They fans too?"

"No, don't get sidetracked by pop culture."

Crowley laughed. "Mate, I'm joking. I'm a historian too, remember?"

"Right. Well, shut up and listen then. The Sons of Ragnar still worship the old Norse gods. They're trying to bring that worship back into the mainstream. They want to make the Norse religion the official national religion of Scandinavia, and reunite all the Scandinavian countries back into a single kingdom."

"A kingdom? Like with a king. Not a unified republic?"

"Wait, reading." Cameron breathed down the line for a moment and Crowley watched the streets of Rome slide by out the window, then the cab moved onto the highway heading for the airport.

"Okay," Cameron said. "It's all a bit complicated. They want a united Scandinavia, no longer any part of Europe, to be run like a kingdom but with an elected council in charge. They've got a secret draft charter that we've managed to get hold of. It would take me too long to read through it all now, but I can send it to you. Anyway, the upshot is that it's not just some band of hippy cranks with delusions of pagan glory."

"No kidding!" Crowley said. "The kind of people coming after us have been well organized and well-armed."

"Right. And they're well backed. The Sons of Ragnar is controlled and bankrolled by businessmen mostly, a band of very wealthy people. Some politicians are cozying up to them too, if our intel is to be trusted. Which it usually is. That means they have all kinds of power structures available to them. And it's all managed by one man in particular, an incredibly wealthy businessman."

"Let me guess," Crowley said. "His name is Landvik?"

"You got it. Halvdan Landvik. A notoriously xenophobic man, very well known in Norway for his brutal and cut-throat corporate methods. He's powerful, with many powerful friends. I got a picture of him here, I'll send it over. Tall guy, something like six-three, fit and strong, in his mid-forties. It's not public that he's in charge of the SOR, of course, but that's what all our intel points to. His full name is Halvdan Ragnar Landvik, if you believe that, and he runs the SOR from its secret base on the island of Björkö, in Sweden, not far from the archeological site of Birka."

Crowley nodded to himself. This was why it always paid to have informed friends to help decode information gathered by unpleasant means. "You think the site, this Birka place, is relevant?"

"Relevant to what, mate? I'm not sure what it is you're up to. But you know what? This is a pretty interesting place. Björkö means 'Birch Island', and it's only about thirty kilometers from Stockholm, in Lake Mälaren. Back in the day it was an important trading center, used for goods from all over Scandinavia and Central and Eastern Europe, and the Orient too. Birka, on the other side of the island, is a significant archaeological site with loads of Viking lore attached to it. It's been a UNESCO World Heritage Site since 1993. According to this, a silver ring from a Viking-era grave in Birka is the first with an Arabic inscription from that era ever found in Scandinavia. Think about the significance of that! I'll send all this info over to you. Well, the relevant parts at least."

Crowley blew out a long breath. What did it all mean? It was fascinating stuff, but how did it relate to Rose? He thought about her birthmark, like the result of the blood eagle torture. And didn't Ragnar Lodbrok die that way? He'd need to check his history books again, but it was all too far-fetched and complicated to figure out now. Regardless, whatever the deeper reasoning, he had a lead. "Bless you, Cam. You're worth your weight in gold. Looks like I'm going to Sweden then. Can you figure out the best way for me to get to this island of Björkö? I'll fly to Stockholm on the next plane out of Rome."

There was silence from the other end for a moment.

"Cameron? You still there?"

"You're really going up against this Landvik and his people?"

"Don't try to lecture me now, Cam. I don't have any choice. He's got Rose and I don't think he means to treat her well."

"And you say you're enjoying a bit of action in the field again?" There was a slight longing in Cameron's voice now.

Crowley laughed. "Sitting at a desk starting to get to you, mate?"

"You fly to Stockholm, Jake. I'll meet you there."

CHAPTER 37

Rose had no concept of how much time had passed. The drug had worn off slowly, leaving her muddle-headed for a long time, but she had regained her senses and her fury focused as her thoughts did. Still tied to the dentist's chair, she had been moved into more of a sitting position and the pressure of the bindings had eased marginally. She still couldn't move much, but at least her blood flowed.

The large blond man returned, carrying a covered plate. She smelled the hot food immediately, rich and savory, and her mouth watered instantly. She realized she was famished.

"You will need your strength," the man said. "Eat."

"You going to feed me like a baby, or do I get a hand free to hold my own fork?"

He smiled and slit one binding with a shiny silver pocket knife, then handed her a plastic fork. He set the plate on her lap and stepped away.

Rose set the metal covering aside and saw a large pile of stew, chunks of lean-looking red meat, carrots, potatoes, peas. It smelled amazing and, despite her reservations, she dug in. The first few mouthfuls she barely chewed, and as they hit her stomach she slowed down, took a few breaths and began to eat more normally. She needed to make a break for it, but she would eat first. She needed the strength.

"My name is Karl," the blond man said while she silently shoveled the food in. "Once you have finished your meal, you will be untied and taken outside. A vehicle is waiting there, and you are to be transported somewhere else. If you comply, it will all go more easily for you."

Rose's stomach turned, a wave of nausea threatening to send the meal straight back up again. "Easier for me? Seriously? This is my last meal and you want me to be a meek little lamb?"

Karl frowned. "Not your last meal."

"You said there's something inside me and you have to take it out. I can't see that going particularly well for me, can you?"

Karl shrugged, looked away. "It's not like that. The process will be… unpleasant, perhaps. That's all."

Rose swore at him and went back to cramming food into herself, desperate only for the energy it would give her. Once she scraped her plate clean, the man rose and moved toward her. He took the plate and held out his other hand. Rose stared at him.

Karl sighed. "The fork, please?"

Rose sneered and handed it over. "A plastic fork?"

"You kept it, didn't you? Thought maybe you could do something with it? Honestly, I respect you for trying, but I have a job to do. Now, I'm going to untie you. Please don't do anything stupid."

"You're confident, here on your own with little old me," Rose said, giving Karl a sarcastic smile.

He stopped, stood up again and looked down at her. "There are others outside. Should I call them in?"

Rose deflated in the chair. "No. Fine." At least now she knew for sure that he wasn't alone, but she didn't know how quickly the people outside might respond. Or if she could get by them. But forewarned was forearmed.

She didn't move, but watched him closely as he used his small, shiny knife again, first to cut her other arm free, then he crouched for her feet. The moment her second leg was free, she launched herself forward and used every ounce of strength she could muster to deliver a crashing right hook to Karl's jaw. He was a big man, but Rose was a strong fighter, and he reeled back with a grunt of surprise and pain. Her fist flared in pain, maybe broken from the impact with his big, dumb head, but she didn't stop to think about that. Not waiting to see the effect, Rose stood from the chair, ignoring the whine of pain in her legs and the surge of pins and needles, and drove a kick up under Karl's chin. His teeth snapped together and he sat back hard, then collapsed like a scarecrow with the pole removed.

Rose grabbed the knife from where it had fallen and paused. She looked down at him, half of her desperate to remove any threat, imagining herself dragging the knife across his throat where he lay. Is that what Crowley would do? She shook her head. She couldn't do it, not kill in cold blood.

She turned and ran around the chair, heading for the door out of the strange, small warehouse. It was where Karl had come in from, so surely the others would be waiting out there. Or was that a ruse and he was on his own after all? Behind her, Karl groaned and moved weakly, regaining consciousness. No time. Her feet and legs were rubbery from inaction.

She looked frantically around, but there were no other exits except a huge roller door at one end. No way would she be able to get that open easily or quietly. She went to the first door and opened it an inch or so. Outside was a strange twilight sky, mostly cloudy. A cool breeze tickled across the bare skin of her arms as she leaned out to look further. She saw a lot of white houses with red tile roofs spreading away from her up a shallow hill. Water glittered off to her right, dark under the gloaming evening. A few masts rattled and rang with sail lines in the tiny harbor there.

A white panel van was parked just to one side and two men stood beside it, talking quietly. One smoked a cigarette. She could smell the acrid smoke on the otherwise cool, clean air. She slipped from the door as Karl began to moan more loudly behind her. As she ducked past the end of the van, trying to put it between herself and the other two men, Karl hollered something in Swedish. His voice boomed from the still open door and the two men swung around, faces shocked. They saw her.

"Hey!" one yelled and she bolted.

But her legs were still like jelly from who knew how many hours tied to the chair. She stumbled as she ran, her feet sparking painfully with pins and needles. A cavalcade of footsteps rattled up rapidly behind her and she spun around, slashing out with the knife. The two men yelped and leapt back, one slapping a hand to his left forearm, face twisted in pain.

"Bitch!"

Blood leaked out from between his fingers. Rose snarled at them like a caged animal, sweeping the knife left and right as they watched her warily. Then too late she realized they were waiting, not advancing. Karl had come the long way around the van and he grabbed her from behind, clamping her arms to her side. One of the others stepped forward and slapped her hard. Her face sang with the sharp pain of it and her vision crossed. The knife dropped from her fingers though she desperately tried to hold onto it.

The three men were snapping at each other angrily in Swedish, short, sharp sentences. Karl lifted her, feet kicking a foot above the ground, and threw her into the back of the van. He climbed in behind her and slammed the sliding door. By the orange glow of the interior light he stood over her, one fist raised.

"I will beat you unconscious if you don't stop fighting!"

"Like I just beat *you* unconscious?" Rose spat.

Karl laughed weakly, shook his head. "Yes, exactly like that."

His eyes were winced half-closed, as he clearly struggled with the pain in his head, no doubt the nausea of a concussion. He was tough, but she took some pleasure in his obvious discomfort. Just moving fast and taking her back under control was hurting him. But she knew when she was cornered. Better to wait it out now and have another chance to run than give him the excuse he needed to beat her into submission. He was a professional to not beat her anyway out of spite, for revenge. She slumped back against some sacking in the open back of the van and stared daggers at him.

Karl relaxed, visibly relieved. "Good." He turned to the front where the other two had taken their seats and said something. The van roared to life and pulled away.

They only drove for a couple of minutes before the van stopped and Karl grabbed Rose roughly by her upper arm. He slid open the door and dragged her out into the cool air. She was taken across a grassy area, a variety of trees here and there casting deep shadows as the twilight began to turn into night. Up ahead a large, rounded hill of rock rose up. Atop it she saw a square metal fence around a tall monument, what Rose thought of as a Celtic cross. But she was beginning to suspect that she wasn't anywhere Celtic. The dusk had the feel of late night, which meant far northern latitudes. And the Scandinavian accents and language. Was she in Viking country? She was fairly sure the men driving her around were speaking Swedish, but that didn't necessarily mean they were in Sweden. The scientist in her kept gathering information, while refusing to jump to conclusions.

Another group of men were gathered in some of the deepest shadows under trees at the base of the stony hill. They wore long robes with hoods pulled up, concealing their faces in darkness. Rose swallowed hard. Karl pushed her forward and one of the men stepped away from the others. He was very tall.

She began to remember horror movies from her youth—Satanic rituals and maidens slaughtered on stone tables. Her heart raced and her already weak legs wobbled. Violent trembling set in and she could do nothing to still her vibrating limbs.

The man who had stepped forward from the group, well over six feet, stood close enough to tower over her. He threw back his hood to reveal a slim, handsome face topped with short ash blond hair. He smiled, his grin wolfish in a neatly trimmed salt and pepper beard. "Please, try to relax."

"What's happening here?" Rose asked, hating the quaver of fear in her voice. "I don't know *anything!*"

"Ah, but I think you do."

"Who are you people?"

The man looked around the small gathering, the three thugs arrayed behind her, the six others in robes behind him. "We are just a small contingent of the Sons of Ragnar. The people you see behind me are the most powerful of us, the most important. And I, for my sins, am in charge. My name is Halvdan Landvik, and please, if you show me some respect and treat me well, I will do the same for you."

"Are you crazy?" Rose knew she should do nothing to antagonize this man, he was clearly some kind of psychopath, but she simply couldn't help herself. "You chase me all over Europe, you drug me, abduct me! And then tell me you'll treat me with respect? Screw you, buddy!"

Landvik reached out one long, slim palm and gently stroked her hair. "You have no idea of your importance."

Rose cringed away from his touch. "Why don't you just ask me?"

"If only it were that simple." Landvik looked up, addressed the three who had driven her here. "Head back to the base. If I need you again, I'll call. We have our vehicles here."

Rose heard the men walk back across the grass, but didn't dare take her eyes of Landvik. He watched them go for a moment, then returned his attention to her. "Please, sit." He pressed hard on one shoulder, giving her no choice but to sink to the cold grass. She knelt, staring at him in fear and just a little bit of wonder.

"What do you know about past lives?" Landvik asked suddenly.

Rose frowned. "It's a bunch of crap."

Landvik smiled. "Why?"

Rose laughed, shook her head. "You're serious? It's simple mathematics. The human race has grown exponentially. There aren't enough people in human history for everyone today to have been someone else in the past. It's just the kind of nonsense that people who think the stars have some relevance to their lives like to believe in to make themselves feel better. To feel less small and insignificant."

Landvik smiled again, but it was cool, condescending. "You're correct, of course. Not everyone has a past life. As you say, how could they? But some very special people *are* reborn. Again and again. And you, Rose Black, whether you believe it or not, were once someone incredibly special."

Despite her fear, Rose rolled her eyes and made a noise of disdain. "Really? And who am I supposed to be? And don't say Tokyo Rose. I'm Chinese, not Japanese." She narrowed her eyes at him, challenging.

Landvik chuckled. "I don't believe Tokyo Rose was a single person."

Rose shrugged. "You're smarter than you look."

Landvik inclined his head slightly, like he was accepting the compliment instead of seeing the sarcastic barbs Rose tried to throw. The man was infuriatingly calm and superior in his attitude. He was clearly someone used to getting everything he ever wanted and always having his butt kissed.

"You asked who you once were," Landvik said. "Perhaps you have heard of my ancestor, Ragnar Lodbrok?"

Rose surprised herself with a genuine laugh. "Great. You think I'm the guy from the television show?"

"No. I said Ragnar Lodbrok was *my* ancestor. *You* were once King Aella, the man who tortured and killed Ragnar Lodbrok." Landvik's calm demeanor hardened, anger flitting around the edges of his eyes. This was history that he seemed to take rather personally.

Rose was baffled. "And how do you know this?"

"When the person we once were suffers a grievous injury, or dies a particularly painful death, we are often born bearing marks which reflect that pain."

"Marks?" Rose's thoughts immediately returned to her birthmark, the trigger for all of this. It seemed suddenly powerfully relevant that she herself regularly thought of it as a blood eagle, ever since she'd learned of that hideous torture. "And what do my marks tell you?" she asked, nervous once more.

"The sons of Ragnar Lodbrok put King Aella to the blood eagle torture, partly for revenge, and partly to extract information from him. But they failed."

It all came crashing together in Rose's mind. She remembered her excitement in the hotel in Rome, not long before those men had attacked her and dragged her away while Crowley showered. She had researched the strange text beneath the newly discovered sketch of the squatting devil, in the back of the real copy of the *Codex Gigas* they had discovered. She recalled animatedly telling Crowley about the ancient Akkadian language, and what the ritual seemed to be. She heard her own words echo in her mind.

According to this, if I'm right, it not only extracts memories, but causes a person to actually revisit past lives.

A ritual for extracting past life memories. For *revisiting* past lives. And this Landvik lunatic thought that she used to be some King Aella, who had killed Ragnar Lodbrok?

"The information these sons of Lodbrok were trying to extract from this King Aella. You think I can give it to you?"

"You actually helped us enormously," Landvik said. "I've been reconstructing the ritual for years, finding whatever information I could. Then you run off and, while I'm getting angry with you for being so elusive, you're finding the original *Codex Gigas*. And you find the original text of the ritual, take photographs of it and bring those photographs to us when we finally catch up to you."

The weight of it sank onto Rose. "Well, isn't that just the most ironic course of events?"

"You've made it easier on yourself, in fact. I might have got the ritual wrong otherwise. Now I know it's right."

"And you think I'll be able to tell you what this King Aella knew?"

Landvik nodded, smiling once more. "We will soon find out."

CHAPTER 38

The island of Björkö, Sweden

Crowley crept along darkened streets, fueled by anger and a desperate desire to see Rose unharmed. Part of him balked at being her knight in shining armor, coming to save her. If she had proven anything, it was that she was pretty capable of taking care of herself. But against these odds, neither of them had done well alone. If not for her, he'd still be in an oubliette in Prague. So now it was his turn.

Cameron's intel had narrowed it down to several buildings on the tiny island. The town was more like a village anyway, but even a few dozen buildings could take hours to check and Crowley was under no illusion that time was not on his side. Time, in fact, was like a tightening noose, slowly closing.

But he was glad to have Cameron along. The man had met him at the airport, a wide smile in his olive-skinned face, jet black hair a little longer than Crowley remembered, tousled. They were of a height, around six feet, but Cameron was broader, solid in a way that a person could never build in a gym, but only gain from genetics. He had waved as Crowley emerged into the arrivals hall and had got straight to business, detailing the area they needed to cover, the variety of places they would have to check, which buildings Landvik owned, and he had reiterated the strength of the Sons of Ragnar operation.

"These are some bad guys, Jake. And they're connected in all kinds of high places. You get caught here and you could be disappeared very easily."

"As could you," Crowley said. "You're taking a risk coming along on this ride for fun."

Cameron smiled crookedly. "It's not only for the skit, my friend. When you said Rose had been abducted, I got worried. You two had been doing well so far, it seemed. I had no idea what kind of muppets you were up against and figured you were coping. Then when you had me look into these SOR guys, and you said they'd got Rose, well…"

"The balance has kinda shifted, huh?"

"That's what I thought. And I figured you could use my

help."

"You were right." Crowley grasped Cameron's forearm, and Cam returned the gesture, his wide, strong hand closing over Crowley's arm. "It's good to see you again, man."

Cameron grinned. "You too. Like the old days, eh? Come on, I have transport already arranged."

But once they reached Björkö they had to split up. They could cover all the places they needed to check in half the time if they did it alone. A text lit up Crowley's phone.

I'm at the offices. People here, but going to sneak by and look around.

Crowley nodded, sent back a reply.

Be careful. I'm just approaching the storage complex now.

He knew Cameron was more than capable of breaking stealthily into the offices Halvdan Landvik used on the island. He might have been at an intel desk for a lot of years now, but Cameron had a solid history of field work and was a professional in every way.

Crowley concentrated on his own situation. A storage facility which consisted of one large metal warehouse and two smaller buildings, white with red tile roofs like most of the surrounding town. The town was incredible, postcard beautiful, and would have been a great place to come as a tourist. But that applied to pretty much everywhere Crowley had been thus far, and none of it had felt like a holiday.

A white panel van was parked against the side of the large warehouse, right next to a small wooden door. A big roller door filled the front of the building, currently closed. The two smaller buildings were also closed up, and the windows all blank, black squares in the quickly darkening night. It was late, already nearing midnight, but the dusk had only just passed into darkness. This far north, this time of year, the days were long and the hours of shadows very short. But in the gloom, Crowley saw a bead of light beneath the side door of the warehouse.

He stood for a moment, chewing his lower lip. The two outbuildings might offer some good intel, but they were dark and still, so almost certainly wouldn't be where Rose was held. Assuming she was even here at all, even on the island, let alone this complex. But if she was anywhere, the large metal building made the most sense.

Crowley crept along in the shadow of its wall, watching carefully where he put his feet. Everything was still and quiet, no people moved anywhere. As he approached the small door he heard voices and froze. But the voices resolved into music and he realized it was a radio playing somewhere inside. That was good. It would help to conceal his approach.

He moved forward again, and pressed himself to the cold metal wall right beside the door. It was painted wood with a standard door handle and keyhole arrangement, and two small glass squares about three quarters of the way up. He leaned forward to peek in.

A large open space presented itself. At the back he could see the edges of shipping containers, closed up. A wooden staircase climbed over those to a kind of mezzanine level with several offices along the back wall of the warehouse. Two of those were brightly lit, light spilling out of their mostly glass fronts to illuminate the concrete floor below. In front of the containers was a wide open space, desks and machinery around the edges, and a dentist's chair right in the center.

Crowley stared for a moment, confused by the incongruous sight. Then he made out loops of rope around the top of the chair. Its back was to him, so he had no idea if anyone occupied it, willingly or tied in place. He would have to go in to find out. He allowed himself a small smile. It was an ideal candidate for Rose's place of imprisonment.

He moved around the door, carefully scanning the whole interior. It seemed empty but for the voice on the radio, now a host chattering away in Swedish. If there were any thugs here, they were likely up in the offices. It would be sweet if he could slip in, free Rose, and they could both slip out again, unnoticed.

Still scanning carefully inside, he let his hand fall to the doorknob and turned it painfully slowly. His smile widened as the door popped quietly open. He pushed it only far enough to allow him entry, then crouched and quickly closed it again. He listened, tried to filter out the radio and see if any other sounds reached him, but none did.

He snuck forward, staying low, keeping his eyes on the windows of the lit offices above and to his left. He rounded the dentist's chair. It was empty. Someone had been here, the bindings were cut, but whoever it was had gone. Surely it had to have been Rose. Unless these guys regularly abducted people and tied them up. That was entirely possible.

Suppressing a curse, Crowley looked around. A half-smile returned when he spotted a patch of dark brown on the pale concrete not far from the foot of the chair. He knew dried blood when he saw it. He guessed someone had been dropped there, bleeding heavily from a nose or mouth. Maybe even from a small stab wound.

Good girl, Rose, he thought to himself. He had to believe she'd been the one to draw blood, and that he was getting closer.

He would have to sneak up to the offices and see what he could find. And that almost certainly meant a confrontation with whoever was up there. He slipped his hand into his jacket pocket and pulled free a small knife. It wasn't much, and right about now he would much prefer a firearm, but traveling around Europe with a gun wasn't possible. He was handy enough with a knife if he could engage on his own terms, get close enough. He took a deep breath and crept to the stairs.

"Hey!"

Halfway between the dentist's chair and the stairs, exposed in the wide open concrete space, Crowley froze and looked at the door he had entered by. A man stood there, eyes wide. He had a grocery sack under one arm and was trying to reorganize his load to reach inside his jacket, no doubt for a shoulder-holstered weapon.

He yelled out in Swedish but Crowley was already on the move. As the man's hand came free of the jacket, Crowley dove forward toward the man and rolled. The man tried to track him, fired once and the slug bit up a spray of concrete from the ground right beside Crowley as he came back to his feet and drove the knife at the man's chest. The grocery sack fell, cans of beer hitting the hard floor. Some split, hissed and spun as they sprayed white foam across their feet. The man got an arm up to deflect the deadly thrust of Crowley's knife, but Crowley's other arm was already looping around. His fist cracked into the thug's jaw and the man fell limp. Crowley went down with him, snatched the gun from the man's slack fingers, and rolled instinctively away as more gunshots rang out and more chips of concrete flew.

Feet thundered across the landing above and Crowley tried to estimate how many as he tucked in against one of the shipping containers for cover. At least two, maybe three. Well, this had certainly turned bad incredibly quickly. The feet came down the metal stairs, ringing in rapid succession, and Crowley dove out to roll quickly across the open space, firing as he went.

His aim was good, but the movement and not knowing quite where his enemies would be made the move a little too random. One of the men yelped and spun away, clutching his upper arm, while two more ducked for cover behind another shipping container. Crowley used the moment of panic to run behind the dentist's chair and in behind some metal cupboards on one side wall. At least now he had all the enemies in front of him, but he was still outnumbered three to one. The man he had punched groaned and rolled onto his hands and knees. Make that four to one.

Crowley was in no doubt of the trouble he was in and needed to even those odds. He drew a bead on the punched man and, as the thug rose groggily to his feet, Crowley fired twice. The man's chest blossomed scarlet and he fell backwards and lay still.

More yelling in Swedish and rapid footsteps hitting concrete behind the containers. There had to be enough space behind them for the enemy to move around them, trying to gain Crowley's flank. He was pinned down against one wall. He had a closer look at his weapon. Standard automatic, fifteen rounds. He'd just cleared two. Time to start counting. Three enemies and thirteen rounds. Those odds were good, but only if he had time and space to engage. Which was exactly what he lacked.

Memories of raiding houses in Afghanistan came back to him, scared faces huddled in corners, insurgents with furious eyes running madly to attack. Suddenly, Crowley himself was the trapped local. The men moving around him operated like he had with his squad, outnumbering and outmaneuvering. He did not like being on this side of the arrangement.

These guys were pros. He could feel their pincer movement closing in and knew he had little time. From this side of the warehouse he now saw that two cars were parked in the opposite far corner, near the big roller door. If he could get between them he'd be able to move more freely, create better lines of fire. And if he was lucky, one might have keys in it and he could ram-raid his way out of this trap.

He ducked his head out for a quick look and immediately gunfire punched through from the front. Crowley fell back, one hand going instinctively to his head, feeling for blood. He'd felt the passage of at least one of those slugs. He put his hand out, blindly squeezed three quick covering shots and, hoping like hell the guy had ducked from his blind fire, ran for the two cars. He made it halfway before more gunfire boomed in the large space, so he dove sideways and rolled. A line of fire grazed his left calf and he barked a curse, but made it between the cars. No time to check his injuries, he rose over the hood of one vehicle and squeezed off three more shots in the direction of the last attack. Seven shots left and no one else taken down yet. His odds were rapidly dwindling.

Another quickly barked shout of Swedish and someone ran left to right across the front of the warehouse. Crowley took a bead, then immediately, though too late, realized his mistake. Cold metal touched his temple and a gravelly voice said, "Don't move."

Crowley squeezed his eyes shut, let his weapon drop. Idiot! He'd fallen for a decoy run. He felt like a newbie. *I'm sorry, Rose,* he thought.

The man with a gun to his head put a hand under Crowley's arm and hauled him up, pushed him forward. One of the other two was checking their dead friend, while the third, a large, broad man with blond hair and a suit tight over large muscles, stepped forward.

"I should just shoot you where you stand," he said.

Crowley shrugged. He had no answer to that.

"Karl," the kneeling one said.

The blond man looked over and the kneeling man shook his head, said something in Swedish.

Karl looked back to Crowley, his eyes dark. "The man on the ground next to Phillipe? His name was Karol. He was a good man. He has been my friend for over twenty years. And you have killed him."

Crowley lifted his chin. Defiant. "You lot started this! I'm only trying to get *my* friend back."

"You have been more than troublesome, Mr. Jake Crowley."

"Good."

Karl backhanded Crowley and he tasted blood. But he refused to go down, remained standing, staring hard into Karl's eyes. Phillipe moved to stand beside Karl, spoke again in Swedish.

Karl nodded, addressed the man still holding Crowley's arm. That one moved away and carefully lifted Karol's body from the ground and headed for the stairs to the offices above. A large, scarlet pool was left where Karol had lain. Crowley took a moment of perverse pleasure from it. These guys may have got the drop on him, but at least he wasn't going down without some return damage.

"You will not die easily," Karl said. "You will suffer for what you've done. And you will suffer in a uniquely relevant way."

He turned to Phillipe and spoke rapidly in Swedish, not for a moment taking his gun away from pointing at Crowley's chest. And he was just far enough away that Crowley couldn't reach him. If he did lunge forward, Karl would shoot instantly and Crowley would take the shot full in the heart. He almost considered chancing it, but as he braced himself, his leg burned again. He glanced down to see his lower left trouser leg soaked in blood. He flexed the muscle a little and pain blasted up behind his knee. It didn't feel like a terribly bad injury, a flesh wound really, but he was losing blood and it made him slow to move and a little woozy.

Scraping against the concrete floor drew his attention back and he turned to see Phillipe dragging two large metal stanchions over. He stood them about four feet apart and Karl pushed Crowley to stand between them. While Phillipe kept a gun trained on Crowley's head, Karl stripped Crowley of his jacket and shirt, then pushed Crowley to his knees and tied his wrists high on the metalwork, leaving Crowley in a kneeling crucifix position.

"You are by now, I'm sure," Karl said, "aware of the blood eagle torture?"

Crowley grimaced, hung his head. He cursed Karl, and Landvik, and everything that had happened since that day in the museum. This was no way to die.

"Prepare for more pain than you ever imagined," Karl said, and Crowley felt the icy tip of a blade touch the middle of his back.

CHAPTER 39

Night had fallen properly by the time rough hands pushed Rose to her knees on the cool, damp grass beneath the large old tree. She struggled against the bonds that secured her wrists behind her back, but to no avail. The robed figures surrounded her, at least two of them women from the curves Rose saw pushing against the voluminous robes. Though her eyes had adjusted to the darkness, the shadows were inky deep beneath the wide spreading arms of the tree under which they gathered. And perhaps it was only the fear at work, but something felt powerful in this place. The ancient tree seemed to press its age down upon them, the land itself felt soaked in history that rose to meet them like a mist.

Landvik stood before her, his hood still down, piled on shoulders, the only one to have revealed his face. It made Rose uneasy that he was unconcerned about her knowing his identity, made her fairly sure he planned to kill her after this was all done with. She imagined Crowley, maybe still in Rome, frantically trying to track her down. What must he have thought to find her gone? Had he heard the ruckus of her abduction? She had certainly tried to make enough noise to attract his attention, but now all that was academic. He could be anywhere in the world, but he wasn't here. For that, she was strangely grateful. Crowley was, after all, simply a kind history teacher. He had a violent and difficult past, for sure, but he had retired from all that only to find himself caught up in all this. And, like a true gentleman, he had stepped up without question. Rose was pleased he wasn't here to die with her. She didn't want to die, of course, she would take any chance she could to escape when and if one presented itself, but she was glad Crowley remained out of danger. It offered a small comfort as Landvik approached her with a long, sharp knife in hand, glittering slightly in the wan moonlight that occasionally peeked through small gaps in the clouds.

"It is time," Landvik said. "Try not to be afraid."

Rose bared her teeth at him, but couldn't bring herself to speak for fear her voice would be weak with fear.

Landvik placed a small vessel on the grass in front of her. It looked to be made of brass or bronze, strange symbols carved around its girth. The six others in the group arrayed themselves in a crescent behind Landvik as he crouched in front of Rose.

"I'm going to need a small amount of your blood," he said, that wolfish smile still in place. He was clearly enjoying every moment of this.

"You're mad, you know that?" Rose said. "Like, actually insane. This is the really real world, you nutter. There's no magic, no past lives!"

Landvik, still smiling, ignoring her tirade, raised the knife.

"Don't cut me!" Rose screamed, but Landvik held her jaw in one vice-like hand and drew the knife across her left cheekbone. The pain was sharp and electric and Rose whimpered, but Landvik's grip was iron and he didn't let her move.

He put the knife on the grass and lifted the bronze chalice to her face, pressed the cold lip of it to her cheek and watched intently. Rose imagined her blood leaking from the burning wound on her cheek, running into the bowl. After a moment, Landvik carefully put the chalice down again and pressed a handkerchief to her face. He held it there a moment, a look almost of apology on his face, then moved away, taking the chalice with him. One of the others stepped forward, wiped her face with something cold that stung furiously. Then a Band-Aid was carefully stuck to her cheek. She stared straight ahead throughout, ignoring their ministrations. She refused to be grateful for this small kindness given everything else they were doing to her.

Once that person returned to the group, Landvik turned to the crescent of six and held out the chalice to the first of them. Rose saw her chance, his back turned, the others watching Landvik and not her, and gathered her strength to leap to her feet and run. But even as the thought crossed her mind, Landvik turned back, pointed the knife at her. "Be still." His voice was like a gunshot in the calmness of the night and Rose stopped short.

The hooded figure with the chalice produced a knife of his own, nicked the side of his thumb, and dripped a few drops of blood into the chalice. Each of the other five did the same in turn as Landvik watched Rose like a hawk. Then the last returned the chalice to Landvik and he added a few drops of his own blood to the mix. He put the chalice back on the ground in front of Rose's knees and the seven of them moved to stand around her in a circle, with Landvik front and center, staring down.

He pulled a roll of paper from inside his robes and began to speak, in a language Rose could not recognize. His voice was low and sonorous, rising and falling like a chant. The night seemed to grow heavy, as if the darkness itself had a weight, wrapping around her like a cloak. Something cold was pressed to her lips and a thick, bitter liquid cascaded over her tongue. She tried to cough, to spit, but Landvik tipped her head back, covered her mouth and nose and forced her to swallow. More woolly thickness smothered her mind.

All the surrounding small sounds became muted, the gentle breeze stilled. Only Landvik's voice existed as he began to chant again, and then slowly another voice and another were added to it as each of those present began to match his incantation.

Rose shook her head, blinked rapidly, trying to throw off the feeling that descended on her. Surely this was like hypnosis or some kind of stage magic, the power of suggestion and nothing more. Or perhaps whatever drug she had just been given. Her muscles seemed to grow weak and she slumped back onto her heels, unable to prevent her head falling to her chest. Her breath was low and deep through her nose. With a force of pure will, she raised her chin, determined to stare Landvik in the eyes, but he wasn't there.

She saw a large room, like a bedchamber in a stately home, people in old-fashioned clothes moving through it, laughing.

She blinked, a soft cry escaping her lips, and before her was an open field, horses cantering in the distance and a checkered blanket spread out at her knees. A man with a clipped beard and 1920s clothing leaned his head back and laughed, an old car parked behind him.

"Wha..?" Rose's voice was thick and slurred, she felt suddenly drunk. Or drugged, the effects of whatever she had been given flooding her senses. But she also knew, deep in the truest part of her, that what she experienced was far more than drug-induced. Something entirely more real.

A wooden building surrounded her, numerous faces of children and teenagers, miserable and crying. Some were obviously very sick. One tiny infant lay on a cot, clearly dead.

Rose sobbed, blinked again, and saw a small hovel,

thatched roof and wooden walls, in a hilly field. A woman leaned on a broken hoe in front of her, looking more tired than anyone Rose had ever seen. The woman smiled and raised one hand to stroke Rose's cheek and Rose felt her own beard under that palm, realized she was a man.

Past lives? she thought, unable to truly accept the possibility, but then what else could it be?

The images began to spin rapidly by, flickering like a film in fast forward, too quick to pin down. Or, she realized dizzily, a film in fast rewind. So many faces and places, days and nights, towns and countryside, land and sea. Rose became nauseated, swayed on her knees convinced she was going to pitch forward and vomit.

Then she did fall forward, but was held in place somehow, her arms stretched up behind her, secured to something just higher than her shoulders. Ropes bit into her wrists. She pulled her head up off her muscled, hairy chest, tasted blood on her lips that ran into her beard with her sweat and saliva.

"I am a King!" she roared. Cold wind swirled around her naked body.

Leather-armored men with bloodstained weapons stood all around, and Ivar the Boneless, the huge, muscled son of Ragnar Lodbrok, stepped forward. The other sons of that damned Ragnar stood behind, faces like dark thunderclouds of rage and hate. Fires crackled all around, lighting up the night with orange glows, and smoke roiled by.

Rose-Aella grimaced, refusing to show any fear.

Ivar spoke, but his voice was strange. Though Rose looked out from Aella's eyes and saw Ivar, she knew the voice belonged to Halvdan Landvik.

"Tell us what we want to know," he said.

Rose spoke with Aella's deep baritone. "I don't know what you want."

She remembered the battles, the victories. She saw Ragnar Lodbrok die at her hand, cast down into that pit of snakes, and she smiled. Aella's presence swelled inside her and Rose was pushed back deep inside, able to do no more than advise. Or not even that, perhaps only watch. Aella spoke again, his tone defiant. "Ragnar Lodbrok was twice the man you'll ever be."

"And yet here you are on your knees before me," Ivar said. "Tell me where it is."

Aella met the other man's gaze and bared his teeth in a

wordless snarl, not trusting his voice to be strong if he spoke. He could never possibly let Ivar find what he sought.

Rose watched through Aella's eyes, as if from miles away, though she still felt the wind and the heat of the bonfires, still smelled their smoke. But she was fading, Aella's mind taking over, pushing her away and yet, simultaneously, she knew her presence somehow weakened the Briton king, made him more vulnerable to the interrogation. The tiny, scared part of her screamed at Aella to tell Ivar what he wanted to know, to make all this end. Aella's presence resisted, refusing to jeopardize all he had done, prepared to take his place in Heaven if that's what must happen. The strong, defiant part of Rose tried to howl out her own insubordination, tried to lend strength to Aella, but she was a mere conduit, with no more agency than a stretch of desert highway. And that thread of her consciousness only weakened the blockage in Aella, and opened the way for Ivar-Landvik to get the information he wanted.

"Where is Mjolnir?" Ivar-Landvik demanded, and Rose fell backwards into darkness.

Landvik stood before Rose Black's inert form, watching her chest gently rise and fall. The night coolness made the grass damp and it began to darken her clothes.

"Pick her up," he said to one of the robed figures behind her.

"What shall we do with her now?" the figure asked. "Make it look like an accident?"

Landvik pursed his lips, thinking of all he had learned, all he still didn't know. Then he shook his head. "We must keep her alive. It's possible we'll need more information from Aella before this is all over. This ritual is new to us. Maybe I can make a better job of it next time if this information proves insufficient."

"This time it nearly killed her," a female voice said. "She's strong, but whatever she experienced is maybe stronger. If we do it again, it might kill her anyway."

Landvik nodded. "So be it. We won't do it again unless we absolutely have to. But she stays with us, in case. Sedate her and bring her along."

CHAPTER 40

The island of Björkö, Sweden

Crowley winced as the knife point spiked into the flesh of his upper back, then a soft sound rang down from above. Crowley frowned. It had sounded like a stone hitting the roof high above them, as if something small had dropped from a great height.

Phillipe, standing in front of Crowley, looked up, clearly questioning Karl. The touch of Karl's knife disappeared and Crowley breathed a sigh of relief, though he imagined it would be short lived.

Phillipe and Karl exchanged a few words, then Karl called out, presumably to the one who had carried Karol's body up to the offices. There was a pregnant pause, silence growing heavy. Karl called out again, louder this time, and got no response. Crowley allowed himself a small smile.

More words and Phillipe pulled his gun from his jacket and jogged off. Crowley heard his shoes on the metal stairs, quickly at first and then slowing as he neared the top. Karl's knife touched the side of Crowley's neck, like a shard of ice.

"Don't move and don't speak," Karl said softly, but his voice was a little distant. Crowley assumed he was turned away, watching Phillipe make his way along the mezzanine level.

Phillipe called out something, followed by a crash. Karl's knife moved away fractionally and Crowley wasted no time. He hauled himself sideways, further from the blade, using all his strength to drag with him one of the metal frames to which he was tied. A gunshot rang out and a shout, then sounds of fighting. Glass smashed.

Crowley threw himself back and down, the metalwork falling with him. It clanged to the concrete almost on his head, close enough to have brained him senseless if he hadn't twisted his neck to avoid it. But he didn't spare that a thought as he kicked out, high and dead center. Karl was lunging forward, face twisted in fury, the knife raised high, and Crowley's heel slammed into his solar plexus.

Karl woofed out his breath and for the first time Crowley saw a bruise across the man's cheek, a swelling to one side of his mouth. In bizarre slow motion he had the impression this was the man Rose had hit, the one who had bled not six feet away from where he now lay. It drove a crazed laugh from Crowley and he threw his hip over to kick out again with the other leg, this time cracking his booted foot across Karl's jaw. Karl's head whipped to one side and he staggered away, dropped to his knees, his head swaying slightly as he fought to remain conscious.

Two more gunshots boomed from above, then another crash and a scream of pain.

Crowley used all the strength he had to haul himself back to his feet, dragging the two metal stands with him. They stretched his shoulder muscles almost to the breaking point, but he ignored the pain and took one step forward, then another. Then he pulled back one foot and, as Karl looked up, eyes swimming left and right, Crowley swung his kick in like he was punting for a field goal. Karl's head snapped up and back, several teeth flying in a spray of blood, and collapsed onto his back.

Movement on the mezzanine above caught Crowley's eye and he flinched back, restricted by the massive weight of metal hanging off each wrist, then he grinned.

"Need a hand down there?" Cameron asked.

"Phillipe?" Crowley asked.

"The guy who came up the stairs or the one who was already up here?"

"Either now you come to mention it."

"Both deader than flower power and flared trousers, mate."

Crowley laughed. "You're a legend. I see desk work hasn't made you soft."

"Not even slightly, it would seem."

Cameron came down the stairs, watching Karl as he did. The big blond man began to writhe slightly, a low moan escaping. Cameron took his knife and cut the bonds at Crowley's wrists.

"Thanks," Crowley said, rubbing his skin. He found his shirt and jacket and quickly pulled them on.

"You want me to finish this guy too?"

"Not yet, thanks. We need information. I'm glad you came when you did."

Cameron nodded. "When you stopped responding to my

texts I figured you might be compromised. Found a way in over the roof of the building next door."

Crowley crouched beside Karl. "Where is she?"

Karl sneered, his mouth full of blood that ran over one cheek and dripped onto the pale concrete. He said something in Swedish that sounded rather unpleasant.

Crowley took the knife from Cameron and pressed it against Karl's throat. "Where. Is. She?"

"You're going to kill me anyway, I'm telling you nothing," Karl said.

"I can make it very unpleasant for you," Crowley said. "How about *we* do the blood eagle torture on *you*? I know exactly how it works, you know."

Karl's face blanched, his eyes momentarily wild.

"Oh yeah," Crowley said. "And I'll enjoy it too."

Karl let out a humorless laugh. "It's irrelevant, you're already too late. And besides, if they're still there you can't sneak up on someone in open parkland. They'll gun you down from a distance."

"Open parkland? Near here?"

Cameron leaned forward. "Birka?" he asked. "Did they take her to the archeological site?"

Karl's eyes flickered and Cameron shared a nod with Crowley. "I think that's all we need to know."

Crowley smiled. "It is. And I think we need to hurry. Goodbye, Karl."

It didn't take long to reach the site, but it was obvious from a distance that no one was there.

"We too late?" Cameron asked.

Crowley shrugged. "Lots of dark places under those trees. Let's hunt around. We have no other leads."

They jumped from the car and made their way quickly to the foot of the rocky hill with the cross on top, surrounded by a square, spike-topped fence. After several minutes of searching, growing increasingly frustrated, Crowley stopped and let his arms fall flat to his sides.

"That bloody Karl was right. We're too late."

Cameron shook his head ever so slightly, and gestured with a subtle nod to one side. Crowley didn't turn his head, but let his eyes track sideways, searching the darkness. He saw what Cameron had seen; a small shape huddled in the darkness at the base of a large tree, trying hard to hide.

"Oh well," Crowley said. "One last look around, you go that way." He pointed away from the tree. "I'll go this way." He gestured back toward the car.

Cameron immediately took his meaning, knew they could go in opposite directions and circle around behind the tree unseen, to come behind whoever it was in case the person made a break for it. They trudged off through the darkness, then lightened their steps as they quickly doubled back. The man crouching had about two seconds to realize they had flanked him and leapt up to run, but they were on him, each grabbing one arm.

The man yelled in Swedish, struggled frantically for a moment. Crowley braced himself, wincing at the pain in his hastily bandaged calf. The wound was superficial, an annoyance more than a hindrance. He had been lucky. Crowley gripped the man's arm harder, pushed him back against the tree trunk, and the man stilled. He wore a long dark hooded robe, like some kind of monk. Cameron reached up and pulled the man's hood away, revealing a pasty, puffy round face and balding head. The man was in his fifties or thereabouts, and his eyes were wide with fear. He jabbered quickly in Swedish.

"English," Crowley said in a low growl.

The man frowned. "Who are you?" he asked, his English heavily accented.

"I might ask you the same question," Crowley said.

"I'm no one! Just a man enjoying a walk."

Crowley laughed. "After midnight? Dressed like that? Try again!"

"I'm no one. Leave me be!"

"You haven't been conducting any weird occult rituals lately?" Crowley asked.

The man winced, then pressed his lips together, his look suddenly defiant.

"Decided to clam up now, huh?"

Cameron looked at the man with a frown, lost in thought for a moment. Then he smiled. "I know who this is," he said to Crowley. "I thought he was familiar but couldn't think why for a moment, but it's just come to me. When I was researching the Sons of Ragnar for you, this guy came up."

The man's breathing became rapid and Crowley grinned. "Got you there, hasn't he?" he looked back to Cameron. "So who is it?"

"His name is Pietr Nilsson. He's a far right wing politician here in Sweden. Quite a high profile character, aren't you, Pietr?"

Nilsson clamped his lips together again, his eyes flicking left and right as he tried to watch both Crowley and Cameron equally.

"Now then," Crowley said, "as we've established who you are, you can dispense with the ridiculous midnight stroll in your robes story. What are you doing here?"

"Re-consecrating the site of the knowing," Nilsson said, his expression smug, like he expected them to simply not understand.

"That's why they left you behind, is it? To do the cleanup work like a maid?"

Nilsson blanched.

Crowley leaned close. "Where is she?"

"Who?"

Crowley slapped Nilsson hard across one cheek. The politician yelped, his eyes going wide as saucers, bright in the night. The tears standing on his lower lashes indicated he wasn't used to getting roughed up.

"I don't have time for any more games!" Crowley said sharply. "Rose Black, the girl you took from Rome, who you just recently subjected to something here. Where is she?"

"I'm not telling you anything," Nilsson said, but his voice was watery, weak with fear.

Crowley sighed, shook his head. "I am getting so tired of this. I can hurt you, Nilsson. I can make you beg for death. Just tell me what I need to know."

"You wouldn't dare!" Nilsson said.

It was Crowley's turn to widen his eyes. "Oh really?" He slapped Nilsson again.

"We can ruin you too," Cameron added. "We don't need to physically hurt you. Imagine what we could do to your career if we exposed your connection to the Sons of Ragnar. To everything you've been doing here. Not to mention the dirt I'm sure I could dig up on you in no time, should I choose to. You know I'm not lying."

Nilsson began to shake, still looking left and right, fear making him paler than ever. "You're too late anyway! She's gone. Landvik took her."

Crowley leaned very close, his breath tickling Nilsson's

chubby cheek. "Took her where?"

CHAPTER 41

Rose blinked, trying to clear her blurred vision. She sat in the back of a moving car, two armed heavies squeezed in either side of her, pinning her in place. A broad man with a shaved head drove with Halvdan Landvik in the front passenger seat.

She felt yet again as though she had been drinking too much, but this time it wasn't only drugs. She lifted one hand to rub her face and the other hand came with it, her wrists bound together with zip ties. Her head felt full of cotton wool, her ears rang slightly as though she had been at a loud concert the night before. The chance would be a fine thing. She longed for the opportunity to do something as normal and mundane as go to a gig. And to feel this way from actually drinking too much, carefree and happy.

She'd had moments of clarity here and there since the ritual but knew she had been out for hours. The process had left her drained, thoroughly exhausted. Only now was she beginning to feel as though she might be rested enough to start thinking clearly again. She managed to blink her vision clearer and looked out between Landvik and the driver. She recognized the sight ahead of her, as she had been here several times before. Sometimes casually as a tourist, but also in her professional capacity.

Their car was queueing with several others, moving slowly along a narrow roadway that led out across mudflats, water to either side in pools and patches. In the distance was an island. She was looking at the Holy Island of Lindisfarne, off the north east coast of England, not far from the Scottish border. She raked through her memories of the place. A tidal island, also known simply as Holy Island, accessed by this causeway that was cut off by the tide twice every day. Lindisfarne had been an important center of Celtic Christianity under several saints. In the tail end of the eighth century there had been a Viking raid on the island, she remembered that much. After the Viking invasions and the subsequent Norman conquest of England, a priory had been re-established on Lindisfarne. She had fond memories of exploring its ruins with an ex-lover. The small castle atop the island had been built in the sixteenth century. The island wasn't large, maybe three miles long by one and a half wide. Sand and mud flats surrounded it, and across a part of that expanse the ancient pilgrims' path ran. Many people chose to walk that way rather than drive over the relatively modern causeway where she now lined up with her captors. And that was the sum of her groggy recollections. What were they doing here?

They traveled slowly along the mile or so of causeway until the island became clearer ahead of them, all gray rocks and deep green grasses under a lowering sky. One of those classic English days where everything was dull and overcast, even though there may not be rain. She suspected some light drizzle nonetheless, and imagined the gloomy weather would persist for several days. It usually did, especially this far north. The causeway led along the long, narrow spit of land on the island's western side, sometimes out over the mud flats, other times hugging slight green rises. Slowly, the land on their left grew taller and grassier while mud flats persisted to the right. Eventually they gained the island proper, dry stone walls to one side. The whole place remained low to sea level, but now well above the tides. The street became tree-lined, the dwellings of the islands one hundred and fifty or so residents on either side. Then they entered the small town, white walled buildings and lots of gray-brown stone. In the far distance was an aberration in the otherwise flat landscape, a sudden small peak of rock, the castle atop the hill a gray-brown fortification, standing proud over the slate gray ocean. The sea was relatively calm, so there must not be much wind outside. But they had turned south through the town and continued along that way. Rose knew from previous visits that they were headed to Lindisfarne Priory and Monastery. Why?

She tried to piece together the journey, but it was all a blur. She had vivid flashes of the ritual however. Memories of a different life. Of being a different person. And the flashes of excruciating pain. She shut that memory down quickly before it could overwhelm her again. Even secondhand, that agony was mind-destroying. She had, at least in part, lived it. How was that possible? But she *had* lived it, felt and heard and smelled the environs of ancient Scandinavia. She knew the sensation of a strong male body. She knew implicitly the fear of certain death and the equally sure certainty of the impending halls of Valhalla.

She had felt the knife blade open her back, the ax chop at her bones. She gasped, pushed the memory away again. Could it really all have been some trick on Landvik's part? Some strange hypnotic spell? But why? There was nothing for him to gain from any of this unless he believed it completely. Which he certainly seemed to. But what exactly did he believe? She strained her mind back, tried to ignore the solid memories of her historical self and recall what the interrogation had entailed. Questions asked and answers given. And then she remembered one word. *Mjolnir.*

She couldn't suppress a soft laugh at the recollection. Landvik twisted in the seat to look back at her. "You're coming around at last."

"Thor's Hammer?" Rose said. "Seriously? All of this has been about you searching for a freaking mythical hammer? A thing that never existed?"

Landvik smiled softly, shook his head. "It existed. The great king Ragnar Lodbrok rediscovered it, and by its might he rose to power and led his people to great conquests."

"Come on!" Rose scoffed. "That's as much myth as the hammer itself."

"Lodbrok's conquests are a matter of historical record."

"Until he was killed! Why didn't he hammer all his enemies to death?"

Landvik's face hardened. "Ragnar lost the true faith. He was fascinated by Christianity, and foolishly believed that to worship both the true gods and the Christian gods would give him even more power. In fact, his apostasy cost him everything."

"By true gods," Rose said, "I assume you mean the old Norse gods."

"Old maybe, but no less powerful. In fact, only more powerful for their age. Except that only a true believer can harness the power of the hammer."

Rose let her eyebrows rise. "And Ragnar, tempted by the Christian faith, wasn't a true believer?"

Landvik raised both palms. "Just so. But I am a true believer."

He fell silent, turned back to face the front as the car left the mainland behind and started to travel slowly along the causeway.

"True nutcase, more like," Rose muttered. In a louder

voice, she asked, "So why are you keeping me with you now, if I've already told you where to find the hammer?"

Landvik didn't turn around, watching the priory ruins grow nearer. The tourist traffic, both in cars and on foot, was heavy. Rose wondered how easily they might haul her around with her hands bound up in the scattered crowds. Maybe she could scream for help, make a scene to get away. But her curiosity burned. "Why keep me?" she asked again.

Landvik sighed. "You told us one word. Lindisfarne. So that is where we are. But we might need to extract a more specific memory from you yet, if we can't find out why you brought us here. So we'll start at the priory and begin our search. I suggest you do all you can to remember any details that might be lodged in your mind, or we will have to conduct the ritual again. For your sake, you had better hope it does not come to that."

CHAPTER 42

Lindisfarne

Crowley tried to relax in the passenger seat of the Land Rover Discovery while Cameron drove, but it wasn't easy. His brain roiled with worries, concerns that they would be too late for Rose. And that only made him wonder just what it was they might be too late for. What the hell did these people want with her anyway? For all his techniques, the politician, Nilsson, hadn't been all that forthcoming. It quickly became apparent the man actually knew very little and was going to be hardly any use at all. But he'd given them one piece of information that had to be useful, because it was all they had. Lindisfarne.

Whatever Landvik wanted, apparently he believed he would find it on the Holy Island, and Crowley had to believe the man would keep Rose alive until then. So he prayed to gods he didn't really believe in that he and Cameron wouldn't be late.

"Lot of tourists." Cameron nodded ahead at the line of cars under the gloomy skies.

Traffic had been heavy all the way through from the airport, the typical English jams repeatedly slowing them down. Now a single line of vehicles snaked ahead and off over the long causeway leading to Lindisfarne Island.

Crowley scowled. "Might be quicker to leave the car and jog across!"

"Might be, but it's certainly not safer. The cars are crawling, but they're moving. We'll get there." Cameron's voice still had that edge of excitement Crowley had noticed before.

"Even slow moving traffic is more fun than sitting behind a computer, eh?"

Cameron flicked a half grin over, then turned his attention back to the car in front. "You'd be surprised how full on the intel game can be, even from a desk. And it's not all staring at a screen, although there is *so* much data crunching involved. But yeah, getting out into the field properly again is pretty good fun. I've pulled a few days leave though, so I won't be able to stay out long."

Crowley grimaced, nodded ahead. "Let's hope this is the

end of the line and it all finishes here, today."

"Here's hoping. But I also hope there's not too much action. Only two of us, so we'll probably be outnumbered. I'd really prefer not to be killed."

Crowley laughed. "Me too. But it's the *nearly* being killed thing that's so thrilling, right?"

Cameron flicked him another look, a little less amused this time.

Crowley waved one hand dismissively. "Seriously, though, I like our chances here."

"Really? Based on what?"

"No one's managed to do us in yet, have they?"

Cameron blew air out through tight lips. "Dude, everyone's lucky until their luck runs out. That's how it works." He nodded ahead again. "Check it out."

Crowley looked out to see a large white sign beside the road.

DANGER
HOLY ISLAND CAUSEWAY

It warned them to pay attention to the tide tables and safe crossing signs ahead. They passed another sign, bright red this time, with a picture of a large car half drowned by the incoming tide.

WARNING
THIS COULD BE YOU
PLEASE CONSULT TIDE TABLES

"Don't muck around with their signage, do they!" Crowley said with a laugh.

Cameron nodded. "Yeah, but look how low the causeway sits. The water would cover it very quickly when the tide comes in. Can you imagine how many idiot tourists mess it up and get stranded every year? I read a thing that listed the costs of airlifting and sea rescues that happen regularly. Pretty crazy sums of cash."

"No accounting for fools."

"But we're good for now. I checked earlier and we've got a while before the next tide comes in."

They followed the slow-moving line of cars out onto the causeway, mudflats glistening on either side as the sun found occasional breaks in the pall above. Halfway down the mile-long causeway, a light drizzle spattered the windshield, despite the glimpses of sunshine and slices of blue sky.

Crowley looked to the north and saw a heavier bank of darker cloud that way. "Typical English weather," he muttered.

"Four seasons in one day?" Cameron asked.

"Four seasons in one place! That looks like some big rain coming in."

"Yeah, depends on the wind though. It is forecast to get heavier."

Crowley quirked an eyebrow. "You checked that too?"

Cameron laughed. "Of course! Information is my business."

"Even the weather?"

"Even the weather."

The road began to wind along the edge of the island peninsula, grasslands off to their left. As they made their way into the small area of houses, Crowley said, "Not many people living here."

"Only a couple of hundred or so, but it's packed with tourists most of the time. Today is no exception, despite the rain."

People walked everywhere, many strolling obliviously into the road causing cars to beep and brake. The tourists ignored the persistent drizzle, happily rambling around in brightly-colored raincoats or under wide umbrellas.

As they drove slowly into the small town, Cameron said, "It'll be hard to spot Rose or Landvik in these crowds. We could walk right past each other and not notice."

"Yeah, but I don't think they'll be taking in the sights. I've been looking through all the relevant information we've found, trying to figure out just what it is this Landvik is after. And honestly, I still don't really have a clue. But as we've been led all the way to Lindisfarne, I can't see them heading for any other place than the priory or the castle. I reckon we start with the priory. It stands on the spot of a seventh century Anglo Saxon monastery, but was attacked by Vikings in 793. Given all Landvik's return of the Viking gods stuff, I figure we at least start there." He pointed up the road ahead. "That way."

CHAPTER 43

Halvdan Landvik stared for a moment through the rain-spattered windshield, the ruins of Lindisfarne Priory standing ahead of them like broken teeth beyond the neater edifice of St Mary's church. They were parked on a green verge, just past the last houses of gray-brown stone with slate or red tile roofs. To their right, the grassy slope fell away in a shallow decline to the water. To their left, the church, cemetery, and priory ruins.

"What is it about this place?" Landvik asked Rose without turning around. He knew she would answer. No doubt with some smart-mouthed quip.

"You tell me," she said. "You're the one who dug through my brain."

Landvik pursed his lips. No more or less than expected. He would almost certainly have to do the ritual again, but he had nearly lost her the last time. Her experience of Aella's pain had been something quite astounding to behold, though she seemed to not have a strong memory of those events now. Probably for the best if she was to retain her sanity. Perhaps if he gathered some more information, a few more points of relevance with which to conduct the interrogation, then maybe next time it would reveal more. There was nothing scientific about this occult methodology and that bothered him, but he had to play the hand he had been dealt. At least he had the girl now. If the next ritual killed her, well, so be it. He had no other choices at this stage.

He twisted in the seat to address the large man wedged in to Rose's right. "Grigor, you stay here with her. She doesn't leave the vehicle. We won't be long."

"Yes, sir."

"You two with me." Landvik opened the door and climbed out, knowing his men would follow. The crowd of tourists had thinned somewhat, now they had the chance to spread out across the island, but there were still knots of people in every direction. He headed up the road, tailed by the sound of gravel crunching beneath the shoes of his men as they followed.

A low stone wall, rough-topped with patches of moss, surrounded the ruins and the larger church that stood before them. They entered through a narrow wooden gate. Just to their right Saint Mary's Parish Church filled the view, large sandstone blocks with three tall arched stained-glass windows, the tallest in the center framed by thick stone columns. Atop those columns was a bell tower, the silhouette of the bell itself stark against the pale gray skies. But, Landvik noticed, the pale gray was growing slightly darker. The soft drizzle that gusted through the air had begun to take on a heavier feel, as though it might at any minute turn into a downpour. No matter, he thought. That would match his mood. A cemetery surrounded the church and he gestured to the nearest of his men. "Search the graveyard."

The man frowned. "What am I looking for?"

Landvik shrugged. "Anything, I don't know. Runes, carvings of hammers, anything that might hint at something other than the obvious Christian history here. Just look."

"Yes, sir." The man moved away and Landvik led the other along a bitumen path between graves, heading for the old priory behind the church. At the end of the church they turned right and walked another path until they came to the front of the ruins. At their backs rose the end of St. Mary's church, another tall, narrow stained glass window buried in the pale, irregular stonework. Before them was the entrance to the old priory, an arched doorway with rounded columns to either side. One square tower rose almost complete on their right side, but on the other it had all gone, leaving a ragged edge of reddish-gray stone. Beyond, high above the ground, curved the famous rainbow arch, a smooth, shallow arc of stones connecting two narrow, crumbling towers. The underside of the arch was carved with roundels, giving it the look of a strange row of too many teeth, upside down.

Landvik entered and began to stalk around, paying close attention to the walls and stones, trying to see something that might give some credence to their coming here. Some reason beyond the unreliable memories he had extracted from Rose Black. The broken down walls showed many places where double rows of stone left spaces in between, the kind of spot where any number of treasures might have once been concealed. Large archwork with thick brickwork columns, carved with worn chevrons for decoration, cast strange shadows in the wan, watery day. Landvik glanced up and winced as the rain began to increase as he thought it might. Several tourists with them in the space hurried away, presumably seeking the shelter of their cars or buildings in town. He would be glad to be left alone.

Landvik grew more and more impatient with every minute of the search. As he inspected the crumbled walls, it became apparent that anything concealed here was likely found and removed long ago. There were precious few places that something might still be hidden, save for within the remaining stonework. He could hardly start pulling bricks free and kicking the ruins to pieces, though as his impatience grew, the desire to do just that increased exponentially. Perhaps the hammer, if it were here, had long since been recovered and carried away. He paused, looked out beyond the ruins. Was he even in the right place? It seemed most likely, the seat of the island's Christianity, first abandoned after a Viking raid in 793. The timing was right. But even if it were, did the hammer itself maybe lie elsewhere? Rose Black had identified Lindisfarne, she had muttered something about the Christian stronghold, so that had to mean this priory. But there were an awful lot of years between her memories and the present day. Things could be moved around all over the place, yet still remain on the Holy Island. Not to mention the possibility that Aella's knowledge of the place, or his recollections, could have been wrong. The impotence of the searching began to infuriate him. Fear of failure rising, Landvik quickened his pace. If they exhausted every possibility, they would perhaps have to expand their search further. And he had to at least find something with which to target the next ritual with Rose Black. Something to trigger a usable memory.

CHAPTER 44

Rose watched Landvik and his men stalk off into the church grounds as the rain made rivulets on the car windows, growing heavier. People began to hurry out of the site, heading for their cars, grinning and making rueful faces at each other. Classic British stoicism in the face of awful weather. The only people looking truly annoyed about it were probably foreigners.

She looked down at her hands in her lap, wrists still bound tight with a black plastic zip tie. Despite her best efforts, she hadn't managed to loosen it at all. All she had done was make a sore, red band around the outside edge of both wrists. Right now, she knew, was her best chance of escape. The effects of the ritual and whatever drugs she had been given were at their lowest ebb thus far. She wasn't exactly clear-headed, but was as close to it as she had been in a long time. And only one goon sat with her in the car instead of four. Though he was a big goon. Grigor, Landvik had called him. The name suited him somehow.

She saw the slight bulge just under his left armpit, no doubt a shoulder-holstered pistol. She considered the possibility of disarming him, but thought perhaps that was pretty unlikely. And if she did escape, then what? It wasn't like the place was crawling with police, though there must be some around the island, if she could only find them. She doubted any tourist would lift a finger to help her. More likely they would video her desperate attempt to escape and it would be on YouTube before the end of the day. But she had to try something.

She watched Grigor's craggy square head for a moment as he stared mutely out at the increasing rain. After a moment she said, "Hey, Grigor." He didn't look around, didn't even acknowledge he'd heard her. "Grigor? I need to pee."

He huffed a grunt that might have been the beginning of a laugh. Without taking his eyes off the view outside he said, "Nice try."

"Dude, I'm serious."

"Go ahead. I have a baby at home, so it's not like I'm not accustomed to the smell."

Rose cursed him quietly, but loud enough for him to hear. He chuckled softly. She considered calling his bluff just for spite, but knew it would only cause her more discomfort. She didn't doubt he would let her sit in her own piss and enjoy it.

She sighed deeply, angry and frustrated. There must be something she could do, some way to take a chance that had some possibility of success. Once the thug on her left side had got out of the car she had scooted over from the center of the back seat, buying herself some more comfort and leg room. It was a relief not to be pressed up against the solid bulk of Grigor any more. It also put her closer to the door. She surreptitiously cast a glance toward it, pictured in her mind how it would go to grab for the handle with her hands tied as they were. She imagined the process, a quick dive for the door release, pull it and drive her shoulder into the door and roll right out of the vehicle. She might hurt herself, but she was trained to break fall. She could hit the ground on her shoulder, sling her legs over to gain momentum to roll onto her upper back and then gain her knees, then quickly her feet. She pictured it again in her mind, imagined the roll and then a sprint out into the people heading back in the direction of town, holding her bound hands above her head as proof as she screamed about being abducted. So what if it ended up on YouTube, surely among all the people milling about in the rain, someone would help her. And Grigor wouldn't pull his weapon and start firing in such a place. Would he? They needed her alive after all. Her heartrate increased as she quietly began to psych herself up for the bolt. She flicked her eyes back toward Grigor and her stomach fell.

He was looking right at her, grinning widely. "You would never make it."

Fury bubbled up, made Rose grit her teeth. She was tempted to try for the escape anyway. Maybe she could use her tied hands as a double fist and smash his stupid nose first, then roll from the door. The big idiot wouldn't be expecting that.

Then another look passed over Grigor's face, one she'd seen a million times before from a million creepy guys. Her already boosted pulse ratcheted up again.

"Don't even think about that!" she said.

Grigor laughed, a low, guttural noise. "I can do whatever I want, you know."

"Landvik needs me. You don't want to piss off your boss."

"Landvik needs your memories. Your body is a lot more

disposable." He slid one hand up her thigh.

All Rose's frustrations bubbled over and she lifted both her hands, twisting them painfully against the zip tie to drive her right elbow as hard as she could into his ribs.

Grigor winced and grunted, folding slightly against the impact, and that gave Rose another surge of adrenaline, a more positive one this time, but Grigor straightened and grinned. "I like a little fight in my women."

He shot one hand out, grabbed the hair at the back of Rose's neck, and pulled her toward him. He planted a hard kiss, crushing her lips against her teeth. His breath was rank with tobacco and some kind of alcohol. Rose opened her mouth and bit hard against his lips, tasting a surge of salty, hot blood. Grigor roared, jerking back. He put one palm in the center of her chest to drive her back and backhanded her with the other. Her face whipped to one side, her cheek stinging instantly with the sharp pain of it, thankfully the opposite side to where Landvik had cut her.

He pressed the back of his hand to his mouth, the words, "You bitch!" muffled against it.

Rose knew she was in trouble, the man animalistic now with anger. Her back pressed against the door, she couldn't twist around to open it, to dive free, so she took the fight to him. She shot forward, and threw her weight to one side, slamming an elbow across the bridge of his nose. He tried to get his arm in the way and was only partly successful. Rose was rewarded with a dull crunch and Grigor yelped, the sound as surprised as it was angry.

"You like a little fight, huh?" Rose yelled at him, clutched her fists together and crashed them into his head, once, twice, three times. Grigor snarled, covering up with one arm. As he clawed out with the other, she batted it aside and made a move for the car door. She kicked out backwards as she grabbed the door handle and pulled, planning to drive against him with her legs to exit the vehicle even if she landed on her face. She pulled the door handle, adrenaline and exhilaration pulsing through her, expecting cold wet air. Nothing happened. She yanked the handle again. Nothing.

Grigor laughed. "You think we're stupid? Child locks, you idiot." He grabbed her roughly above the knees and flipped her over. The back of her head hit the door as she landed and bounced against the car seat. "You should have gone for the driver's door." Grigor's grin was wide again, leering, all the more terrifying for the blood over his teeth and the rapidly swelling lower lip.

Rose was pleased that she had hurt him, but it was small comfort as he dragged her down and straddled her. Thoughts of violent rape rippled through her and she tried to drive a knee into his groin, but he was ready for that and turned one thigh to block her. Her eyes went wide as Grigor's bloodied, angry face rose over her and he closed both meaty hands around her throat.

CHAPTER 45

Lindisfarne Priory, Holy Island, Berwick-upon-Tweed

Landvik turned on the spot, disconsolate. Rain plastered his hair flat to his head, ran in cold rivulets down the back of his neck. He hadn't known what he might find, but had been sure he would find *something*. After all, others here would never have expected to discover Mjolnir. They wouldn't be looking for clues to its location. But he knew greater truths, and he was a man of great faith. All he needed was a little more indication, some tiny sign. But all he found was wet stone and disappointment. Perhaps he needed to change the way he looked, maybe reconsider what he expected to see. Perhaps there were clues elsewhere on the island.

A short, rotund woman in a green rain coat with *Lindisfarne* stenciled across the back stood in the broken down front doorway to the priory. Her back to him, she hunched against the rain and seemed to be watching out past St Mary's Parish Church. Landvik waved his man over.

"Anything?"

Brushing rain from his eyes, the man shook his head. "Nothing."

Landvik approached the woman in the green jacket. "Excuse me, do you work here?"

The woman laughed, rolling her eyes dramatically. "For my sins! There's a guided tour due to start in five minutes and in this weather I honestly don't expect anyone to show up for it. But you never know, and I have to be here just in case."

"A guided tour?"

"Yes. I lead the group around the priory and surrounds, talk about the history of the island, its place in the development of religion and so on."

"And the Vikings?"

The woman's face brightened. "Oh yes, of course the Vikings. You know…"

Landvik cut her off. "You know anything about any Viking-era artifacts that have been recovered from here?"

"Well, there have been all kinds of archeological digs and

programs. Any number of things from across hundreds of years have been unearthed."

"Yes, yes, but Viking artifacts?"

The guide seemed a little put out by Landvik's gruff questioning. He realized he was being rude, but was too wet and too annoyed to care. "Well," she said, "if you go back down toward the town and turn right on Marygate, you'll find *The Lindisfarne Heritage Centre*. There's an exhibit inside dedicated solely to the Viking influence here and there's a number of artifacts on display there."

Landvik brightened, a thread of hope igniting again. "Right, okay." He began to turn away but caught the flash of a frown pass over the woman's face. "Thank you," he added.

She smiled uncomfortably and nodded.

Landvik whistled once, sharply, caught the attention of his other man still roaming about between the headstones in the small cemetery. "Back to the car," Landvik called out.

Rose fought desperately against the blackness closing in around the edges of her vision. The man's hands clenched her throat like a vice, his eyes wild in his furious face. He had clearly completely lost control, one too many strikes from Rose hurting him enough that he no longer cared about anything except hurting her back. Permanently.

She tried to gasp for breath, tried to tell him that Landvik needed her memories and for that she had to be alive. She wanted to plead with him for her life as the terror of actually dying became an all too real possibility. After everything she had been through since this whole ridiculous drama had begun, it was surely impossible that she was about to die now at the hands of an ignorant, musclebound idiot.

Darkness closed in further, her vision narrowing to a pinpoint showing only Grigor's grimacing, blood-stained face, and Rose's consciousness, her very life, ebbed away.

The iron pressure of Grigor's grip suddenly vanished. Still blinded by lack of air and panic, Rose could only gasp, her chest tight, her throat on fire. She heard a cry of surprise, a fleshy thwack, as she gasped again. Through blurred and swimming vision she watched Grigor dragged backwards through the now open car door on his side. She caught a glimpse of Crowley's face, hair slicked to his scalp by rain, mouth twisted in a snarl of rage, but refused to believe it was real. Surely she was hallucinating from lack of oxygen to the brain. Was this some strange fantasy of rescue, her brain softening the agony of her last moments before death? But she felt the cold wind coming into the car, heard the rain more loudly, spattering against the bitumen outside.

The other back door behind her head popped open, more cold, wet air gusting in. She dragged more life-saving breaths into her straining lungs. A strange man with deep olive skin and black hair as wet as Crowley's called her by name. She twisted in the seat to see him more clearly, trying to order her thoughts. Unsure who this stranger was, she scrambled forward anyway, desperate only to be out of the car, with a chance to get away from all of this.

"I'm with Crowley," the man said. "My name is Cameron. Come on!"

Too woozy to argue, she stumbled into his waiting arms. He held her up and produced a small pocket knife that he flicked open with the hand holding it. A wash of panic slipped through her, and then he dragged the blade up through the plastic of the zip tie around her wrists. It fell away and her arms swung free. Nothing had ever felt so good. She vigorously rubbed at each wrist with the other hand, moving her elbows and shoulders as she did so.

Over the roof of the car she could see Crowley tussling with Grigor. It really was him! Where had he come from? The thug was bigger than Crowley, but not gaining much ground against Crowley's trained skills. A number of tourists milled around, faces stunned in expressions of shock. At least two were pulling phones from their pockets, pointing them at the action.

Crowley and Grigor ducked and moved, Grigor throwing out a heavy looping punch that Crowley caught on one forearm as he ducked in and delivered a rapid double uppercut to Grigor's liver. The big man grunted in deep pain, folding over Crowley's fist, then a voice cut through the wind and hiss of rain.

Landvik came running from the gate of St Mary's, water slashing up from the recently filled puddles in the gravel path. His other two heavies were right behind. One of them pulled an automatic from his jacket, raised it over Landvik's shoulder and fired. The low popping of its report hinted at a silencer, but still the gawking crowd began screaming and running randomly left and right, all generally heading back down the road away from the ruins.

The first two shots hit the car, shattering windows.

"No wonder," Rose thought distantly, the idiot firing a handgun at range while running. But he was getting rapidly closer.

Cameron dragged against her arm and turned her toward a large white Land Rover Discovery parked behind them, with both front doors open and the engine running. It must be the car Crowley and Cameron had arrived in.

Crowley ducked and caught Grigor across the jaw with a fast jab. As Grigor stumbled, Crowley slipped behind him and lopped one arm around the man's neck. He dragged Grigor backwards as a human shield as he came around Landvik's car, heading for the Discovery.

Rose dove into the big white car and scrambled into the back seat as Cameron jumped into the driver's seat. Another bullet kicked up dirt at Crowley's feet, then she heard two wet thuds, strangely loud, and Grigor cried out in pain and fell limp. Crowley dropped the dead weight of Grigor's corpse and leapt into the passenger seat as Cameron gunned the engine and the Discovery skidded in a wide arc and began to power away down the narrow road. Cameron ducked as his side window shattered and showered his lap with glass.

"Are you hit?" Crowley yelled.

"No." Cameron's voice was tight, his focus entirely on driving.

Tourists leapt aside, many screaming and shouting, as another couple of bullets pinged against the car's bodywork. The rear window suddenly burst into a crazy field of glass cubes, made Rose cry out in surprise, but it didn't fall, then they were gaining speed back between the houses.

"That guy would make a great Stormtrooper, right?" Rose quipped, her adrenaline a furious rushing in her ears.

Crowley laughed, his face flushed from his exertions as he looked back from the front seat. "Sounds like you're okay then?"

"I've been better," Rose admitted. "But I have never been happier to see someone in my entire life!"

CHAPTER 46

Lindisfarne, Holy Island

Cameron drove expertly through narrow streets lined with stone walls, small shops and buildings built right up to the edges. Tourists milled about, some cars moving slowly, causing Cameron to brake and downshift to roar past at the first chance. People angrily shook fists and yelled abuse as they went. Crowley had watched Landvik's car skid around hard and come powering after them, but lost sight of it quickly. He knew they were not at all far behind.

A small red car with its hazard lights blinking and the hood up appeared as they rounded a shallow bend. Traffic in the other direction blocked the way. Cameron stood on the brakes, the tires squealing, making several people jump and hurl fresh abuse.

"They're right behind us!" Crowley said tightly.

Cameron nodded. "I know." He revved up and forced the Discovery into an unbelievably tight turn given the size of the vehicle and headed into a right turn.

"That was the only road back to the causeway," Rose said. "There's no other way off the island."

"Again," Cameron said with a tight smile, "I know. Going to have to try to go around."

He continued to wind too fast through the tiny village, steering subtly left and right, trying not to kill pedestrians. Crowley trusted the man's driving skills, but not so much the likelihood that a member of the public wouldn't do something stupid. People tended to react in bizarre ways when they were scared. He was tense, sitting forward, hands on the dash. He leaned back repeatedly, watching for Landvik in the wing mirror, but couldn't see the man's large black Lexus.

Cameron made a hard left, presumably attempting to double-back toward the causeway, but braked hard. Landvik's Lexus was parked a hundred meters ahead, facing them. The passenger door popped open and one of Landvik's heavies rose up, leveling a gun at them as he did so.

Cameron spat an eloquent curse and slammed the Discovery into reverse. He hammered backwards, grabbed the handbrake and made a skillful bootlegger turn, especially impressive in such a narrow space. As the Discovery slewed around, the shattered back window exploded inwards in a ringing shower of glass as a bullet whined into the car and tore up the ceiling fabric above Crowley's head. Crowley ducked reflexively and Cameron cursed once more. A knot of wide-eyed tourists and stationary cars blocked the way to their right, which led back to the causeway in the direction they had first tried to go. Crowley saw Landvik's car powering up behind them as Cameron turned a sharp left, heading away from the village.

As they went, some of the cars began to move again and there were screeching tires on the wet road and shouts of abuse as Landvik's car was momentarily blocked. As the people shrank with distance, Crowley saw Landvik's man waving his gun around, tourists fleeing, and the cars once again trying to back up, but getting in each other's way in the small available space.

"Why is he so desperate for you?" Cameron asked, eyes focused on the road ahead. "Crowley said he didn't want you, just information."

Crowley turned again in his seat to see Rose. "That's right. Did you give him anything?"

"Apparently I did," Rose said. "Honestly, I can't remember much of the ritual. It's all a weird blur. But I gave him enough info to bring him here. He's keeping me around in case he needs to delve deeper into my memories."

"For what?" Crowley asked. "Have you found out yet what the point of all this is?"

Rose let out a small, humorless laugh. "He thinks I can help him find Mjolnir. You know, Thor's Hammer?"

Silence fell in the car but for the rush of tires on the rain-soaked tarmac.

Cameron eventually let out a chuckle and Crowley said, "Seriously? Thor's Hammer? That's some serious comic book bollocks, isn't it?"

Rose shrugged. "Is it?"

"It has to be. It's a ridiculous idea!"

"Well, normally I would agree," Rose said. "But then again, a few days ago I thought the idea of extracting past life memories was ridiculous."

Crowley stared at her for a moment, having to accept there was some truth to what she said. "That really happened?" he asked.

She nodded. "Something happened. I experienced things I simply have never known about before. I didn't just remember them, I re-lived them. It was uncanny. Terrifying." She winced and Crowley realized there was a memory of considerable pain in there somewhere too.

The road they followed cut across a wide open space, grassy fields to their left, water to the right. They were fast approaching a lonely crag, the silhouette of a castle standing atop it, striking against the slate sky.

"This road is a dead end," Rose said.

Crowley's eyebrows rose. "Seriously? No junctions?"

Rose shook her head. "I've been to the island a few times, I know it quite well. This road leads there, to Lindisfarne Castle, and nowhere else." She narrowed her eyes. "But you know what? I'm feeling strangely drawn to it. The feeling I had during the ritual, a kind of visceral longing… I can't explain it, but I'm feeling it again now."

"Well," Crowley said. "Looks like we have no choice but to make a stand there."

CHAPTER 47

Lindisfarne, Holy Island

Landvik leaned from the passenger window and yelled at the halfwit in his employ. "Hurry up, Levi! This place will be crawling with police soon."

Levi nodded and went back to yelling at drivers. One woman had leapt from her car in a panic and run away down the road, leaving Levi to move her car himself. Most other pedestrians had long since followed the frightened woman and only a couple of cars remained, blocking the way to follow Rose Black and her interfering friends.

Landvik returned his attention to the tiny dot that was their Land Rover Discovery, heading out to the castle atop its lonely crag. "The hammer must be hidden up there, eh, Jarn?"

Jarn's grip on the steering wheel didn't falter, but his shoulders shrugged. "You think so, sir?"

"They seem to be heading that way."

Jarn shrugged again. "The castle was built long after the Viking invasion."

Landvik grinned, wishing he'd thought of this simple fact before now, but no matter. He was reminded of it now. "Yes, but the castle was partly built from the ruins of the old priory. Besides, there must have been something up there before. A wooden fort, a lookout, some structure would surely stand on that single raised piece of rock in this otherwise flat and dull island. Look at that place, how it stands above everything else, proud over land and sea alike. What man wouldn't build something atop a place like that, hmm? You don't think it feels right? A gateway to Valhalla."

"I suppose that's true," Jarn admitted reluctantly.

Landvik felt a warmth inside, despite his cold, soaked clothes. A sensation of completion had begun to settle over him. "I'll wager Rose remembered something about the castle, and was doing her best to keep it from us until her boyfriend could arrive. Or perhaps it's only just come back to her now. Either way, it's worked out for them this far, but we will soon catch up again."

"Or perhaps that's simply the only way they *could* go, given that we cut them off," Jarn said.

Landvik laughed. *Always such a pragmatist, young Jarn.* "Well, maybe so. Either way, she said Lindisfarne, and she's led us this far. Now she leads us there. So it's there that we go."

The road ahead was clear and Levi slumped back into the rear seat. "Let's go," he said uselessly as Jarn gunned the engine and the powerful car leapt forward.

"We left Grigor's body lying in the rain back there," Landvik said. "And there are many people in a panic, all making calls. This island will be alive with police soon, so we have little time. Whatever happens, I think it will end one way or another up there." He nodded toward the crag and castle, the car with Rose Black and her friends lost from sight for the time being. "Be ready for anything."

CHAPTER 48

Lindisfarne Castle

Cameron raced through an open wooden five-bar gate, the tires buzzing over a short section of cobbled road. To their left was a small grassy area with a few cars parked on it. A handful of people jumped and looked around at Cameron's speedy entrance, many frowns forming. But Rose knew they wouldn't say anything. That British polite disapproval was as far as they would go. It seemed strange that these people had no idea of the mayhem and carnage just a kilometer or two behind them.

Cameron parked and they jumped from the car and jogged up the path leading to the castle. From this angle, the rocky outcrop with the castle atop looked like a giant ship had plowed into the island, forcing up a bow wave of grass and stone before it. The path immediately forked, the left side staying low and skirting the craggy rise. The other path went shallowly up to the right side of the castle. Crowley and Rose ran side by side up the right hand path, Cameron on their heels.

To their right lay a narrow grassy verge, then a low three-bar wooden fence. Over the fence, rocky beach extended a little way before the water lapped against the stones. The sea looked cold and uninviting, but the darkness of the clouds had lifted a little, the rain easing back to a gusty, intermittent spray. After the confines of cars and planes, Rose exalted in the cold wash of it, the salt scent of the ocean, and the aroma of fresh grass. The wind had a biting edge of cold to it that reminded her she was alive, her heart racing. She had come so close to death, Grigor's hands around her throat, and now she was running, breathing deeply of the wide open world. She felt exhilarated.

The dirt path turned to cobblestones, a new wooden fence to their right to prevent people slipping down the steepening grass to the rocky beach. The craggy grass in front of the castle gave way to steeper, broken rock on their right, the mossy, gray stone walls of the castle itself looming high above them.

They hurried past a small group of tourists ambling ahead of them, and then the path turned sharply back on itself. Beyond, the land was flat and grassy, and then seemed to drop off a large step to more grass and the ocean beyond.

"Down there are the island's famous lime kilns," Rose said, remembering previous trips. "Right on the water's edge. We're above them up here." She barked a short laugh as another recollection came to her. "The lime kilns at Castle Point on Holy Island are among the largest, most complex and best preserved lime kilns in Northumberland," she quoted. "Honestly, it's ridiculous the kind of information my museum brain retains!"

"Impressive," Crowley said. "But I think we need to go the other way."

To one side were four wooden sheds. One large and regular shaped, the other three designed like half boat hulls flipped upside down. The smoothly cobbled way that doubled back on itself became a series of irregular long steps, climbing steeply up against the castle wall. The largest, normal-shaped shed was the reception and ticket office. Cameron ran ahead of Crowley and Rose, pulled money from his pocket.

He returned with three tickets and they hurried up. The castle had but a single external entrance, a door in the south side of the building. As they reached the door, something flashed through Rose's mind, momentarily blinding her. She heard screams and howls, saw flames flickering against a night sky, then the sound of rapid footsteps on stone. Voices shouted. Her vision swam into a dark corridor, vaguely lit with the flickering orange light of flaming torches. Nausea rose and her knees buckled.

She felt hands grab under her arms, haul her back upright.

"Rose!" Crowley's voice was sharp, concerned.

"Landvik and his idiots have just pulled up next to our car," Cameron said.

Rose's vision swam back. She saw Cameron looking out over the small area with cars down below, Crowley's face much closer to her, his expression one of stress and worry.

"I'm all right," she said. "Sorry. Something happened. I saw... something."

"You can carry on?" Crowley asked, the unspoken problem clear in his tone if she said she couldn't.

"Yes, I can. Let's go."

A large wooden door, with vertical bands of black iron, stood open before them. Stone steps under an arched ceiling led up a few meters to the lower battery of the castle. They ran up onto a wide open, flag-stoned area, crenellated walls with old gun emplacements making a curve of one end. Behind them another door led to the entrance hall.

"Come on!" Crowley ran for it, Rose and Cameron on his heels.

"Won't we be trapped in here?" Rose asked, though she knew, somehow, that they needed to be here.

"We might be," Crowley admitted. "But what choice do we have?"

"Did Landvik and his goons see us?"

They pushed past another small group of tourists, muttering apologies as they went.

"Who knows? Regardless, they won't have much trouble figuring out where we've gone. The question is, what can we do while we're here? And how can we make a stand against them?"

CHAPTER 49

Lindisfarne Castle

Thick stone columns divided the entrance hall into three distinct areas, white-painted ceiling arching above. Over the large fireplace almost filling one end of the room was an ornate wind indicator. It depicted Lindisfarne Island with a compass over the top, marked into sections with ships sailing all around. One hand like a clock's pointed currently just past North West.

Off to one side of the entrance hall lay a large kitchen, and beyond it the scullery. From the doorway, Rose saw a mechanism for lowering the portcullis that she knew from previous visits could still be used to bar the entrance below. It was an appealing idea to keep Landvik and his men at bay, but the tour guides nearby would certainly not allow it.

She blinked, dizzy at flashes of strange visions, bubbling up through her mind like air bubbles from a SCUBA diver's regulator. Strobe-like flickers of memory flashed before her eyes. Crowley and Cameron hurried through the castle, looking for places to hide, to set an ambush, ignoring the bemused looks from the handful of other tourists enjoying the sights. They talked about what they might improvise as weapons, something better than the simple knives they both carried. For Rose, every room, every passageway, sparked a new memory. A sudden string of images made her stagger, flashes of descending beneath the castle, interspersed with more recent memories of the ritual Landvik performed on her.

"I've been here before," she whispered, but the others didn't hear her.

The castle accommodation formed an L-shape and they hurried down the long arm of the L, through a passage that seemed almost carved from the rock of the crag itself. They ran to one side, into a vaulted dining room, dominated by a large fireplace at one end and a wall painted bright blue at the other. A large oval table filled most of the space. Like all the rooms so far except the entrance hall, this one was small, almost cramped. This was a castle of urban home dimensions, like a castle in miniature. But nowhere seemed to afford a good place from which to mount their assault against men with guns and murder in mind. Crowley and Cameron grew increasingly frantic.

Rose staggered again, more flickering memories obscuring her vision. She called out, falling against one wall lest she collapse to the floor. Crowley and Cameron rushed back, crouched either side of her as she slid down the stone to sit on the cool ground.

"Are you okay?" Crowley asked.

"I've been here before," Rose said again.

"What?"

She grimaced, frustrated at Crowley's bone-headed focus and her own inability to order her thoughts. "I have been here before," she said for a third time, injecting more certainty into her tone.

"That's good," Crowley said. "Any idea where we might hide?"

She shook her head, and then stopped when it only made her dizzier. "That's not what I mean. I'm talking about previous lives. Yes, I've been here as a tourist, and as a professional researcher, but I'm having different memories now, ancient ones."

Crowley sat back on his heels, lips pursed. "Rose, I'm not sure we have time for this."

She shrugged. "I think it's important. I'm generally as skeptical as you are, but I have no other explanation for this. Landvik's ritual brought the memories back, and like I said before, they were more than memories. They were lived experiences. And it's happening again. But different. I see Ragnar Lodbrok, but I have Aella's life memories, not Ragnar's. Of course, I know his intent, from the things he told me during the blood eagle." She winced, the recollection of pain flooding her again, and arched her back with a soft cry.

Crowley put a concerned hand on her shoulder.

"I'm okay. I remember the things Ragnar told Aella, I mean. What he wanted. And what I subsequently told Landvik. At least, some of it."

"So what exactly do you know?" Crowley asked. "Can it help us now?"

Rose breathed deeply, tried to calm her mind.

A castle guide came over, face creased in worry. "Everything okay here? Do you need an ambulance?"

Cameron stood quickly, guided the concerned young man

away. "No, no, it's fine. She just came over a little dizzy. Thank you, though."

Rose closed her eyes, tried to grab at thoughts that flitted through her mind like moths around a bright light. "My memories are Aella's," she said quietly. "And I'm certain, at least I think I'm certain, that this is where he sealed up the hammer."

"It's real?" Crowley asked. "And how can you know that?"

"It's somewhere down below. Ragnar's sons killed me…Aella, but that was because Aella had been the one to kill Ragnar. But before Ragnar died, Aella got the location of Mjolnir from him. And because it was, in Aella's mind, an evil and dangerous pagan thing, though he was tempted by its power, he tried to ensure that it would never be found. I know, I *remember*, that the hiding place was here!"

Crowley looked nervously at Cameron, who stood near the door keeping an eye out. Cameron raised his hands, Crowley shrugged, so Cameron came back to them. "We need to get ourselves organized," he said.

Crowley nodded. "Rose, what can we do?"

She squeezed her eyes closed in concentration. "Ragnar's apostasy from the Norse religion cost him everything, that's what Landvik told me. Aella was sure the hammer itself would lead *him* to ruin, because he was a pious Christian man. He feared what it could do. I have his memories of learning that this is where Ragnar hid it, and of Aella coming here to seal it up, but I can't see clearly. I can't see where, apart from it being somewhere low, somewhere dark."

"How is that possible?" Crowley asked.

Rose flashed him an angry look. "How is any of this possible?"

"It's all feasible," Cameron said, looking slowly around himself. "The crag this castle stands on would have reminded someone like Ragnar of the special rocks and hills in Scandinavia where the dead were believed to dwell. He might have even thought of it as an entrance to Valhalla. It's a good place to hide something of such importance."

Rose frowned. "Isn't Valhalla supposedly in the sky? Like Viking heaven or something?"

Cameron shook his head. "Valhalla, or 'hall of the fallen' derives from *valhallr*." He spelled it out. "That means 'the rock of the fallen'. I think Ragnar would have found in this place a connection to his gods."

"Okay," Rose said. "So it makes sense that Ragnar would hide it here, and it's just as good a place for Aella to have sealed up Mjolnir forever."

"If that's the case," Crowley said. "If the hammer is actually a real thing, and it's really here, we can save our lives if we find it first."

Chapter 50

Landvik, Jarn and Levi hurried along the cobbled path and went to enter the gate leading up to the castle entrance. A young man ran from the wooden shed they had passed.

"Excuse me! You need a ticket."

Landvik paused, sucked a breath in through his nose, and turned to the young man.

Jarn leaned close. "Best to keep as calm as possible, sir. The trouble back there will catch up soon enough."

Landvik allowed himself one curt nod. The young pragmatist was an asset in this instance. "You're right. Thank you." He turned a smile to the ticket officer. "My apologies. How much?"

A few moments later they were on their way up the long, uneven cobbled steps.

"I feel like I've just been robbed," Landvik said.

Jarn laughed. "That's these kinds of attractions for you. They gouge the populace to keep them open."

A few small groups of tourists were braving the inclement weather and Landvik moved impatiently around them. The rain had eased again, back to a gusting drizzle more like a thick mist than anything that could really be called a downpour. But he was already soaked, his skin wet and icy. A soft shiver kept rippling through him and all he wanted was to be somewhere warm and dry. All this running around after Rose Black and her incessantly annoying boyfriend was beginning to shred his nerves. But a little more patience and they'd have them. This was a dead end, and it had the feeling of an impending conclusion.

They climbed the steps to the lower battery and paused to get their bearings. A tourist tapped Landvik on the shoulder.

"Excuse me, could you take a photo for us please?" He pointed to a woman and three children standing against the battlements, the gusting rain and ocean behind them like a Turner seascape.

"No, I could not!" Landvik said and turned away.

He heard the man mutter, "Well, how rude!" then he was

striding into the main entrance hall.

"You think Rose has been holding out on us?" Levi asked. "Like, she knew all along it was here?"

"No idea, but it must be here. Why would they run here otherwise?"

"Perhaps they were just running."

Landvik paused, shook his head. "No. Something has drawn all of us here. Fates are at work this day. We are meant to be in this place, at this time. I'm sure the hammer is hidden here somewhere."

"But I checked the history," Jarn said, his voice nervous. No doubt he knew he was on thin ice contradicting Landvik's conviction. "The first recorded structure here on this rock was built in the sixteenth century."

Landvik turned to him, one eyebrow raised.

Jarn paused, and then continued. "This rock, it's called Beblowe Crag. The first recorded structure here is Beblowe Fort, not built until 1548. That's nearly a thousand years after Ragnar Lodbrok's time."

"You think nothing was here before?" Landvik asked. He gestured forward. "That way. Look for Miss Black and her friends."

They moved on. "Well, history says…" Jarn began.

"History is written by the winners and by politicians. This island was raided by the Vikings in 793. They had a presence here and they would have established various places of habitation and worship. They absolutely would not have ignored a rock like this, a possible gateway to Valhalla."

Tourists blocked one room and Landvik turned the other way, stalking along a narrow passage.

"So if the hammer was hidden here, then the castle was built on top of it, you think the hammer was moved?" Jarn asked. "Taken away? Hidden in the new construction?"

Landvik shook his head. "I've been researching thoroughly. This is my life's work. I'm certain the hammer has never been discovered. It must be hidden beneath the castle, perhaps in the remnants of the old fort that stood here." He paused, thoughtful, then shook his head. "It's somewhere here."

"How can you know for certain, sir?" Jarn asked. "That the hammer has never been found, I mean. No one knows what it looks like, right?"

"If it had been found, the world would know," Landvik

said. "That's surely true, because there's none like it. Now move. We must find them quickly!"

CHAPTER 51

Lindisfarne Castle

Crowley led the way into the castle's "Ship Room" at the far end of the corridor. They were fast running out of places to search or hide. A large model of a Dutch ship hung from the ceiling above, presumably giving the room its name. The room itself was not unlike the hull of a ship turned upside down, the walls rising and curving in to meet high above in a slight point rather than a smooth arch. Deeply recessed windows let in wan light to either side, the floor a herringbone of red bricks, like most places throughout the castle.

Crowley looked about the room, thankfully empty of tourists. People seemed to be heading off, perhaps about to join a tour outside or something. It worked for them, allowing more freedom of movement, but they had little left to explore. And he was increasingly concerned about Rose's state of mind. She was plagued by these flashes of memory. They had a physical impact on her, made her dizzy and uncertain on her feet. Whatever that bawbag Landvik had done to her, it seemed to have long-lasting effects.

"This room used to be the fort's ammunition store," Cameron said, reading from a small plaque by the door.

"What if we can't get below from anywhere?" Rose said, her voice shaky. "What if this castle construction has blocked off anything that was here previously?"

Crowley frowned, shook his head. "It's possible, but I don't buy it. This place was built for defense, so wouldn't you want an avenue of escape when under siege? Otherwise, your enemies could starve you out."

"He's right," Cameron said. "Remember the only external access is the door we came through at the top of the path? No way is that the only way in and out. There must be others."

Voices sounded from a short distance away and the three of them froze. They were male voices, the words unclear but the lilt of a Scandinavian language unmistakable.

"We'll be trapped in here!" Rose whispered, eyes wide.

Cameron looked left and right. Some large brass plates

were mounted on one wall, heavy-looking. He pointed. "We could hide on either side of the door and jump them. Brain them with those. But it's three men with guns versus two with knives and brass dinnerware. Not great odds."

Crowley couldn't help but agree. This was a bad place to be cornered, not much room to move around, only a table and chairs, a few armchairs, nothing to afford real cover from flying bullets. He looked to the fireplace, thinking to arm himself with a stout iron poker or other implement. He frowned, looked closer.

One stone in the back of the hearth looked out of place, darker and coarser than the others. It made him think of volcanic stone. Heart racing, hoping for a break, just one small piece of luck, he gave the stone a shove with his fist. It shifted a little, but not much.

"They're coming closer!" Rose's whisper had an edge of panic to it.

Refusing to be beaten, certain there was something up with this brick, and losing all other patience besides, Crowley slammed his booted heel into the dark square of stone with all his might.

A muted clack echoed behind the hearth and the stone gave way. The sound reminded Crowley of a tumbler in a lock sliding into place. With a scrape of stone, the back of the fireplace slowly slid sideways, revealing a low, dark tunnel. He turned a grin back to the others and saw them both staring with mouths hanging open.

"Come on then!" he said. "No time to stand around gawping!"

The three fell to their hands and knees and crawled inside. Crowley, bringing up the rear, heard the voices as though they were almost on top of them. Shadows moved in the corridor outside the door to the ship room, voices urgent and talking over one another in frustration. Crowley spotted a small metal lever to one side of the gap. Hoping desperately it would work, he pulled it. The false back of the fireplace slid closed, plunging them into utter darkness.

"That," Crowley said with relief, "ought to buy us some time. Now, let's see what's down here. And quickly, in case they figure out what I did."

CHAPTER 52

Beneath Lindisfarne Castle

Crowley, Rose and Cameron all flicked on the flashlight apps on their phones. The small space behind the fireplace was cramped, but the passage led away from them, descending at a shallow decline. Crowley took the lead, on his knees and one hand, holding his light up with the other. They knew instinctively not to talk, not drag their shoes or make any other noise. If Landvik did discover the secret entrance, which Crowley assumed he would eventually, they didn't want him to do so just yet by giving themselves away with noise.

As he traveled further, Rose behind him and Cameron coming last, the ceiling began to rise as the slope continued down. After about twenty meters he was able to stand, albeit hunched over so as not to bang his head on the rough rock.

He eventually came out into a small, low-ceilinged cave, hewn roughly from the rock. One side, low down, was smooth like maybe that had been natural, with the rest mined out by human hands. As Rose and Cameron arrived beside him, adding their lights to his, he saw several other passages leading away. The space was like a rocky hand, the tunnel they had crawled down being the wrist, with five dark fingers leading away, spread almost evenly apart. On the far right, the tunnel was only about a meter in diameter and their lights showed that it quickly narrowed to something even a small child would have trouble navigating. The other four passages were all big enough for a grown adult, though a couple would require crawling once more.

"We should split up," Rose said. "There's no telling how much time we have. If Landvik finds the secret door, we're in trouble. At least if we find the hammer, we've got a bargaining chip."

Crowley opened his mouth to reply when Rose gasped and staggered. He ran to her side, grabbed her arm. "You okay?"

She made a noise of anger, almost a feral growl, and hauled herself upright. "I'm fine. Honestly, thank you. These memory flashes are disorienting, but I won't let them weaken me."

Crowley grinned, impressed again with her strength. "So

can your memories tell us which tunnel to take?"

She shook her head. "That's what I just tried to do, to remember where Aella had been, but it's too dizzying. We'll just have to check, I think. Quickly. Separately."

"Yes, okay then," Crowley reluctantly agreed. He pointed to his left. "I'll take to the one on this side. Rose, you want to take the other side?"

"Sure."

Cameron held out a shining bowie knife. "Take this. Don't be squeamish about using it if you have to."

"I won't. Thank you." She hurried over to the passage beside the one too small for access, then paused. She flicked a look back over her shoulder and grinned. "Good luck!"

"You too. Scream if you need us!"

She nodded once and vanished into the tunnel's dark mouth.

Crowley pointed to the remaining two passages in the center. "Take your pick."

"I'll take the left one first," Cameron said. "Whoever's out first can check the last one if necessary."

Crowley grabbed his friend's forearm, squeezed. "Good job. See you soon."

Cameron returned the pressure on Crowley's arm, then ducked away into the darkness. Crowley dropped to his hands and knees and scooted as quickly as he could along his tunnel. At intervals, it rose high enough that he could crouch and crab-walk along, but was otherwise narrow and featureless. His light quickly shone back to him from a dead end of rock.

"Nothing," he muttered, shining his light around to be certain, then spotted an iron ring set in the ceiling. Surrounding the ring was a circle of stone, maybe a little over half a meter in diameter. He frowned. An old-fashioned kind of manhole? He put his phone on the floor, light shining up so he could see, and worked at the ring, trying to work the stone loose. He pulled out his knife, ran the blade point around the circular edge, then shook and pushed and pulled at the ring again, hoping he wasn't about to bring the round slab of stone down on his head.

After some muscle and grunt, the stone shifted, turning in its seat and raining grit and dust down onto his face. Crowley blinked and coughed, but pushed upwards with all his strength. The stone tipped up and he put both hands beneath it and slid it sideways as cold, damp air rushed in.

He grabbed the edges and hauled himself up, his head rising inside a gloomy building. Watery daylight shone in through stone arches that looked out onto broad swathes of green, the cold ocean not a stone's throw away.

He remembered Rose's museum brain moment on their way up to the castle and realized he must be inside the old lime kilns. He seemed to have discovered the escape route he had postulated. He dropped back down into the passage, wondering if this was all some ridiculous wild goose chase. Could he honestly believe that such a thing as Thor's mythical hammer really existed? And that they might find it here? But what other choice did he have right now than to continue as if it were?

He retraced his steps and soon emerged back into the central cave. The others were nowhere to be seen, everything quiet and still. It felt as though the cave itself were waiting for something. Only one passage left unexplored, assuming Rose and Cameron hadn't found anything. It was the lowest and narrowest of them all and Crowley bit down on rising claustrophobia as he squeezed his bulk through the small opening and crawled forward.

CHAPTER 53

Landvik emerged into a small cavern, Jarn on one side of him, Levi on the other. Several more tunnels were ranged out before them.

"Well, well," Landvik said. "You really did find something of interest here, Jarn. You have an eagle eye."

Jarn nodded his thanks. "You told us to look for anything out of the ordinary while we tried to find Rose Black and her friends. Besides, that scraping sound tipped me off. It must have been the secret door closing behind them."

"Even so, you did better than myself or Levi. Well done. Now, we can assume that Rose Black and her friends are down here somewhere, and we can't discount what they may have found should we run into them. So I want them alive. You find anyone, you bring them back to this spot and you call out for me, understand?"

Jarn and Levi both said simultaneously, "Yes, sir."

Landvik pursed his lips. "Right, well let's each choose a passage to explore. Let's make this quick."

Crowley had crawled for what felt like a couple of hundred meters, worried he was traveling down a stony throat which might swallow him, when the ceiling above him finally began to rise higher. He stood, moving cautiously further ahead. After another twenty or thirty meters, he stopped, crestfallen. Before him was a wall of rock. A dead end. He shined his light across it and saw that between the stones there seemed to be leaking sand. He frowned. This wasn't solid rock, but stones stacked and mortared in. A long time ago, it would probably have appeared like nothing more than an actual rock face, the dead end he had first assumed it to be. But time had caused the mortar to crumble, the stones had settled a little. The whole thing had the appearance of a tired wall rather than a rock face once he paid enough attention.

Cautiously, Crowley put one hand against the higher rocks, and pushed. They shifted slightly. He pushed harder and a couple moved, slid against each other with hollow knocks. One tumbled free, falling into a space behind. With a smile, Crowley pushed harder, putting his back and shoulder into the effort. Once he had started the movement, the wall lost its integrity and tumbled to a pile at his feet. It still blocked the lower meter or so of the passage, but he could easily climb over it and get through the gap above. He moved on, the air drier and more still than it had been before. Or was he just imagining that?

After another several meters, the passage flowered out into a wider tunnel. He froze at the sight of figures moving around ahead of him.

Holding his breath, he smothered the light with his arm and stood motionless, ears straining. No sounds of movement, no shouts of challenge. As slowly as he could manage, Crowley took his knife from his pocket and then began to reveal a tiny portion of his light. Under its weak illumination, now that he was still, he realized he had seen not actual people, but life-sized carvings. He unveiled the light entirely, panned it back and forth.

Figures in all manner of friezes were carved into the rock walls of the widening passage in which he stood. He moved closer, recognizing many. He strained his brain to recall his history lessons on Norse mythology, trying to place the characters and settings. Winged Valkyrie ferried the dead to Valhalla, wolves flanked the god Odin who stood with a raven on his outstretched arm. Beautiful Freya, on a mighty steed, rode through fields of corpses. Ice giants roamed, and there was Loki, causing mayhem. And finally Thor, his hammer held high, about to crash down on the world below him. The carvings were incredibly detailed, unlike anything Crowley had seen in his life before. He moved his light slowly, made the deep shadows flicker and shift as though the scenes before him were truly alive. He had found something incredible here.

He moved along further and the passageway ended with a small opening, a lower tunnel once more. Crowley sighed, fell back onto his hands and knees, and crawled along. It was only three or four meters before the cramped way opened into a small square room hewn from the rock. As Crowley lifted one arm to see more clearly, the light of his phone glinted on something metallic.

CHAPTER 54

Beneath Lindisfarne Castle

Rose's tunnel had gone on for so long that she began to wonder if it would ever end. Admittedly, she was going cautiously and watching all around herself, so it probably wouldn't seem nearly as far on the way back. But surely it had to go somewhere.

She did her best to ignore the rapid flashes of memory that repeatedly flickered past her vision. They were not only disorienting, but hard to decipher, confused and opaque. And while their frequency seemed to be enduring, their clarity faded with every passing minute. Perhaps the effects of Landvik's ritual were finally wearing off completely.

She paused, listening. A sound, distant and roaring, worried at the rock somewhere ahead. She kept her light high, hoping her phone battery wouldn't fail her. She was terrified of being lost in the complete darkness of underground. As she moved further forward, the sound resolved itself slightly and she realized she was hearing the sea. There were no great waves around Lindisfarne unless the weather was stormy, but she definitely heard water, and the soft rush of the ocean further out.

She came around a shallow bend and her light reflected back off a solid surface and she stopped, disappointed. The end of the tunnel had clearly been sealed up, rocks piled and jammed together. There was a vague outline of the original tunnel mouth that seemed to be the beginnings of an opening into a cave. *Clever bastards,* she thought to herself, imagining the builders of this place finding a sea cave far from the foot of Beblowe Crag. She could picture them digging the tunnel from the cave system in the crag itself, working their way along until they met the sea cave, thereby having an exit like Crowley had suggested. An escape if they were under siege, or a way to smuggle people and supplies into the castle from the water, with only a small cave to defend, or the tunnel itself if the cave were taken.

She smiled, shook her head. Interesting history, but useless to her now. There was nowhere here to hide a mystical hammer. She turned off her light for a moment, plunging herself into stygian blackness. She breathed deep against the nerves that immediately rippled through her. She would need to preserve her battery, in case they needed to explore further. Who knew how far the other tunnels might go? She knew for a fact that it was one single passageway back to the cave where they had split up, so she could walk carefully trailing one hand on the wall for stability and get back with some of her battery preserved.

She took another deep breath, telling herself to be calm, then froze. She had heard something. No, not something. She knew exactly what it was. The scuff of a shoe on the rock floor. She knew instinctively that it wasn't Crowley or Cameron. They knew she had come this way, they would call out her name or something, not creep along like that. A light danced around the shallow bend back the way she had come.

There had been a fissure in the rock beside the blocked-up cave entrance, a kind of fold as if the rock had been creased by some giant hand. Rose quickly, as quietly as she could, backed up, feeling behind her as she went. As the approaching light brightened, her hand fell into the gap and she pressed herself in.

The gap was narrow, but she forced her way. The leg of her jeans snagged on a sharp protuberance, but she drove herself against it, pushing deeper in, ignoring the cold rock against her flesh, the knife Cameron had given her gripped tightly in one hand. Her heart beat so hard it filled her ears, slammed against the inside of her chest. She drew breath as quietly as she could, but the rock closed her in, stopped her lungs from expanding. She fought against panic, trying not to hyperventilate.

The scuffing shoes came nearer, the light ridiculously bright now. Was she far enough in to be hidden from view?

Landvik appeared around the shallow bend, his face a mask of fury in the stark light from a small penlight torch. He grunted a sound of annoyance as his light splashed on the blocked dead end. He shined it around, looked up and down, and scanned the ceiling above. He muttered something in Norwegian that sounded almost certainly like a curse and turned, took a few steps back the way he had come.

Trembling from nerves and the cold, Rose was about to release a quiet sigh of relief when Landvik stopped, then turned back.

CHAPTER 55

Crowley pulled himself into the small space, a seemingly prefect cube hewn from the rock. In an alcove on the far wall, a second, miniature cube, sat a hammer.

He shook his head, staring in wonder. Even with everything else they had uncovered, Crowley had never really believed they would find Mjolnir, Thor's Hammer, but this had to be it. It seemed to glow slightly, or was that just his phone's light reflecting off the impossibly silver surface?

The hammer had a rectangular head, on which it stood, about the size of a shoebox. The metal seemed almost unearthly, silver, but not silver. Like an alloy, perhaps, with a smoothness like aluminum, but a brightness like diamonds. The haft of the thing, made from the same metal as the head, stood straight up from it, maybe half a meter long, a little thicker than a broom handle. Crumbled bits of old leather strapping lay across the hammer head and around it on the stone shelf.

Norse runes surrounded the square alcove, two rows all the way around like a double frame around a painting. The inside set of runes were inlaid with silver, the outer ring just carved into the stone. Around those was a convoluted carved pattern, twining lines and stylized animals. Crowley flicked up his camera app and took a series of quick photos, showing the hammer in place, then closer up, moving the camera around it from several angles. He made sure the runes were clear in the shots.

As he got closer he saw there were runes and sigils on the surface of the hammer head too, though not carved. More like laser etchings he had seen, but how was that even possible? He laughed softly. How was any of this possible?

He took a deep breath, held it for a moment, then slowly let it out as he reached for the hammer's haft. As his cold fingers and palm closed around it, an electric spark pulsed into his flesh and he whipped his hand away with a quiet yelp. He had knocked it slightly sideways as he pulled his hand back and thought he had seen sparks flicker underneath it. It had shocked him! What the hell could this thing be made from that it could generate such static electricity? Or store it?

He had noted before the dry air in the passageway behind the wall he had knocked down. It seemed only more so here, tinder dry, which was incredibly weird for a subterranean cavern so near the ocean in northern England.

He pulled a handkerchief from his pocket and carefully wrapped it around the handle, careful not to touch the metal, and picked Mjolnir up. He had braced for the weight, thinking he would probably need both hands given its size, but it was light, like aluminum. He gently drew one edge of the hammer head across the stone and watched incandescent blue and purple sparks flicker and dance around it. The glow he had thought he saw before was more in evidence now, not unlike a kind of phosphorescence like krill in the ocean. The thing hummed slightly in his grip. He couldn't hear a sound, but felt it buzzing ever so gently against his palm.

Curious of its potential power, he drew it up a few inches and struck down against the edge of the alcove where the hammer had rested. A flash momentarily blinded him and the stone shattered, sending up a spray of fine particles. Crowley grunted in shock, blinking the rock dust from his eyes as his vision slowly returned to normal. "This thing can literally store energy," he whispered to himself, keen to hear the sound of his own voice for some measure of sanity in the suddenly bizarre situation in which he found himself.

He lifted the hammer. *Is this truly Mjolnir?* Enraptured, he started at the sound of a distant cry, and then the unmistakable crack and echo of a gunshot.

CHAPTER 56

Beneath Lindisfarne Castle

Crowley doused his light and moved back toward the small exit from the hammer's secret chamber. There was the short, narrow crawl, then the tunnel with the carvings that would eventually lead him back over the broken down wall and all the way back to the main chamber. He crouched at the small exit tunnel, straining to hear something, anything, but no further sound was forthcoming.

With a shake of the head, he prepared to crawl back through, hoping he wouldn't find anything distressing when he finally made it back to the cavern. But given they were unarmed and he had most definitely heard a gunshot, it did not bode well. He scrambled back from the small tunnel as light danced around on the walls near the carvings of the Norse gods. Someone was coming. He moved to one side, still on his knees, and peered carefully out. His view was restricted by the three or four meters of narrow passage, but he saw a glimmer of light, bobbing as whoever carried it walked briskly along. Probably a flashlight, Crowley thought, or even a phone light like he had been using. Bloody stupid of this person to not realize the light would be a beacon signaling his position and approach. But Crowley was glad for the man's idiocy. It gave him a moment to plan.

But plan what? He was in a perfectly empty cube of rock, trapped behind the narrow throat of the square passageway out. There was nowhere at all to hide. And as soon as that goon spotted anything, he would start shooting.

Levi paused to shine his penlight over the impressive carvings on either side of the tunnel. He had never seen anything like them. This place had some pretty amazing secrets to give up, but he had really had enough. Running around like fools, chasing after this fabled artifact. He tried to be a believer, tried to take the word of Halvdan Landvik for truth, but it all sounded faintly insane to his ears. The sooner this particular escapade was over the better.

The passage ended in a tiny square opening, maybe a meter

across. Great, more crawling around. He was tempted to forget it, go back and claim he had found nothing. But if somehow Mr. Landvik learned he had left any corner unexplored, well, Landvik would kill him. It was as simple as that.

He dropped down, put his penlight between his teeth and crawled forward on one hand and two knees, holding his pistol out in front of his face. He realized this particular tight passage was only a few meters long and then seemed to open out into a small room. He paused, took his light in hand and shined it left and right, leaning and craning his neck to see in. He couldn't see it all, would have to go all the way in and check. With a sigh he returned the light to his mouth and scrambled forward the last few feet.

Something tingled in his hindbrain, some sixth sense of caution. He paused, just before the opening and moved his head to shine his light left and right again. He could almost see the entire small, square space, except for the nearest wall and the two corners closest to him. He would only be able to see those spaces once he emerged from the cramped tunnel, which he was suddenly reluctant to do. If someone was waiting just inside, he would be rather compromised as he tried to pull himself in. Compromised enough, at least, for that person to get the jump on him.

But he couldn't leave the place unchecked. Could he wait out whoever might be in there? Maybe, but if there wasn't anyone inside he'd be here forever. He had heard one gunshot already, so either Mr. Landvik or Jarn had run into some drama, but that didn't mean all of them were caught. Or even the most important one, Rose Black herself. And Levi knew very well she could handle herself if necessary. He would have to take a chance, but not without a distraction.

He set himself up for a fast scoot into the room, legs braced up underneath his hips, one hand hovering ready to grab the edge and pull himself forward. Quick as he could, he thrust his gun hand out into the room and fired quickly, two shots hard left, two shots hard right, then launched himself into the room. Anyone waiting either side of the opening would surely have caught at least one of those bullets.

Something heavy landed on him. Levi's breath was forced from him in an explosive rush, his flashlight skittering away across the rock floor. He flailed, reflexively pulling the trigger of his pistol again, sending bullets ricocheting around the tiny space, the sound deafening, pounding his eardrums. Something smashed into his skull and everything went black.

CHAPTER 57

Crowley stood in shock, checking himself all over. The bloody idiot had fired so many bullets, surely he was struck somewhere. His calf still burned from the flesh wound he had caught back in that warehouse. He really didn't want any more injuries. He had used the hammer to strike out a handhold above the tunnel and hung there one handed waiting for the thug to emerge, so he had avoided the man's first attempts to shoot either side of the opening. But the fool had taken so long thinking about his plan that Crowley had nearly fallen from numb fingertips.

Thankfully the man emerged just before Crowley's grip gave way and he had managed to fall onto the thug's back. More wild gunshots started pinging around until Crowley had caved the man's head in with Mjolnir. He wondered how long it had been since the hammer had been used in battle. It seemed to sing in his hand, thrumming with renewed energy, almost pulling at his grip like it wanted more skulls to crush.

Crowley's jacket had a couple of fresh holes and a hot line burned along his right outer thigh where a bullet had grazed him, but it barely bled. Almost more a burn than a wound. He had been lucky once again.

He took the man's gun from his limp hand and ejected the magazine to check the remaining ammo. Three bullets left. Better than nothing, and better than a knife. He crawled quickly from the secret chamber and hurried back along the passageway, fearing for his friends. The single shot he had heard before was concerning enough, but now the multiple shots fired by his victim would have taken away any element of surprise he might have had. But he had to get to them, try to help them. He hefted the hammer, somewhat comforted by the bargaining power it ought to buy him. Though he was reluctant to let it go, this amazing thing that surely would set the historical and scientific worlds on fire once it was revealed.

He put out his phone light and pocketed it, clipped Mjolnir against the wall periodically as he hurried back up toward the cavern. Its sparks and flashes helped to light his way while he kept the pistol in his right hand. He felt the thing humming, storing up energy every time it struck a surface, charging itself, aching for battle.

He slowed as the tunnel began to narrow again, knowing he would have to crawl the last couple of hundred meters on hands and knees again. He was mightily sick of cramped, cold stony places. He kept the pistol in one hand, crawling on his knees and the elbow of his gun hand, careful to keep Mjolnir clear of the rock with his left hand. He didn't want sparks and flashes to give him away now in case anyone was waiting in the cavern ahead. He might have a chance to squeeze off a couple of shots if he was quiet enough.

Finally nearing the end of his crawl, he paused near the mouth of the passageway. In the light of a slowly moving flashlight he saw two sets of feet.

"Come out very slowly, Mr. Crowley," Landvik said, his voice tight. "And if I see a weapon, Miss Black dies."

CHAPTER 58

Crowley closed his eyes and swallowed. This was a bad place to be, with Landvik in complete control. He slipped the pistol into the back of his belt, and pulled his jacket over it. The man wouldn't see it, but no way was Crowley leaving it behind. The one bargaining chip he had was the hammer, and he would have to try to leverage that.

"I'm coming out. I do have a weapon, but I think you might be quite interested to see this one. Just stay cool, okay?"

He crawled out of the low tunnel, careful to hold Mjolnir ahead of himself in plain sight. He heard Rose's sharp intake of breath and Landvik's sigh of pleasure. He stood slowly, holding the hammer in front like a shield.

Landvik stood behind Rose, one arm around her neck, holding her tightly to his chest. That hand held a flashlight, blindingly bright as it swept across Crowley's face, making him blink rapidly. Landvik's other hand held an automatic pistol, the barrel pressed to Rose's temple. Rose had both hands on the arm around her throat, like she would pull it away any moment, though Crowley doubted she would have the strength to do so in that compromised position. He saw blood on Landvik's hand, a slash in the flesh of his wrist. Rose had not been captured without a fight and had cut him, but he had subdued her nonetheless. Her lower lip was bruised and swollen, her left eye blackening, the same side as the grubby Band-Aid on her cheek. And both her eyes were wide with fear.

Landvik's eyes were wide too, though avaricious. There was no fear in him. "You found it!"

Crowley lifted Mjolnir, an unnecessary confirmation of Landvik's words. "Let Rose go and I'll give it to you."

Landvik grinned, shook his head. "Hammer first."

"Don't believe him!" Rose said. "He'll kill us both once he has it. You know he will."

Crowley nodded. He knew she spoke the truth. Landvik would gladly shoot them and leave them down here to probably never be found. Their bones would remain as mute testimony to their failure. But he couldn't see any other possibility. He measured up the odds, tried to play through the possibilities in his mind. No way he could draw and fire the pistol before Landvik killed Rose. Even if Crowley also killed Landvik, Rose would be just as dead and that was the worst failure, something he simply couldn't allow. Besides, the way Rose was being used as a shield made it a hell of a risky shot, even though Crowley's marksmanship was pretty top notch. In the weird low torchlight as well, he couldn't guarantee a hit, let alone a kill. And still, Landvik would pull the trigger in reflex.

"Fine, the hammer is yours." He took a step forward and Landvik dragged Rose back a step.

"Stop there. Slide the hammer over to me."

Crowley smiled, though he tried to continue conveying disappointment. Holding Landvik's gaze, he slowly crouched and laid the hammer on the ground. Still keeping Landvik's gaze fixed with his own, he let the handkerchief fall to the floor, and flicked it back into the shadows of the cramped tunnel behind him. He stood, placed one booted toe against the hammer head, and shoved it hard. It slid across the rough stone, sending up a shower of flickering bright blue sparks and chips of rock as it went. Landvik and Rose gasped in unison, blinking against the sudden strobing brightness.

Landvik pushed Rose to her knees. "Stay there!"

He put his flashlight between his teeth, still directed to watch Crowley, switched his pistol to the now free hand and reached down for Mjolnir with the other. Crowley braced as Landvik's fingers closed around the haft of the hammer. The man yelped in pain and surprise as the electric shock shuddered up his arm. His flashlight dropped from his mouth as he cried out, smashing on the rocks, plunging the cavern in utter blackness. Then quick sparks and flickers as Landvik grabbed the hammer again, but Crowley had already whipped the pistol from his back. He fired slightly up and to the left of the flickering hammer, but the shot ricocheted off a wall. Knowing he was at risk, he dodged aside just as Landvik's gun barrel boomed light and sound, the bullet tearing past Crowley's ear with a hot whine.

Crowley drew a bead on Landvik's muzzle flash and fired again, but once more the bullet hit rock, not flesh. The man was fast. He only had one shot left. He hit the ground and rolled, yelling, "Stay down!" to Rose, as Landvik fired again, three rapid shots that all buzzed over him into the rock walls.

Ears ringing, eyes stained with after-images from the muzzle of Landvik's gun, Crowley spotted the spark and flash of the hammer as it was lifted and carried away, back toward the tunnel leading up to the Ship Room in the castle. Crowley aimed and fired his last bullet. He heard a satisfying grunt of pain, had a tiny moment of elation, but the flickering hammer kept going as Landvik ran with it, obviously not wounded enough to be stopped. The Norwegian fired another couple of random shots back as he disappeared up the passage.

Crowley cursed eloquently, knowing full well he'd be a sitting duck if he followed the man up the narrow tunnel. Light flared as Rose turned on her torch app and Crowley's attention turned entirely to her. He looked her up and down, desperately hoping there was no blood.

"I'm okay." She rubbed a hand at her throat where Landvik had held her vicelike in the crook of his elbow. "I'm a little beat up, but I'm okay."

"The hell is happening down there?" Cameron's voice was weak, but held an edge of anger, coming from the tunnel he had first gone down when they split up. "Come this way and fight, you mongrels!"

Crowley laughed, relieved his friend was still breathing. Since the first gunshot he had heard, he had been doing his best not to consider the worst. He and Rose hurried into the dark passage, Rose's light dancing and skipping ahead of them. Not far down, they came across Cameron on the cold floor, his left leg covered in blood. He pointed a pistol at them, face set in determined fury.

"It's us!" Crowley said, "Don't shoot!"

Rose angled the light so Cameron could see them clearly. He slumped, lowered the gun. "I thought you were both dead."

"I thought the same about you!" Crowley shined his own light around. One of Landvik's thugs lay on his back in a pool of blood, dead from numerous stab wounds.

"He got me in the leg, but then I got close enough to use my knife." Cameron's face was split in a satisfied grin.

"How bad is it?" Crowley shined the light on Cameron's leg. There was a lot of blood, but he'd bandaged the wound using strips from the dead thug's shirt.

"It'll be okay if I can get to a doc fairly soon. Hurts like a son of a bitch, but I'm all right. Had worse."

"And that's his gun?" Crowley gestured to the weapon in Cameron's hand.

Cameron handed it over. "Yep."

Crowley took the weapon, checked the chamber.

"There's a dozen left in there," Cameron said.

Crowley nodded, drew in a deep breath. "Okay, sit tight until I get back."

"Where are you going?" Rose asked. "We should carry Cameron out to get help."

"I'm not lugging his great carcass around. I'll get help and bring it here."

Rose shook her head, eyes narrow. "You're going after him, aren't you?"

Cameron grinned, threw over the keys to their car which Crowley caught one handed and dropped into his jacket pocket.

"Sit tight," Crowley repeated, and ran back up the passage, gun in hand.

CHAPTER 59

Crowley emerged from the small round hole into the lime kilns behind Lindisfarne Castle, immediately met by the cold, wet breeze. It felt good. Landvik had a head start, but the man had to get up to the secret door in the fireplace of the Ship Room, then down through the castle. And hopefully he would be slowed by whatever flesh wound Crowley had scored on him. There was a chance Crowley could catch up.

He made a dash for the small parking area where they had left their car, hoping to get there before Landvik, but the Norwegian was just ahead of him. There was a deep scarlet stain across the man's hip. It looked like Crowley had winged him in the love handle on the right side of his body. Lots of blood, but nothing life-threatening. Though Landvik had one hand pressed hard against the wound, and the other hugged tight to his body, no doubt cradling Mjolnir inside his jacket. Crowley raised the pistol, blinked the rain from his eyes, and fired just as Landvik dived for his car. The bullet pinged off the black vehicle's roof, the handful of tourists braving the weather screaming and scattering in horrified shock.

Landvik pointed his weapon back and squeezed off more shots without looking, making Crowley dive for cover, then the Norwegian was in the driver's seat and the engine gunned into life.

Landvik's car sent up a spray of mud and gravel as it carved a sharp turn and sped out onto the narrow road back across the island. Crowley ran for the Land Rover and gave chase. Flickering blue lights were heading their way and he realized the mayhem back at the priory was catching up. Three police cars were hammering along, heading directly for Landvik's car.

Crowley smiled, thinking the man was caught now, but the smile withered as Landvik's arm emerged from the driver's side window and his gun kicked and flashed. The police cars braked and swerved, one windshield shattering into a crazed web of safety glass. Landvik skidded onto the grass and drove hard around them all, fishtailing as he went. Cursing, Crowley followed. As he powered past the police cars frantically trying to turn back, he reached out of his own window and fired off two quick shots, managing to shoot out Landvik's rear screen, but the man drove on.

They sped back among the buildings of the small village, faces of shocked tourists zipping past all around as they leapt aside from the speeding vehicles. Crowley gritted his teeth and dropped the pistol into his lap. Too much chance of hitting an innocent bystander to fire from a moving car now, so he put both hands on the wheel and concentrated on sticking close to Landvik's tail. The flickering blue lights of the three police cars, one with its shattered screen now kicked clear, filled his rearview mirror as they joined the chase. The faces of the two officers of the car without glass were pictures of pure fury, concentrated in their pursuit.

They shot through town and along the beginning of the causeway, the grassy hill to their right as they approached where the low-lying roadway crossed the mud flats. But it wasn't mud flats any more. Crowley grinned, finally letting himself relax at the sight of the ocean on both sides, already washing hard across the road. Small white wavelets kicked up and foamed, the level of the causeway itself lost under the churning dark water.

"Dead end, you bastard!" he cried.

But his pleasure was short-lived. Landvik either didn't see or didn't care, and drove the black car hard along the causeway, water spraying up from the wheels to either side in two wide fans. Crowley shook his head, stunned the man would take such a risk, and followed him. Crowley's car was large and designed for off-road use, at least, but Landvik's wasn't. The water rose up faster, Landvik's car sending up walls of spray to either side, but he kept going. The water curved up over the hood as well now, drenching the car, almost obscuring it completely. Crowley felt the drag of the ocean against his own wheels and decided not to risk his life any further. He stopped, hit reverse, and backed up as quickly as he could. The vehicle shifted and bucked uncertainly, then his tires rose back onto dry road. He watched in amazement as water slowly engulfed Landvik's vehicle. The blue lights of the police cars filled the road behind and Crowley climbed from his seat into the pouring rain, arms held high to show he was not a threat. He left his stolen pistol on the passenger seat.

Landvik's car slowed to a stop and the door popped open

as the vehicle was lifted and turned by the tide. The man clambered out, still clutching the hammer, his face a mask of concentration and determination. He tried to swim for it against the rapid current. The last thing Crowley saw was the man's blond head sinking out of sight beneath the churning waters.

CHAPTER 60

In a private hospital room in the Royal Infirmary Edinburgh, a little over an hour from Lindisfarne, Cameron sat smiling in bed, post-surgery. A police guard outside his door was a formality, but they remained until all the details of the bizarre recent events could be ironed out. It was going to take a while for everything to be recorded and cross-checked.

Crowley sat one side of the bed, Rose on the other.

"So you're going to walk okay?" Crowley asked.

"Yep. I've got some muscle damage, and apparently the bullet chipped my thigh bone, but nothing that won't come good again with time to heal and some rehab exercises."

"Seeing as you live your life behind a desk now, it shouldn't matter anyway right?"

Cameron laughed. "Well, I did tell you I didn't want to get shot. Maybe I *should* go back to my desk."

"You only got shot in the leg. Halfway right."

Cameron twisted a wry smile. "How come I got it? You got away scot free."

"Not true! I was shot twice."

"Two grazes, buttercup. Hardly worth even mentioning."

"Are you two really comparing bullet wounds?" Rose asked, though her voice was amused. "Honestly, you boys are such clichés."

Crowley pouted. "Cliché? Oof!"

"I will have to go back to my desk, though," Cameron said. "If I want to keep my job. But I enjoyed our excursion all the same."

"Me too."

"You going back to the classroom?"

Crowley let out a soft laugh, shook his head. "It'll be hard after this, but I need to keep my job too. At least for now. I have mortgage payments to make." He looked over the bed at Rose. "And you in the museum?"

"Same. I'm glad all this is over. I'll actually be glad to get back to work. It was exciting, in hindsight, but I've had enough excitement for a lifetime, I think."

Crowley shrugged. "We'll see. Excitement like this does tend to be a little bit addictive."

"Is it over?" Cameron asked.

Crowley paused, thoughtful. "Well, Landvik's body wasn't found, or the hammer. Just his empty car. At least, that's the official word from the police. Apparently it's possible for currents to carry things, even cars, a long way. So it's entirely possible his body and the hammer may never be found."

"Or he may have escaped," Cameron said. "With the hammer."

"It's possible. But either way, he doesn't need Rose any more and presumably has no need to track us down again."

"Unless it's purely for revenge."

"True, but Landvik's not an idiot. A smart man would take his win and move on. But we don't even know if he lived or..."

"Either way," Rose interrupted, "for my own sanity, I'm declaring this whole thing over and done with. All of it. Finished."

Crowley made a sad face, deliberately overacting. "All of it?"

Rose laughed. "Well, I could possibly be persuaded to see you again. If the situation were just right."

Crowley grinned. "I'll have to think of something."

Cameron waved a hand in each of their faces. "Take it back to London, you two! Some of us are trying to recover from actual gunshot wounds here."

They laughed and Crowley caught Rose's eye over Cameron's protesting form. She gave him a quick wink. He smiled. Maybe it wasn't all over just yet.

END

ABOUT THE AUTHORS

David Wood is the author of the popular action-adventure series, The Dane Maddock Adventures, and many other works. Under his David Debord pen name he is the author of the Absent Gods fantasy series. When not writing, he co-hosts the Authorcast podcast. David and his family live in Santa Fe, New Mexico. Visit him online at www.davidwoodweb.com.

Alan Baxter is a British-Australian author who writes dark fantasy, horror and sci-fi, rides a motorcycle and loves his dog. He also teaches Kung Fu. He lives among dairy paddocks on the beautiful south coast of NSW, Australia, with his wife, son, dog and cat. He is the author of the dark urban fantasy Alex Caine trilogy and many other titles. He won the 2014 Australian Shadows Award for Best Short Story and the 2015 Australian Shadows Paul Haines Award for Long Fiction. Visit him online at www.warriorscribe.com.

50905330R00155

Made in the USA
San Bernardino, CA
07 July 2017